THE WALLS CAN TALK

A Lucky Bat Book
The Walls Can Talk: A Bad Vibes Removal Services Novel
Copyright ©2017 by Noreen M. Cedeño

ISBN-10: 1-943588-54-6
ISBN-13: 978-1-943588-54-1

Cover Artist: Brandon Swann
Published by Lucky Bat Books
10 9 8 7 6 5 4 3 2 1

Discover other titles by the author at nmcedeno.com

N. M. CEDEÑO

THE WALLS CAN TALK

Lucky Bat Books

DEDICATION

This book is dedicated to Mary Elizabeth Graham, because she wanted more Bad Vibes stories, and to my parents, my children, and my husband for their continued support and encouragement.

"If you want to find the secrets of the universe, think in terms of energy, frequency and vibration."

$\sim$*Nikola Tesla*

Chapter 1

"Kamika, we double-covered the walls, but I still feel a chill of anger or bitterness. I don't know where it's coming from," said Lea. She squatted next to her equipment bag and frowned at the walls around her, vexed by the unsuccessful results of their labors.

Kamika studied the eggshell-white-painted walls with a thoughtful but wary look, as if concerned that something unpleasant might emerge from them. "Could it be static from another room, or," she hid the twinkle of mischief in her eyes and adopted a serious tone, "one of your *dead* friends coming to see you?"

Lea jumped up. "They aren't my friends! I don't want to see them!"

Kamika giggled.

Lea realized she'd taken the bait and laughed. "Thou art a general offense," she said without rancor.

"Throwing old quotes at me won't solve the problem with this room. Seriously, what do you think is going on in here?" said Kamika with a grin.

Lea returned to packing the equipment bag. "I have no idea. The feeling of anger is stronger in the area around the closet. I haven't seen any lingering dead residents in here, but I haven't walked through the whole house. The owners specified that we reset *this* room. If they wanted the whole house done, they should have requested it."

"So no foul on us?" Kamika raised her dark, delicate eyebrows.

"Not unless we missed something in here."

Kamika turned her lean body three hundred sixty degrees, looking like a music box dancer in slow motion. She repeated the turn, looking up and again looking down as she carefully examined the walls, ceiling, and floor trim. "We didn't miss anything, except the closet, and they told us not to touch that because it's crammed full of junk and locked." She stood with her hands on her hips, biting her lower lip in front of the locked closet door. "I bet it's the closet. They've got something nasty in there. With our luck, it's the body of their murdered, wealthy auntie whose bank account they're emptying."

Lea rolled her eyes. "Don't be melodramatic. We could do a reading to pinpoint the source . . ." Lea's voice trailed off. A reading would take time and push them behind schedule. "How does the room feel to you?" she asked, turning to Kamika.

Kamika closed her eyes and stood still for a moment. Then her eyes popped open, and she laughed. "It feels like any other room. What do you think? You're the one with the spook sense."

"Provided the owner isn't as sensitive as I am, we should be fine." Lea finished packing her equipment, still bothered by the room. She paused. "What if the problem is under the floor or behind a wall? That would explain why I still feel it. The house has been remodeled. Walls were moved, removed, and added. Doorways have been moved and stairs rerouted."

"Well, we can only treat the surface. We can't tear into walls. And we don't have time to waste," said Kamika with a pragmatic shrug of her delicate shoulders. "I can add a note to the report advising the client to examine the structure of the walls and empty the closet if the room is still uncomfortable. That should cover our butts."

"Okay, do it. We have to go to the next customer." The failure irked Lea, but she tried to dismiss the matter. She and Kamika reset the emotional atmospheres of rooms to her satisfaction 99 percent of the time. The few that didn't meet her standards were rare but did crop up on occasion. Even so, the residual emotion in this room felt more intense than in any other room that they'd failed to reset. The only other time they had failed this badly, the distressed ghost of a teenaged girl had been present, rendering their work ineffective.

Kamika saved her recommendations to the customer's file and emailed the customer a copy. On the way out, she slapped the preprinted description of the services they had completed onto the kitchen counter with the finality of a judge banging a gavel.

Lea entered the owner-supplied temporary code into the house's security system to allow them to exit. The system logged them out and locked the house behind them.

They stowed their equipment into secure compartments in their van. After a final, annoyed backward glance, Lea hopped into the van. The vehicle advised the women to buckle their seatbelts and identified the preprogrammed route to the next customer.

Kamika reviewed the services they would be completing next on her monitor. "We're going to Dr. Gomez's office. He runs the physical rehabilitation clinic on Arlington Street. We were there six months ago."

"A regular medical reset?" Lea asked as she tucked a heavy, jet-black lock of hair into the band of cloth wrapped around her head. She liked this simple, ancient Roman hairstyle. Of all the fashion practices from ancient civilizations that she'd tested while studying them, this one was by far the most convenient for her day-to-day work activities.

"Yep."

Lea glanced at the time. "How many calls after that?" It was already mid-afternoon. Sometimes Miguel, the routing and scheduling guru, crammed too many calls into a Friday afternoon because of his desire not to put off customers who insisted that they needed services before the weekend.

Kamika scrolled down on the monitor. "Only two more on the schedule right now. Miguel better not add any more," said Kamika. "With travel time, we should be done at five-thirty, right on time." She tapped Lea's arm. "Guess what! I have a double date. My cousin Lusa is in town visiting colleges, and her boyfriend is a student here, and he's got a friend. We're going to dinner, followed by clubbing."

"Sounds great."

Kamika shot Lea a look of surprise. "You hate clubs. You'd rather stay home and read about ancient dead people's lives and mounds of dirt in Kazakhstan for your masters' thesis."

"Great for *you*, not for me." Lea suppressed a smile. "Okay. Let's go."

Lea looked forward to their next customer. She liked resetting the atmospheres in medical offices. Studies had shown patients recovered more quickly in a positive environment. Over time, the built up negative energies could give the room a feeling of tension or stress that impeded the patients' healing process and affected the staff's efficiency. The doctors, nurses, and therapists were happier, so fewer medical mistakes occurred. Her work helped heal people because she eliminated the negative emotions—stress, pain, and fear—released by patients and absorbed into the walls.

Some people were more sensitive to the atmospheres in buildings than others. Lea fell into the extremely sensitive end of the spectrum. She'd been uncomfortable in certain rooms and buildings her whole life. She enjoyed working for Bad Vibes Removal Services and being able to reset houses for new owners, apartments for new tenants, and spas for those in need of relaxation. Removing lingering negative emotional deposits from buildings improved life for a lot of people.

Lea's phone rang. "Uh-oh," she said, giving Kamika an apprehensive look. She tapped the phone's screen to answer. "Hello."

Montgomery's voice came across as vivid and bursting with energy. "Lea, I need you and Kamika to come help with an investigation. The structure calls for your expertise."

While Lea preferred to obliterate the record of emotions and sounds left in walls, the equipment used to do readings of the sound and emotional energy patterns left in walls was useful for the inventor's other business endeavor. Mr. Montgomery, creator of the process for both reading and eliminating embedded sounds and emotions in buildings, owned both Bad Vibes Removal Services and Montgomery Investigations. He spent his days running the investigations business and left the removal services to his employees.

"Is this another murder case?" Lea asked, curious in spite of her dislike of investigations. She much preferred resetting atmospheres to working investigations, but she also knew that no matter what she said, Montgomery would get her involved. She intentionally refrained from asking about the structure because she knew he was trying to pique her interest.

"No, we aren't trying to solve a murder. The client called me because small items were being moved around the house, sometimes in the middle of the night. They hired me to catch the perpetrator."

Lea threw Kamika a look of surprise before replying to Montgomery. "This is about theft?"

"Not exactly. Nothing has been taken, yet. Someone is searching the house for something."

"So you didn't call me because you think they have a ghost?" Lea asked with exasperation. Montgomery knew that she could see ghosts, and he had relied on that ability to solve several cases in the past.

"Your lack of interest in dealing with the dearly departed has been duly noted. However, you love historical locations. The client lives in a historical house. You do all the readings requested by the historical groups. You have more than double the experience doing readings in old buildings of anyone else. You're doing graduate studies in history. This one is right in your skill set. This building is older than any other structure in Texas. Please, Lea. Come and give me a hand."

Lea noted the confidence in Montgomery's voice, barely disguised by the persuasive tone he was using. He knew she'd be intrigued and wouldn't turn him down, darn him. And he hadn't answered her question about whether he thought they had a ghost. "Okay. Call Miguel and have us rerouted. Kamika and I will come."

"Thanks, Lea. I appreciate the help," said Montgomery. Lea could almost hear him smiling into the phone. She ignored Kamika, who was gleefully dancing in her seat, and stuck her phone back in her pocket.

Kamika continued dancing. "We've got a new case. This is going to be fun!"

Forty-five seconds later, the van's monitor beeped. Kamika pressed the answer button on the screen, and Miguel's round face appeared.

"Hey, Miguel," said Kamika, deploying a wide grin at the face in the monitor. She enjoyed meeting his sour mood with a joyful one.

"The boss is rerouting you two again." He looked and sounded annoyed. As the dispatcher, his job was to set the routes for each team of atmosphere resetters and designers for Bad Vibes Removal Services. Rerouting Lea and Kamika to an investigation meant shuffling schedules and calling clients, which was extra work for Miguel.

Kamika cheerfully ignored his morose demeanor. "Montgomery asked Lea to help him."

Miguel shot an icy look at Lea from the screen. "I'm sending you the new address. Montgomery said to meet him there immediately. Miguel out." The screen went dark.

"Well, he's got himself in a snit. It's not our fault. Montgomery owns both companies. Montgomery calls the shots," said Kamika.

"I could have said no," said Lea diplomatically. "After all, Montgomery hired me to work for Bad Vibes Removal Services, not Montgomery Investigations."

"Yeah, right. Montgomery would have kept talking until he changed your mind. Since when has he ever let the word *no* stop him from getting something done the way he wants it?"

"He is persistent," said Lea.

"Persistent? He's like that Greek guy rolling that rock up a hill. He doesn't give up no matter how often you shoot him down."

Lea laughed. "Sisyphus had to do that as a punishment for deceit and arrogance. The wasted effort was meant to frustrate him. If you want a mythological reference, Montgomery is more like a phoenix, forever rising from the ashes, regenerated and full of new life."

Kamika giggled. "Or like that bunny with the drum in those old commercials that keeps going and going that I heard about in advertising class?"

Lea laughed aloud picturing Montgomery in a giant bunny costume banging a drum. "Not exactly a mythological reference, but yes, that works too. So where are we going?"

Kamika looked at the navigation system. "The address is 15000 Katydid Lane. It's in an unincorporated part of Williamson County. We're going to one of those crazy neighborhoods in the middle of nowhere. Seriously, where do these people shop?"

Lea tapped the address into her phone. No news articles appeared. The thumbnail showed something gray obscured by large trees. Lea tried to expand the picture, but the signal in the area was weak and the image wouldn't load. After a few minutes, she gave up.

"I can't find anything about it on my phone. We'll have to wait for Montgomery to explain."

Lea switched over to read, as she always did between jobs. She covered a lot of reading material and even wrote papers for her graduate courses while riding in the van. Kamika checked social media sites on her phone.

Twenty minutes later, the van turned onto a street lined with wide-spreading oak trees whose majestically curved branches fanned out like octopus arms. Kamika glanced up and squealed.

Lea jumped at the sound, startled out of her reading.

CHAPTER 2

"WHAT'S THE MATTER?"

Kamika pointed out the windshield. "Look at that thing! Why would someone build that there? Do people *live* in it?"

Lea's eyes widened and her mouth dropped open slightly. A thrill of excitement passed through her as she saw what Kamika had seen.

It was a castle keep, complete with parapets and rounded corner towers, built of heavy stone. Lea estimated it to be four stories tall, double the height of its nearest neighbors on the street. The van came to a stop by the curb.

Lea scanned the stone edifice. "Well, it's got electrical wiring, or it wouldn't have that porch light or those brand new security cameras on the towers."

Kamika stared in awe at the massive stone structure. "Why would someone live in a castle in the middle of Texas?"

Lea shook her head. "Who knows? Some people have more dollars than sense." She peered at the structure.

"This isn't a full castle though, only the great tower, or keep, within the fortified walls. A full castle would have had walls with towers surrounding it and outbuildings. This is only the central building, the part of the castle where the nobleman who owned it lived with his family and conducted business."

"If you say so, professor. I'm still calling it a castle."

They parked the vehicle in front of the castle. Lea and Kamika climbed out, staring at the forbidding walls of stone looming over them. Definitely not a fairy tale castle, it rather looked like a fortress meant to withstand an attack by marauding Vikings.

Lea pointed to the boxy, gray air conditioner condensing unit sitting on one side of the castle. "At least they added amenities. If they have air conditioning, the owners didn't want authentic castle discomfort to go with their authentic castle."

"This place is for real?" asked Kamika, startled.

"Yes," said Lea, sensing a disjointed flow of the emotions felt by centuries of people radiating from the stones. The whole building emanated atmosphere and history. "It might be medieval, but from what country, I couldn't say. I haven't studied castle architecture."

"Of course it's genuine," said their boss, Montgomery, from his position by a heavy oak door high above them. The main entrance was up a stone flight of stairs that led to the second floor. Enthusiastic, tall, and rotund, with a balding patch on the crown of his head, Montgomery only needed brown robes and he could have played Friar Tuck on Halloween. "The current owner's great-grandfather had the whole thing moved here from Ireland and reconstructed stone by stone. It was a rescue project. The place was falling to ruin in the 1920s, when old Mr. Hanover visited it and decided to save it. The walls protecting it had crumbled. Local people dragged away the stones to reuse in bridges and buildings in a nearby town. Hanover had discovered a family connection to the place. He'd made a pile of money as a captain of industry, so he could afford to do as he pleased. It pleased him to buy a castle and ship it here."

Catching that he was withholding something, Lea's heart dropped. "Who died here?"

Montgomery gave her a contrite look. "Old Mr. Hanover died in 1929 in the castle. The new owner, his great-grandson, has questions he hopes to have answered about the old man's death that may, or may not, be tied to why someone broke in and searched the castle."

"You said this case isn't about murder," said Lea in an accusatory tone.

"The old man's death certificate says he had a heart attack at the age of 64," said Montgomery. "For the time, that was pretty typical, medically speaking."

"Then what kind of questions does his great-grandson have?" asked Lea.

"The old man died under a cloud of suspicion. He would have been indicted if he hadn't conveniently died when he did. More than a million dollars went missing from his company right before his death. He was suspected of embezzling the money and defrauding his investors. This all happened in late September 1929."

"Not long before the stock market crashed the next month," said Lea. "Why would he steal from his own company? Was he in debt?"

"I don't have all the details of that incident. I've been focusing on the current problem of breaking and entering. All I know for certain is that, according to family lore, Old Hanover's widow insisted that he was innocent until her dying day," said Montgomery. "And whoever broke in is definitely searching for something. Although, so far, the intruder hasn't taken anything."

Kamika gave Montgomery a confused look. "If nothing has been taken, how do they know someone broke in and searched?"

Montgomery trotted down the stone staircase to join Lea and Kamika by the van. "Drawers have been rifled. Closets and cabinets have been opened. Mrs. Hanover's phone and tablet were moved in the night."

Lea frowned thoughtfully and pointed at the security cameras visible on the exterior of the castle. "Didn't the security cameras record anything?"

Montgomery shook his head. "Those were installed yesterday. The electrical system in the house was from the 1920s and wouldn't support today's electrical needs. Several rooms only had one outlet. The electrical wiring required to install the cameras was completed, but some areas are still being upgraded. The rest of the security system—alarms, door and window monitors—should be completed today. The castle hasn't been occupied since it was closed after the widow's death in 1952. The current owner, Ryan O'Dwyer Hanover IV, took an interest in the property when he inherited it. He's updating the utilities now: wiring, plumbing, air, heat, remote system access, the works. Some upgrades aren't complete yet, but the current Mr. Hanover, his wife, and their eight-year-old son, Jack, moved in two months ago."

Kamika raised an eyebrow. "No portable cameras, nanny cams? You have an arsenal of spy equipment."

Montgomery smiled. "I set them up when the client first contacted me, but no more break-ins have happened since I was called."

"Maybe the intruder gave up," said Lea.

"Maybe so," agreed Montgomery. "But the client still wants the rumors about this place laid to rest. The castle was sealed, locked by the current owner's grandfather after the widow's death. Ryan Hanover's father and grandfather, who were also named Ryan Hanover, didn't have the money to reopen and modernize the place. Inheritance provisions prohibited them from selling it. When he was a kid, our client and his friends used to tell stories about what was locked away in the castle: dead bodies, the missing million dollars, treasure, stolen jewels, whatever they could imagine. The neighborhood gossip mill is rife with rumors about this place. Someone might be breaking in to look for treasure or simply out of curiosity."

Lea gave Montgomery a perplexed look. "Why would someone search the place now? Wouldn't it have been easier to break in while the castle was unoccupied?"

Montgomery shrugged his wide shoulders. "The renovations and the reopening of the place caused the old rumors to resurface. A local interest story appeared in the news when the renovations started. The news article mentioned the history of the castle, including the story about the first Ryan Hanover and the missing money. I'm also looking into some other possible reasons for the break-ins. However, we are going to search this place because the client wants us to do it. And if the old man's ghost happens to be here and happens to want to communicate with Lea, well, that would make things easier."

"Are we looking for the money? Is this a treasure hunt?" asked Kamika, excited by the prospect.

"We're looking to see if we can find anything, including the money."

"If we find money, that would prove his ancestor was guilty of embezzlement," said Lea. She scanned the area around her, noting the signs of recent landscaping and improvements to the property. "Did the current owner come into some money? A place like this will need a boatload of cash to modernize it."

"Ryan Hanover recently sold his business to an Internet giant who was anxious to acquire his software," said Montgomery. "The purchase went very well for him."

Lea nodded toward the castle. "This place exudes ancient emotional history, but the stone is too rigid to have retained sound patterns. The sound waves would have reflected instead of being absorbed. Are the interior walls stone, too?"

"Most of the rooms are partially paneled to hide wiring. They added drywall in some places to cover plumbing. The doors are heavy hardwoods, mostly oak. We can get a few solid readings in each room," said Montgomery, rubbing his hands together in eager anticipation. Although he was always animated, working cases with his pet technology made him positively effervescent. He rocked back and forth, from his heels to his toes.

"Each room?!" said Kamika with a suspicious look. "How many rooms do we have to do tonight?" She shook her head in disbelief as she took in the immensity of the castle. The place was a fortress that had once housed the functions of a regional seat of government and a large family. It was easily five times the size of any house that they typically reset.

"Ten rooms, maybe more," said Montgomery, one hand tapping the door frame of the ancient structure thoughtfully. "The client wants to start the search in the larger rooms that were used most frequently back in his great-grandfather's time. The place has lots of rooms, though, so if we don't find anything in the first ten, we can continue on to the others tomorrow. If we start now, we should get a good portion finished before midnight. Let me help you with the equipment." He flung open the side doors of the van and began yanking out equipment bags.

"Midnight." Kamika's nostrils flared, and she cursed in Swedish. She stood with both hands balled on her hips.

Lea grabbed Kamika by the elbow as she opened her mouth to protest. "It's no use arguing. Let's get it done. If you have plans tonight, you can go and leave me here with Montgomery."

"Of course I have plans. I told you; I have a date. It's Friday, and my cousin is in town. Treasure that's been hidden forever can wait until tomorrow or Monday. It's not like it's going anywhere." She shook her head in annoyance but turned to pick up an equipment bag to carry into the castle.

Inside the castle, Montgomery introduced Lea and Kamika to Ryan O'Dwyer Hanover IV, a personable, forty-something man in jeans and a t-shirt. The shirt looked to be a freebie given out to runners who had participated in the ubiquitous 5K and 10K runs held around Austin every year. Though his hair was thinning on top, Ryan looked healthy and active. His eye passed appreciatively over Kamika's lovely, exotic features but moved quickly on to study Lea.

Lea could see him examining the way she'd tucked her thick, black hair around the cloth band tied on her head. He glanced at her tunic and leggings with leather sandals but didn't comment. He could see dozens of more outlandish styles than her current Ancient Roman attire in Austin on Sixth Street any day of the week. The tunic was based on a Roman design, just as Lea's hairdo was. In the last few months, she had tried togas, sandals tied with leather, and stola like those seen on sculptures and described in various ancient Roman documents. She had also studied a wide variety of Roman hairstyles that she couldn't replicate without sewing the hair in place as the Romans had had servants or slaves do.

"Can I watch you work?" he asked, turning back to Montgomery with an interested look on his face. "I love new technology. Can you give me a quick overview of how you intend to find out if anything is hidden here?"

His enthusiasm brought a smile to Lea's lips. Central Texas was full of computer guys who loved technology, making it a birthplace for a variety of new gadgets and software. The castle was outside the city of Cedar Park, an easy commute into Austin if one took the train.

"Yes, you can watch. If you have any questions, just ask," said Montgomery. He loved to show off his inventions. "By reading the walls with my sound scanners and emotional energy scanners, we can look for signs of guilt and conversations about hiding money, which might help determine where to search. We can also locate voids behind walls—hiding places or safes."

Ryan looked intrigued. "How does that work?"

Montgomery gave the short version of his speech on how his equipment worked. "You know how the earliest sound recordings were made on wax cylinders? Essentially an engraving of the vibrations caused by the sound waves as they traveled through a diaphragm?" asked Montgomery.

"Yes," said Ryan.

"My sound-reading equipment works off the principle that the sound waves moving through space make an imprint in materials they pass through at the atomic and even subatomic level. The stone mostly deflects the sound waves; they bounce off and echo around the room. Softer materials, such as wood and drywall, absorb a certain amount of the sound. When that happens, the impact of the waves causes minute changes. My equipment reads the patterns left behind by sound waves. Yelling, screaming, and loud sounds like gun shots come across well. Lower-volume sounds are more difficult, sometimes impossible, to decipher."

"And the closer to the source the better?" asked Ryan.

"Yes, the patterns will be fainter when farther from the source, like ripples in a pond when you throw in a rock. In softer materials, like wood and wall board, the waves can travel into and leave a pattern at the atomic level. My equipment can read and analyze those patterns. We can tell the direction the sound wave came from and how far away the sound originated as the waves dissipate, like ripples of water. Emotional energy is slightly different. It can be laid down in bursts or over a long period of time. The energy waves emitted by the emotion leave a pattern, just like the sound waves do. Unlike sound, however, everything absorbs emotional energy, giving a location a sense of atmosphere."

Lea nodded. "This castle exudes centuries of atmosphere. Think of it this way: Certain places have a certain feel. Have you ever been in a house with a couple who are fighting and you could feel the tension in the air, even though the people are in the other room and you can't hear them? Or have you been someplace that felt serene, calm?"

"I guess so," said Ryan thoughtfully. "My wife doesn't think I'm particularly emotionally sensitive."

Montgomery laughed. "That's okay. Neither am I. However, Lea is on the other end of the spectrum from us."

Ryan crossed his arms on his chest. "Do you think you can find evidence of conversations and emotion from a hundred years ago? Wouldn't more current sounds get in the way?"

Kamika stepped forward. "Lea's our expert, the queen, at reading old buildings. She can sort layers of sound better than anyone, except maybe Montgomery."

"Oh, no," said Montgomery. "When it comes to really old locations, Lea's done even more readings than I have. She has me beat easily."

Lea blushed a little at the praise. "I've done readings at historical locations for a variety of groups, mostly history buffs. Some of those buildings date back to the Republic of Texas era. Provided nothing explosively loud happened in the same location at a later date that could have obliterated the older record of sound, we can still find evidence of loudly spoken conversations, particularly those that were yelled. It builds up in layers that we have to sort. This is probably the oldest structure we've ever examined, but the wood inside isn't as old as the stone. The wallboard and wood panel only date back to the 1920s, and we've analyzed wood far older than that."

Ryan look impressed. "Are the police interested in the technology? I imagine knowing what was said in a crime scene would be a powerful tool in finding the guilty."

Montgomery sighed. "Well, that's trickier. When I invented the scanners, I'd hoped to sell them to law enforcement agencies to help solve crimes. However, they've been unwilling to take a risk on anything that doesn't have a proven track record in court. I'm working to convince the various agencies of the efficacy of the equipment and the trustworthiness of the science behind it. I started Bad Vibes Removal Services to get the technology into the public sphere, since the removal services have the widest application to the general public. So far, I've only been allowed to consult on one cold case that stumped the police. On that case, with Lea's help, we demonstrated the usefulness of my inventions and helped resolve a quadruple homicide. The police are still reluctant to use my techniques in current crime scenes, but other customers are eager to put the technology to use in private investigations. Using the equipment with the citizenry raises awareness of its capabilities. It's only a matter of time before I get a good judicial test case."

Ryan nodded his understanding. "Shall we start at the top?"

"That's fine," said Montgomery.

"Okay." Ryan studied the equipment bags Lea, Montgomery, and Kamika were carrying. "We can send the equipment up the dumbwaiter. That would be easier than carrying it all."

Kamika looked at Lea in confused concern before mouthing, *"Dumb waiter?"*

Lea winked and whispered, "You'll see."

Montgomery gave him a doubtful look. "Will it hold the weight of all this equipment?"

"We rebuilt the mechanism last week. My great-grandfather installed the original back in the 1920s after he had this place brought over from Ireland and rebuilt. The parts had rusted and locked in place, so we had to disassemble the whole thing and start from scratch. My wife wants to use it to move laundry down to the washroom from the upper floors, but with all the renovations, we needed to use it to move heavy equipment, too—either that or put in an elevator. This seemed easier. The system is rated for up to five hundred pounds."

Ryan led them into the kitchen, a long room with sparkling new appliances at one end and a dining table that could seat eight on the other end. He opened what looked like a cabinet and helped Montgomery put the equipment bags inside. Closing it, he pushed the number four and pressed start on a touch screen.

"Now we can go up to the game room and get it all out," said Ryan, gesturing for them to follow him.

Lea followed slowly, studying her surroundings. "You've converted the great hall into a kitchen, dining room, and living area?" she said, gazing around her at what had previously been one high-ceilinged room that was now divided into separate rooms. Signs of construction littered half the space where a wall had been partially demolished.

"When my relatives rebuilt the place, they broke this room into sections by adding interior walls. We want to create a more open floor plan, return the sense of grandeur to the space. We're adding a high, open archway where the kitchen doors were and removing the wall between the dining area and the kitchen."

Montgomery surveyed the construction. "Do you have plans for what the castle looked like before the 1920s changes were made?" He glanced at Lea, giving her a shadow of a smile.

Ryan stopped and turned. "We've been reviewing the plans as a guide for our renovations. Would you like to see the blueprints for the castle? I've got them out right now."

"Absolutely," said Lea, grateful that Montgomery had asked and knowing he'd done it for her.

"With as much as we have to do, you want to waste time on floor plans?" Kamika hissed with annoyance into Lea's ear.

"Come on. I want to see what this place looked like before it got attacked by the Roaring Twenties," said Lea.

Kamika shrugged and shot her an exasperated look.

Ryan led them out of the main room to another that was being used as a workroom for the construction crew. Tools, piles of supplies, paint, and the rest of the necessities of a huge remodeling job were piled everywhere. A folding table in the center of the room was covered with rolled tubes of paper, blueprints, and a stack of yellowing documents set off to one side.

A young woman sat by the table with a cell phone to her ear. She said, "Yes, ma'am, I'll work on that next. Ryan is here with some people. I have to go. Yes. Goodbye." She slid the phone into the pocket of her jeans as she rose from her seat. Her jeans were form-fitting, showing the narrow hips of youth. Her casual pink t-shirt and ballerina-style flats made her look like a teenager, but Lea guessed her to be in her early twenties.

"Hi, Ashley, is Wendy keeping you busy?" asked Ryan.

The young woman smiled politely. "Yes, sir, she is."

Ryan turned to Montgomery and said, "This is Ashley Olafsen, my wife's assistant. Ashley goes to the local community college in the mornings and works for Wendy in the afternoons five days a week. She's studying business." He turned to Ashley. "Ashley, these are the people who are going to look into the break-ins that we've had."

Ashley turned sharply to Montgomery. "Someone was definitely in the castle. Wendy would never leave her tablet in the car. Someone moved it there."

"Ashley is the one who found the tablet after we searched the whole castle for it," said Ryan.

"If she would never leave it there, why did you look there?" asked Montgomery.

"I wasn't looking for it when I found it," said Ashley with a look of concern on her face. "I'd gone to put the new registration sticker on the car. When I opened the door, I saw the tablet in the driver's seat. Someone put it there."

"Why do you think someone might do that?" asked Montgomery.

She glanced at Ryan Hanover.

"Say what's on your mind, Ashley," said Ryan.

"Ryan thinks someone is looking for information about hidden treasure," she said hesitantly. She stood and gathered some papers and a tablet from the table. "I can't think of any other realistic reason someone would move things like they did. Please solve this. It's been worrying me. Wendy needs me to finish some things for her." She nodded and walked out of the room.

Lea wondered what Ashley was withholding. She had the impression that the young woman had said what Ryan Hanover wanted to hear, rather than what she thought. Lea glanced at Montgomery, whose eyes were still on the door through which Ashley had exited. Lea guessed that Montgomery had picked up the young woman's hesitance as well.

A moment later, Lea stood engrossed in the yellowing, hand-drawn architectural plans of the castle. Foxing on the pages made them hard to read in some places. One set of blueprints showed the castle as it had stood before it was deconstructed for removal to the United States. The second set showed modifications and modernizations done in the 1920s when the castle was rebuilt. From cellar to top floor, not counting the roof, the castle had five levels: the underground cellar, the ground floor, the main great hall floor, the nursery/chapel floor, and the owner's floor at the top.

Lea read the notes for each room. In medieval times, the roof might have held pigeon houses and perhaps space for the guards stationed up there. The guard towers on all four corners were marked out. Beneath the roof, the top floor held chambers for the lord and lady of the castle, a smaller room that was a servant's quarters, and a rain storage tank. The modern plans showed that a large bathroom had been installed where the rain storage tank had been. The medieval toilets, with only a long shaft to the ground beneath them, had been converted into closets on the different floors.

The next floor held a nursery complex for children, including space for servants' quarters, bedrooms, and a schoolroom. A linen storage room had been converted into a bathroom on this level. Alongside the nursery complex was the household chapel. Lea wondered what it was used for now. The plans didn't say. The main floor where they'd entered the castle was the second floor. It had been the great hall and was divided into the kitchen, living room, dining room, breakfast nook, pantry, and a powder room or lavatory for guests.

Circular stairs ran up two of the corner towers and connected the floors. The ground floor, with open archways at the front, back, and sides of the castle, had been a storage area and a large open workspace for ancient castle residents. Lea's mind wandered to who could have toiled away there, perhaps a stonemason or laundress. The modern plans showed a laundry room, a game room with a ping-pong table and exercise equipment, and a storage room for gardening equipment. The rest of the ground-floor space was now the garage, with parking for two cars and assorted bicycles.

Beneath the ground floor, the cellar level was small, not half as large as the footprint of the keep's exterior walls, with one stairwell leading to it. A note on the original plans indicated a well had once existed in the cellar, but the rest of the cellar lacked notations. This could have been the dungeon, or root cellar, or more storage.

Lea looked on the table for modern cellar plans but didn't find them in the sea of documents before her. If she didn't get to tour the whole place, she'd poke her head into as many rooms as she could while they worked. With any luck, she'd see the whole building and not find any wandering souls.

Chapter 3

T HE TOP FLOOR ROOM WHERE THE dumbwaiter stopped was paneled in pine. Plaster moldings in complex knot shapes decorated the ceiling line. A large television and sound system equipment filled one wall. Comfortable, overstuffed, leather couches stood grouped in front of the television. A second wall held an empty wet bar. Ryan opened a cabinet by the wet bar that matched the one in the kitchen, revealing the equipment bags inside the dumbwaiter.

"You haven't watched any movies in here yet, have you?" asked Montgomery in a low voice. "Sound clutter in the paneling will be a lot higher if you have. We can filter the layers, but loud sounds—explosions in movies at full volume, for example—can obliterate older patterns in small, enclosed spaces, especially with all of this stone for the sound to bounce and echo around."

"The electrical work in this room hasn't been completed yet. I didn't want to risk power surges on the new equipment from the old wiring," said Ryan. "No movies played in here yet."

"Good," said Montgomery.

While Kamika started up the equipment, Lea surveyed the room. The paneling and plaster work dated to the 1920s. The heavy oak door to the room was a salvaged piece from some other old building. The carvings on it were not Irish or medieval but eighteenth century. "We can do a reading on all the paneling, but I'd recommend skipping this door for now," Lea said to Montgomery while pointing at the door. "It could have hundreds of layers of sound patterns that will take time to sort. From a historical perspective, I wouldn't mind trying to get to the deepest layers, if only to test the limits of the equipment."

"We'll save the door as a last resort if we don't find anything in the paneling," said Montgomery. He turned to Ryan, "Is there any particular reason you want to start here?"

"My great-grandfather was found dead in this room."

Kamika looked up quickly from her equipment and turned to Lea with an unspoken inquiry on her face.

Lea moved her head from side to side a fraction of an inch. She didn't see or feel any lingering spirits. The room itself felt neutral, a solid mix of lots of emotion over a long time. She turned around to find Montgomery observing her with an expectant expression. He raised his eyebrows in silent question.

Lea frowned at him in exasperation and vehemently shook her head *no* again.

Montgomery grinned at her.

Ryan watched their silent exchange with a quizzical look on his face.

Montgomery scooped up his scanner. "Well, let's get started then. Embedded sound first."

Lea picked up her gear. Kamika had the tablet ready to process the incoming data. Montgomery started by the door and worked his way left. Lea started on the other side of the door and worked her way right. They met up in a corner by a window overlooking the neighborhood. Out the window, Lea saw two small boys chasing each other across a playscape in the yard, absorbed in their own world. She smiled at the sight and walked back to join Kamika and Montgomery. The data from their scan of the room was beginning to appear on the screen of the tablet.

Lea pointed to the emerging pattern and analysis. "Look. Hooray!"

"What is it?" asked Ryan, frowning at the pattern, which resembled a sonar map or even a sonogram and required training to interpret.

"This place was empty for so long that there's a sharp demarcation in the embedded sound patterns from your great-grandmother's time to today. That will make it easier to shuffle through the layers," said Montgomery.

"Oh, good," Ryan said, still frowning at the pattern and trying to see what Lea could see. After a moment, he gave up and stepped back. "Could you explain how the output is interpreted?"

"After we detect the patterns, we can compare whatever we find to a database of the patterns for a phonetic alphabet and to a database of frequently screamed words." Montgomery paused to see if Ryan understood.

Ryan was concentrating on the explanation but looked a little puzzled. "Okay. That makes sense, but how do you know what words are frequently screamed?"

"Curse words," said Kamika. She enjoyed the spark of recognition that lit people's faces when told the equipment was good at finding curse words.

Understanding lit in Ryan's eyes, and he laughed. "Makes sense. So, then, the emotional energy analysis will work similarly?"

"Yep," said Montgomery. "A strong burst of emotional energy will leave a mark, like a loud sound will leave a mark. However, unlike sound, we can also detect long periods of sustained emotions, like sadness, depression, or anger, which have absorbed into the walls. The energy emitted by the person feeling the emotion leaves an imprint, like the sound waves do. My other company, Bad Vibes Removal Services, uses an infusion of white noise to cover and obliterate the embedded sound in a room. We can also infuse positive emotional energy to help neutralize or improve the atmosphere of a room. Investigations clients usually want readings of the histories of rooms rather than atmosphere neutralization."

"I'm impressed. That is some brilliant technology," said Ryan, nodding his head in respect to the genius beneath the friendly giant exterior. "This equipment is like nothing I've ever seen before."

Montgomery beamed with pride. "The system is proprietary. I've been contemplating an upgrade on the analysis and interpretation portions of the program. Right now, only people I've trained to understand the data can interpret what this means. If I'm going to expand usage of the equipment, I'll need to make the results of the scans more user-friendly. After we're done, perhaps you and I could discuss the best way to do that."

Lea could see that Montgomery had caught Ryan Hanover's attention. Mentioning a new software challenge made Ryan focus all his attention like a laser beam. Lea could almost see his brain whirling.

"You bet," Ryan said. "I'd need to review your current software as a starting point. Then I can give you some ideas on compiling the results more efficiently."

Lea called their attention back to the data on the screen. "Let's examine the area I scanned near the window. We could get something there."

"I see it. That's promising." Montgomery initiated the language analysis program. "Here we go."

Lea looked at Ryan and pointed to the screen. "We have the pattern for a forceful discussion or argument showing up here. We'll get the loudest phrases from what was said. We rarely get full sentences, but it's possible. So far we have what looks to be a woman's voice, higher pitch, and a man's voice, lower pitch. The woman said 'help out my nephew,' 'second chance,' and 'we have plenty money.' The man said, 'no' at triple her volume, followed by 'no principles,' 'nephew is . . . drunk . . . thief.' The woman said, 'he didn't steal. I gave him . . .' and 'mine to give.'"

"Does any of that mean anything to you?" Montgomery asked Ryan.

"No. I don't know anything about my great-grandmother's family other than that her mother was an Irish immigrant who arrived in the United States in the 1870s."

"How old was she when her husband died?" asked Lea.

"She was younger than he was, about 50," Ryan said. "Is there anything else in the data?"

Lea looked at the patterns and pointed to another area. "I'd bet this is singing."

Kamika stared at the spot. "Is that what that pattern means? I've seen that before."

"Looks like singing. Want to bet on what it is?" asked Montgomery with a twinkle in his eye. "I say it's 'Happy Birthday.'"

Lea smiled and shook her head. "No bet, but you're wrong. My guess is 'Auld Lang Syne.'"

Montgomery directed the program to analyze the area. "You win. Let's try this area next."

They waited, but this time the language program returned an error code.

"That's too jumbled to be analyzed. What was in that corner of the room?" asked Montgomery, pointing to the corner nearest the door.

Ryan stared for a moment at where Montgomery was pointing. "An old telephone was attached to the wall there."

"Lines then weren't always the best. People yelled to be heard, so we have jumbled noise left behind," said Lea.

Kamika had been studying the overall patterns and tapped the screen. "Mr. Montgomery, what is this spot here? It doesn't look like anything around it. It almost looks like a hole in the data. Was something hung on the wall there, blocking the sound absorption?"

"Huh. That's odd. The sound passed though and didn't experience the same bounce back or backscatter from the stone behind it." He paused, frowning in thought. Then a huge smile split his face. "I know what that is. It's a void. The data's telling us that the wall isn't solid behind the paneling there. It's a hidden compartment or a safe." He gave Ryan a questioning look. "Ever heard of a safe in here?"

"I've heard so many tales about this place, who knows what is true. We used to think the place was honeycombed with secret passages. Where is this hidden compartment?" Ryan scanned the paneling on the walls around him.

Lea pointed at the wall. "Tap the wall on your right, above the counter in the bar area, between the two middle shelves. The space looks like it measures twelve inches by twelve inches square."

Ryan began to gently rap on the paneling with the knuckle of his index finger.

"More to the left," Montgomery said.

Ryan obliged, and the sound of his tapping took on a hollow note. "Here! How do you think it opens?" He began pushing and probing the area with both hands.

"Look for a switch, button, or likely knothole," said Montgomery, looking over Ryan's shoulder for any possible mechanism.

Ryan ran his hands lightly over the surface of the shelf and then did the same on the underside. "I feel something." He bent to look beneath the shelf. "It's a latch. There. I got it."

He and Montgomery looked at the paneling expectantly, but nothing happened.

"It wouldn't be automated or electric. Try pushing on the panel or sliding it sideways," said Lea.

Ryan pressed the panel. It depressed inward slightly. He let go, and it popped open, swinging out on tiny hinges.

"An elegantly designed, spring-loaded door," said Montgomery, delighted.

"What's in it?" asked Kamika, dancing on her toes, trying to see around Montgomery's bulk and Ryan's height.

Ryan reached in his hand and pulled out a stack of slim books. He wiped the dust off the covers and opened the top one. "Diaries. This top one is from the 1950s, right before my great-grandmother's death."

"Does one cover the time of old Mr. Hanover's death?" Lea asked.

He flipped through the pile, looking at the starting and ending dates for each. A few dusty pieces of newspaper fell to the floor. "This one covers 1927 to 1932. It doesn't look like she wrote in the books daily. More like once or twice a month." He leaned over to pick up the papers that had fallen. "This is fabulous. This is my great-grandfather's obituary, and . . . this is an article about the embezzlement. Grandmother Mae clipped articles and put them in the diaries." He turned his amazement-filled eyes to Montgomery. "I can't believe we found these. Wait here. I want to show my wife." Ryan turned and trotted out of the room with the stack of dusty books in his hands.

While Montgomery and Lea were still watching Ryan's receding form vanish down the hall, Kamika moved closer to examine the compartment. "Hey, y'all. He missed something. I can see a small box. It must have been behind the stack of books." She reached her hand into the compartment and removed it.

The box was only about two inches square and hinged in the middle, like a jewelry box. Kamika forced the box open. Its rusty hinges resisted her efforts but finally gave way, popping open to reveal a large ring. An enormous red stone twinkled from a gold filigree setting.

Kamika jumped excitedly over to Lea. "Oh! Oh! I found treasure! Look at that ring. That stone is as wide as my finger. Is it a ruby?"

"I'm no gemologist, but it looks like one to me. The ring is old fashioned. It most likely predates lab-created gemstones," Montgomery said. "Those may be diamonds on the band, too." He pulled the ring out of its dusty box to look at it more closely. "The setting is 14-karat gold, according to the markings. Lea, check and make sure there's nothing else in that compartment." He gently reinserted the ring into the box.

Lea felt around the entire opening in the paneling, wiping the sides, top, and back wall. The space was a void created by removing a roughly square block of stone from the wall. The sides of the void were all stone. "Nothing else is in here."

Ryan's excited voice drifted into the room. He was coming back up the circular stairs talking quickly to his wife.

Wendy's disembodied voice said, "Show me where."

A moment later, Ryan and a stylish thirty-something woman with brown, wavy hair entered the room.

Ryan steered his wife to the shelving. "Look. Right there." He closed and reopened the hidden compartment.

"How great is that!" said his wife.

Montgomery interrupted Ryan as he started to show his wife how to manipulate the mechanism to open the panel. "We found something else." Montgomery held out his hand with the ring box open on it. "This was behind the stack of books."

"Holy . . . cow!" Ryan said in the manner of a dad who's trained himself to avoid cursing.

Wendy gently lifted the box out of Montgomery's hand and tugged the ring from inside. "That's . . . that's huge! Is it real?" She looked carefully at the stones in the band and at the brilliant, deeply red stone in its filigree setting.

Montgomery pointed to the markings on the band. "If you look here, you'll see that it says it's 14-karat gold, but I don't know anything about gemstones. You should get it appraised."

Wendy passed the ring to her husband to examine and turned to Lea and Kamika. "I'm Wendy Hanover." She offered them her hand and a pleasant smile. Lea and Kamika introduced themselves. Wendy returned her attention to her husband, who was still studying the ring. "We can take the ring into Austin and have it evaluated. I'll ask Ashley to do it."

Ryan looked up as if struck by another thought. "Did I miss anything else in the compartment? Or is this it?"

"I checked. It's empty," said Lea, enjoying the couple's enthusiasm.

Montgomery gestured to the books now in Ryan's hand. "Please skim or read the diary. Anything your great-grandmother wrote about her husband's death might be helpful. Look particularly at the time right before he died. See if she mentions any troubles they might be having, any money issues or debt.

Ryan glanced at the dusty volumes in his hand and then passed them to his wife. "Honey, would you care to read these? At least the volume from the late 1920s? You're a faster reader than I am. It may help solve our mystery here."

She accepted the stack and flipped one open. "Great-grandma Mae had lovely penmanship. I'd be happy to read them. A peek at life in the 1920s might be interesting. Do you think there's more to solve? Could our nighttime visitor have been looking for this ring? It could be valuable."

"Maybe," said Ryan. "We need to keep looking. Who knows what else might be in this castle?"

"Perhaps we should do a systematic search of all the rooms," Montgomery said.

Ryan surveyed the room around him with a speculative look. "Yes. With all this paneling, we could have hidden compartments in every room."

CHAPTER 4

MONTGOMERY GLANCED AT RYAN HANOVER. "Do you want us to do the emotional reading on this room? It might not add much to what we already know, but sometimes it can be useful."

Ryan nodded enthusiastically. "Go ahead. I wouldn't want to miss anything important."

Wendy walked toward the door and held up the books in her hand. "I'm going to take these books downstairs. I've got calls to make and work to do, but I'll make time to review them tonight." She looked at Montgomery with a satisfied smile. "I'm trying to sell my business—really the software I created, though they want my customers too—to a large conglomerate with interests in charter jet company software. They are considering a few other companies as well, but I think I have the strongest product. We're pretty sure my software has more functionality than the other options the buyer is considering, but we can't say for certain because we haven't seen the competition. Ashley and I are preparing to present my software."

Montgomery smiled and said, "Congratulations!"

Ryan winked at his wife. "You have this deal in your pocket. Your presentation will knock the others out of contention." As Wendy left the room, Ryan turned back to Montgomery. "How long do you think it will take to scan all the paneled areas in the castle?"

Montgomery did rough calculations in his head. "All of it? A couple days. If I bring in more equipment and we split up, we can cover the area faster."

"I can't wait to see what else we find." Ryan stood with his hands on his hips and smiled with satisfaction.

Montgomery turned to Lea. "Well, Lea, looks like we get to see the whole castle." He grinned at her, knowing he couldn't have offered a sweeter treat to a history buff who didn't have the time or money to go to Europe and see a castle in situ.

Lea rejoiced internally but held back her enthusiasm for Kamika's sake. Kamika looked as if she'd been offered torture instead of a gift. Lea suppressed a smile. "I'm happy to stay and help this evening if you need me, but Kamika has plans."

Montgomery burst out laughing at the look of horror plastered on Kamika's face. "It's Friday. Work until your shift ends, then go home."

He was rewarded with a relieved expression from Kamika. "Thank you," she said.

"Are either of you free to work tomorrow?" Montgomery looked questioningly at both women.

"Yes . . . ?" said Lea with an open question in her voice.

"Yes," said Kamika with less enthusiasm.

Montgomery turned and asked Ryan, "What time can we start tomorrow?"

"On Saturdays, we're slow to start in the morning, unless my son, Jack, has an early baseball game. Hang on a second." Ryan whipped out his phone and began to look for the information he needed. "Tomorrow Jack plays at 11:20 a.m. If you arrive by ten, we'll be ready for you. Either Wendy or I can take Jack to the game while the other stays here."

Montgomery glanced at Lea and received a quick nod of agreement from her, followed by a reluctant nod from Kamika. "That works for us. We'll start at the top and work our way down. I'll do the emotional scan on this room while Lea starts the sound-pattern scan on the next room. Kamika, I have a second set of equipment in my car. Could you bring it up?" He turned back to Ryan. "If you'd help her get the things in the dumbwaiter, we could complete a few more rooms before we call it quits for the day?"

"Happy to help," said Ryan.

Kamika inhaled sharply. "Whoa. Wait, wait, wait. Hang on a minute here." Her green eyes were popping out and a look of panic sprang to her face.

"What's wrong, Kamika?" Lea looked at her in surprise, wondering what had upset her friend. She barely finished the sentence before Montgomery chimed in, "What's up?"

Kamika focused on Ryan's face. Her corkscrew curls trembled on her shoulders. "Does this place have a dungeon? You know, one of those horrible holes in the floor where prisoners were left and forgotten. I saw this movie once where people's bones were left to rot in a dungeon under a castle."

Lea understood Kamika's sudden horror. Kamika was claustrophobic. "You mean an oubliette, a dungeon prison with only a trapdoor entrance in the ceiling above."

Kamika nodded.

Lea remembered the movie Kamika had mentioned. It was a sweeping historical epic that they'd watched together one Friday night. The dungeon scene in that historical drama had scared Kamika more than any nightmare creation inflicted upon a viewer during the goriest of horror movies, more than any carefully orchestrated suspense scene.

Ryan laughed, showing his bleached-white teeth, but Lea noticed that his eyes didn't join in. He looked uncomfortable for the first time since they'd found the diaries, his enthusiasm vanishing under a cloud. He looked away from them all before answering Kamika in a slow voice that sounded like a recitation of fact, with opinion withheld. "No, no dungeons. We have a wine cellar and an underground level to the building. As you may know, the Texas Hill Country sits on top of limestone into which groundwater has cut caves."

He paused, and Lea and Montgomery nodded assent. Kamika was still waiting, unconvinced about the dungeon.

Lea detected a sharp change in Ryan's mood and wondered what had caused it. Something about the basement bothered Ryan.

Ryan said, "When my great-grandparents brought the castle over, they had excavation done to install the underground level. The construction crew blasted out the limestone and found a natural cave right at the edge of the area they were clearing for the basement. They called in inspectors and engineers. When the cave was declared safe from collapse, they had a door from the basement added to access the cave. That area's the wine cellar since it's naturally cool. It's the only part of the building that wasn't original to the castle. One area of the basement may have been a prison, but it's not a hole in the ground and never was."

Lea could feel tension radiating from Ryan. He was trying to assuage Kamika's fears, but he was definitely withholding something regarding the basement. She asked, "What was the basement used for in 1929?" She was looking for a way to approach the issue obliquely, hoping a historical question wouldn't shut down his response.

"The basement was only used for storage in my great-grandfather's time. We think that he kept a large stock of black market alcohol there during the Prohibition era. We still need to replace the old electrical wiring down there. Until the work is done, my family and I are avoiding that space. Between the lack of light and rough floor, it's dangerous." Ryan relaxed as he answered Lea. She could see that whatever he was withholding didn't concern how the basement was used in the 1920s. Still, the basement was a topic of concern to him.

"I don't suppose the old man used the cave as a speakeasy for the locals like they did in Longhorn Cavern in the 1930s?" asked Montgomery with a laugh.

Ryan laughed, genuinely this time. "Not that I'm aware of, but I don't have anyone to ask. It might be large enough for a small party." He turned to Kamika. "Shall we retrieve your extra equipment?"

Kamika nodded tensely, not completely reassured about the basement.

Ryan led Kamika out of the room and down the well-worn stone stairs back to the ground floor.

❈

Lea walked into the master bedroom carrying the sound-scanning equipment and studied the room. The high-ceilinged space included a stone fireplace with a modern fireplace screen in front of it. A king-sized, antique-replica, four-poster bed was centered against one wall. Three walls in this room were stone. Paneling had been added to one wall with the light switch and a single electrical outlet. Ryan would have to add more wiring if he wanted more electrical access for gadgets and devices. On the ceiling, a black, thick cord emerged from the paneling and ran to a many-branched chandelier in the center of the room.

Lea was happy to be alone, however briefly. She took a moment to close her eyes and try to feel anything that the ancient stone might whisper. The imprinted history of the space enveloped her in an embrace. The room had seen many lives and many deaths. Lea sensed powerful men, centuries of them: youthful and mature, intelligent and obtuse, abstemious and indulgent, ambitious and indolent. This had been the personal domain of the lords of the castle.

The energy of each personality was layered in the stone, exuding a comforting ambience into the room. This wasn't the dwelling place of a long line of wicked, morally corrupt men. The men of the castle had apparently been overwhelmingly ethical with a personal code of honor, in spite of their various faults. They'd died of disease, injury, and old age in the room where they'd slept, at a time when death was a familiar fact of life, not something hidden away in hospitals and hospices.

Setting up the sound scanner, Lea worked methodically from one end of the paneled wall to the other. The analysis didn't take long. The room hadn't been used much in the time between the first Ryan Hanover's death and his wife's death more than twenty years later. The couple may have kept separate bedrooms, giving Mae no use for his room after his death. Finding the layer of sound Lea wanted was easy, but most of it was muddled, low-volume static. Little stood out for further analysis. Only by the door to the room did the data show a likely area for the language program to sort. In that area, a deep voice, male most likely, was found to have yelled, "can't find . . . cufflinks!" Lea decided that wasn't relevant to the issue at hand.

Kamika entered the room carrying an equipment bag. "Montgomery didn't find anything useful in the emotional energy scan on that first room, only a little furtiveness around the hidden compartment and general frustration around the desk. Ryan says he thinks his great-grandmother settled the household accounts in there at the desk, which explains the frustration. Did you get anything in here?"

"Not unless you count someone yelling that they couldn't find their cufflinks. I haven't done an emotion scan yet."

"I'll help. Montgomery is going to scan the kid's room next door." Kamika began extracting equipment from the bag and held out the emotional energy scanner for Lea to take. Lea repeated her slow sweep of the paneled wall, this time for emotional energy, while Kamika began the processing program.

"What do we have?" asked Lea as she finished the scan and returned to Kamika's side to watch the results appear.

"It says the 1920s layer shows anger, disbelief, and frustration. Maybe that's what old Mr. Hanover was feeling when he found out about the missing money."

Lea studied the data. "No guilt in the mix. That suggests he didn't steal the money himself, unless he was one of those people without a sense of guilt."

Montgomery popped his head in the door. "Lea, would you look at an analysis for me?"

"Sure. What's wrong?"

"I did the emotional energy scan in the son's room, which was Mae Hanover's room. The scanner is showing heavier levels of negativity than I've ever seen. I think it's picking up interference or backscatter from somewhere."

Lea took one step into the room Montgomery had been scanning and stopped as if she'd been slapped. "Oh!"

"What is it?" Montgomery scanned her face for clues.

Lea took a second to respond, taking in the wall of emotion that had hit her as she entered the room. "This room belonged to the lady of the castle, to generations of ladies of the castle. Is the scanner picking up grief, loss, sorrow, and pain?"

"Yes, and nothing else," said Montgomery. "How did you know?"

"After we're done with everything else, we should try a reset on this room. It won't work well on the stone, but even a little would be useful. The Hanovers should get some positivity infused into the paneling, too." She paused as the emotion in the room threatened to engulf her, causing her to clear her throat to keep her voice from cracking. Heat behind her eyelids forewarned coming tears. Lea forced herself to focus on Montgomery, who was waiting with a troubled look on his face.

Lea inhaled deeply to get herself under control. "This room saw dozens of women laboring to give birth without medication of any kind. Infant and maternal mortality was high, so this room saw lots of pain and death: babies born dead or who died minutes after birth, mothers who died in childbirth or within a few days of giving birth, and the pain of extended labor. There's great joy, too, but the babies who survived were outnumbered by the ones who died. Throw on top of that the stressed midwives, maids, and lords of the castle witnessing the death or viewing the dead bodies. It's a powerful emotional stamp."

As she spoke, Lea could see a basin of bloody water sitting by an ancient, low bed. An exhausted woman screamed in pain, trying to give birth. A gray-haired woman with bloody hands worked desperately to help deliver a baby in breech position. The vision passed quickly, but the emotions expended remained.

Kamika hung back outside the door. "Are there a ton of ghosts?"

"No, but so many horrifically painful and sorrowful scenes have played out in this room that it's like they're embedded in the space. The emotion is so powerful that I can see flashes of the people who felt them, though they're long gone."

Ryan trotted into the room. "Anything new?" His excitement and smile faded as he glanced from face to face and took in the worried expressions around him. "Did you find something bad?"

"Unsettling would be more accurate," Montgomery replied. "It's an atmosphere problem."

"What do you mean?" Ryan asked.

Lea noticed that Ryan was suddenly on edge, as he had been when they had discussed the basement.

"I'll let our historian explain," said Montgomery, nodding to Lea.

"Before we get into that, is your son comfortable sleeping in this room?" Lea asked.

Ryan looked surprised by the question. "No. He hasn't adjusted to the move yet. Most mornings we find him curled up at the foot of our bed. Why do you ask?"

"Your son may be having an issue with the room rather than trouble adjusting to the move," said Lea. She explained the history of the room and how the embedded emotions might be affecting the boy who slept in it.

Ryan paced a few steps and ran a hand through his thinning hair. "Can anything be done?"

"Yes," said Montgomery. "Situations like this are why I started my other company, Bad Vibes Removal Services. I can get you a list of services that we perform to make a space like this more livable for the current occupants. That's Kamika's specialty."

Ryan stared at the floor with his hands on his hips. He started to speak then stopped. Finally, he said, "Do you think you could tell me if something like that is the problem in the basement?"

Lea could hear the effort it took for him to speak and sensed the worry she'd noticed before when they had discussed the basement.

"What kind of problem are you having?" Montgomery spoke with a curious lift in his voice, alert. "You didn't mention anything previously."

"I was afraid you wouldn't believe what I said. I don't . . . I didn't believe it myself at first. But it's affecting my wife and son. My son says he won't go to the ground floor anymore because he's scared. He said something bad is down there, and it wants to hurt him. And Wendy has to force herself to go to the laundry room." Ryan looked at them, waiting for them to disbelieve him, but instead he found sympathy. Encouraged, he continued, "My wife says she saw a woman, too. The woman was dressed in old-fashioned clothes. She was crying and running down the stairs to the basement. Wendy saw her twice. The lighting is poor down there, and the floor isn't level, but that isn't what's keeping Wendy and Jack out of the basement."

Montgomery clapped Ryan on the shoulder. "Okay. We'll look into the matter. Lea here has a gift for detecting that kind of thing. We might be able to help. In the meantime, I'd have your son sleep in your room with you and your wife until you decide what you want to do about this room."

"Is the master bedroom okay?" Ryan asked. "If this room has seen such sorrow, wouldn't the other room be bad, too?"

"No, I've checked it," said Lea. "Although that room saw life and death and everything in between, the life outweighs the death. The good outweighs the bad. Your room has the comfortable ambience of the personalities of generations of ethical, powerful, and morally stable lords of the castle seeping from the walls. The men had their joys and sorrows, but the room reflects a good mix. Stepping in there is like putting on your favorite old slippers or sweater: old, tattered from having been through good times and bad, but comfortable."

Ryan heaved a sigh. "That's a relief. I'd hate to think Jack'd be uncomfortable everywhere in the castle." He looked around and surveyed the room. "This was Grandmother Mae's room. You didn't find any hidden compartments in here, did you?"

"Not so far. I need to take a look in that closet." Montgomery gestured to a door on the far wall. Drywall had been added, cutting a few feet off the width of the room in order to create a long, narrow closet. "We've only scanned the exterior of it so far. She may have had another safe hole built in there. We'll finish up in here. After that, it's up to you what you want us to do next."

Ryan glanced at his watch. "I need to explain the issue in here to my wife. She may have questions for you. I'll be back in a few minutes to let you know." He waved to them as he left the room.

After Ryan left, Montgomery turned to Lea. "What do you think of this story of a crying lady? Do you think it's a ghost?"

Lea shrugged. "I don't know. They may be seeing the energy imprint left behind by the woman. Someone crying, traumatized, running in fear would have expended a huge burst of emotional energy that may have imprinted itself on the castle. Wendy may be sensitive to the echo left behind. I noticed Ryan didn't mention that he'd seen the woman. He's not even mildly sensitive to imprinted emotional energies if this room had no impact on him. If I see the woman myself, I'll let you know what I think."

CHAPTER 5

As THEY FINISHED SCANNING THE INSIDE of the 1920s closet that had been added to the lady of the castle's chamber, the Hanovers returned.

Montgomery greeted them both with a nod. "We didn't find any additional information in this room. No hidden spaces or helpful conversations."

Wendy's worried glance wandered over to the stone walls of the room. "My husband says this room has, well, emotional problems. Hearing that makes me feel better about how tense I get when I come in here. I thought I was letting my imagination get the best of me." She smiled ruefully at them. "I've arranged for Jack to spend the night at my sister Carol's house, so you can stay and work as late as you want. She should be here to get him in twenty minutes or so. If you don't mind looking at the basement next, I'd appreciate it. This room makes me tense, but the basement makes my skin crawl. If residual emotional energy is the problem, the sooner we get it solved the better."

Montgomery gave her a reassuring smile. "We'd be happy to help. Lea's our specialist on diagnosing problem rooms, and Kamika's our expert on resetting and redesigning the emotional atmosphere in rooms. I've got a pamphlet you can look at to give you an idea of our services and how they work." Montgomery pulled the Bad Vibes Removal Services flyer of available package treatments for dwellings and businesses out of his equipment bag and handed it to her. "Given the stone construction, we won't be able to eliminate all traces of the past. Our techniques work best in more pliable substances, like wood and drywall. The history of a place like this is what gives it atmosphere and makes it unique. You wouldn't want to remove all traces of the history. However, it should be comfortable for you to live in it."

"If the stone holds energy history, why can't you eliminate it?" asked Ryan.

"The stone has absorbed energy over hundreds of years. We can add a top layer, but it would be sort of like painting over knotholes in wood without using primer. What's underneath will bleed through and overpower what little we put on top. Wood and wallboard are softer, and our static layer can permeate into them. Natural stone isn't as easily infused."

Wendy gave him a perplexed look. "So what can you do for us if the underlying emotions will always bleed through?"

"We can give a room an emotional interior design overhaul. Some people ask us to neutralize old emotional energy, leaving a room a blank slate. Here, since we can't give you a blank slate on the stone, we should be able to insert positive emotional sensory indicators to balance out the negative. We may even be able to overwhelm the negative and give the space a general sense of well-being by infusing positive emotion, adding scents, sounds, and color."

"Balancing the negative with positive sounds good to me," Wendy said.

Lea could see the worry still crinkling the corners of Wendy's eyes.

Kamika stepped forward. "Wendy, I'd be happy to figure out a reset for this room right now. I hate to think of your son having to be uncomfortable in here. I can write an estimate with options for you to review. Then I can do the reset tomorrow while Lea and Mr. Montgomery continue the investigation of the other rooms."

Relief flooded Wendy's face. "Wonderful! That would be perfect."

"I'll get to work here while y'all see to the basement," Kamika said cheerfully. Then as Ryan and Wendy began to study the atmosphere reset options in the pamphlet Montgomery had given them, she whispered to Lea, "I'm not sure I want to go down there until after the diagnosing work is done anyway."

Ashley appeared at the door. "It's five o'clock. I'm leaving for the evening, Wendy. I'll see you Monday."

"Okay," said Wendy. "Wait. Ashley, does this room bother you the way the basement does?"

Ashley stepped into the room and stood considering it. "This room? I haven't spent much time in here. The basement is creepier by far."

Ryan glanced at Lea, who thought he looked uncomfortable even discussing the matter. He said, "The room has . . . problems. We're going to try to fix that. They have equipment that they can use to make the room's atmosphere better, eliminate the bad vibes. We're going to see if we can fix the basement as well."

A look of recognition came into the young woman's face. "Oh! I've heard of that. Bad Vibes Removal. A friend told me that her mom had her apartment reset."

"That's my company," Montgomery said.

"Cool," said Ashley. "I thought you were a detective."

"We do both. You'd be surprised how often the two go hand in hand," he said.

Ashley nodded and turned to leave.

Wendy called after her, "Goodbye, Ashley. Thanks for your help today."

"Bye," Ashley said over her shoulder.

Montgomery rubbed his hands together. "Shall we proceed to the basement?"

Kamika was tapping away at her tablet but glanced up as he spoke. "Y'all go ahead. I'm staying right here."

Lea, Montgomery, and the Hanovers descended the spiral stair to the ground floor space that had been converted into a garage. Ryan led them past his parked, plugged-in electric car and beyond the ping-pong and pool tables to a narrow stairway.

Lea noticed a newly installed railing that would prevent them from walking off the edge into the hole in the floor made by the stairs' opening. The stairs themselves were barely wide enough for one person to go down. A large man like Montgomery would have both shoulders almost rubbing the stone on either side as he descended.

Near the head of the stairs stood double doors leading, if Lea remembered correctly, to the laundry room. If the crying woman had run down these stairs, it was no wonder that Wendy was nervous about coming into the laundry room. "Does the dumbwaiter come all the way down here, Ryan?" she asked.

"Yes, it ends in the laundry room over there." He pointed to the double doors, confirming Lea's memory of the plans.

Wendy stood behind Lea and Montgomery, as far from the stairs as she could get but still be close enough to converse. Lea could see her glancing nervously to the stairs and back to her husband.

Lea could feel the heavy history of the building, the imprint of hundreds of people who had lived and worked in the ground floor, pressing against her. She could see that Wendy was nervous but didn't feel anything that might cause such a reaction. Puzzled, Lea moved closer to the top of the narrow stairwell. She set one foot on the first step, preparing to descend, and a wall of emotion hit her. Here, radiating up into her face, was panic, fear, and, most strikingly, death. While the ground floor workspace belonged to a world of workaday life, the space beneath it was something else entirely.

Lea stepped back quickly, away from the stairs, and found Wendy watching her.

"You feel it too, don't you?" Wendy said. "Going down those steps makes me feel ill, uneasy, and even queasy. I break into a sweat the second I step right where you were standing. Ashley says it makes her uncomfortable, but not anywhere near the degree it bothers me."

Lea took a deep breath to shake off her fear and attempted to smile. "I feel it too. You must be almost as sensitive to atmosphere as I am."

"I'm the opposite, then," said Ryan. "I don't feel a thing on those stairs."

"Not everyone does," Mr. Montgomery said. "I invented the equipment to find and identify the energy signatures left behind by speech and emotion

53

as a crime-solving tool, looking at the issue in terms of energy, frequency, vibration, and the movement of waves through space. The human aspect of it didn't occur to me until later. I've only been uncomfortable in a room once or twice in my whole life. At the time, I didn't understand the cause. Once I realized that the imprinted energies were a tangible, daily problem for some people, I started Bad Vibes Removal Services to put my equipment to use while I work to get law enforcement agencies to accept the technology for its effectiveness in solving crime."

Ryan stood with his hands on his hips and nodded appreciatively. "Getting the public familiar with the technology can only help in your battle to get law enforcement on board, too."

Lea turned from the stairs and looked around the huge, open ground floor space. "Where were you when you saw the woman, Wendy?"

Wendy pointed at the closed doors to the laundry room. "I was starting a load of laundry in the washing machine with the doors to the laundry room open. I had an impression of movement out of the corner of my eye, as if someone were running across this space and toward these stairs. I thought it was Jack playing, so I turned to tell him to stay out of the basement until we add better lights. As I turned, I saw the back of a woman vanishing down the steps. I heard a sobbing cry. When I opened my mouth to ask who she was—at first, I thought she was a real person, someone who had run into the garage from the yard—she turned as if to see someone following her. She was terrified, her eyes so big I could see the whites all the way around the dark pupils. The pupils were so dilated that I couldn't see an iris around them. Her dark hair was braided. Her headscarf or kerchief was falling off, exposing her hair. She wore a brown dress, with layered skirts. Her mouth was open in a wild, screaming wail. Then she vanished on the stairs into the darkness below."

Lea was stunned by the amount of detail Wendy had given. "Could you actually hear her?"

Wendy shuddered, hugging her arms around her torso. "I don't know. I sensed terror, and with her mouth open, maybe my mind filled in the rest."

Montgomery peered into the dark space at the bottom of the stairs. "Can we go down?"

Ryan spread his hands toward the stairs in a welcome gesture. "Go ahead. There are two single, bald bulbs hanging from the ceiling, from electrical wiring added in the 1920s. We want to upgrade the wiring and install several fixtures to improve the lighting. As I mentioned before, the floor is stone and isn't level. It's a tripping hazard."

"We have extra lighting equipment in the van. If it's too dark, we can set up portable lights," said Montgomery.

"Is the entire space stonework? Is there woodwork or drywall?" Lea asked.

"They added a door between the original basement and the limestone cave used as a wine cellar. Other than that, the walls, floor, and ceiling are all stone in the main room. The limestone cave has a hardwood floor and shelving my great-grandfather added. Is that a problem?" Ryan asked.

Montgomery shifted his bulk, squatting to look down the narrow stairs. "Well, it means we won't be able to get anything from the sound reader in the main area.

The emotional energy scanner may pick up too much interference to distinguish between different periods. We can scan the floor and shelves in the cave for anything related to old Mr. Hanover's time."

"Can you do anything about the woman?" asked Wendy, tucking her wavy, brown hair nervously behind her ears and frowning pensively.

"I don't know yet. We'll have to see. That's Lea's area of expertise."

The Hanovers both looked at Lea with questioning expressions. Lea froze a little under their scrutiny. She hated discussing the work she did with ghosts. She patted her dark hair, reflexively checking to see if any strands had escaped the Roman-style cloth on her head. "If I can do anything, I'll let you know. Do you mind if I go down now?" Lea pointed to the darkness below her.

Wendy stepped back as Lea moved forward. "Be my guest."

Lea walked into a dense wall of panic and fear that got more uncomfortable with each step she took. Her skin began to crawl, and the hair on her neck stood up. Montgomery followed behind her with the Hanovers at the rear.

As she reached the bottom step, Ryan called from above, "The wall to your left has a light switch."

Lea put out her hand and felt cool, smooth stone and moved forward into the basement, sliding her hand along the wall in search of the switch. At last her hand found the switch plate. She flicked on the light, which was a single, low-watt bulb hanging above the base of the stairs. It illuminated only a fraction of the space before her. Beyond the ring of light, Lea could tell that the space extended, but she couldn't see how far.

Ryan brushed past Lea into the darkness. "The next switch is on the far wall by the door to the wine cellar section."

A second later, another bulb lit, adding another modicum of light to the basement.

With both bulbs lit, Lea could see a circular pattern on the floor on one side of the room. These stones didn't match the rest of the floor. "Was that where the well was in the original castle?" she asked, pointing to the spot.

Ryan walked over and stood on the circle of stone. "Yes. Since they didn't need to put in a well when they rebuilt the castle, they got some local stone to fill in the space."

Wendy emerged from the narrow stair and stood on the bottom step. "This place gives me the creeps. Look, I'm getting goose bumps." She held out her arm.

"This space even makes me a little uneasy," said Montgomery with a note of surprise.

Lea felt along the wall with her hands, moving out of the lighted area to try finding the end of the room. "Montgomery, do you have a flashlight?"

"Yes, hang on." Montgomery unsnapped a small but powerful light from his belt and gave it to Lea. "We're going to need the portable lights in the van. Those two bulbs are almost useless."

"Definitely." The narrow beam illuminated small areas of the wall intensely. Lea studied the stone walls, examining holes and markings. "This side of the room was a dungeon. A place to punish criminals and hold captured enemies. I'm almost certain people were chained here. See these holes in the stone?" She pointed the light at several spots running along the wall at about the height of her head. "The rust stains on the stone indicate something iron was bolted in there. Bits of broken metal are still embedded in the wall in some places. I suspect that people were whipped here and left chained for long periods. The negative emotional energy output would have been extraordinary: fear, hate, pain, humiliation, with a desire for vengeance and a touch of sadistic pleasure. The history of the room is quite dark," Lea said to Montgomery.

He looked at Lea with his eyebrows up. "Any ideas for our crying woman?"

"She isn't here right now. If it isn't a ghost but an imprint of an event that Wendy is sensing, we may not be able to do much but cover over it with positive. We could add infused flooring, infused wallboards, and give the stone a good coat. In any case, only generations of positive emotion could cancel out what's down here. For the time being, annual reinfusions of positive energy, soothing scents, bright colors, good lighting, and cheerful music would reduce the creepy factor and make the place usable," said Lea before turning to Wendy. "You said Jack felt something, too?"

She nodded, "He felt like something was coming in the garage. He won't play ping-pong with friends anymore. Ryan thinks he freaked himself out, that he's being anxious, but I felt it, too, when I saw the woman."

"Okay." Lea considered the matter. Maybe both mother and son were sensitive to echoes from the past, the imprint of an emotional scene left for all time, but to varying degrees. Jack wasn't sensitive enough to see her, but he felt her. Then again, the ghost might not be confined to the castle. "I'm going to have to give this one some thought. If you see the woman again, note the time and where you see her. If it's a pattern of some sort, something time dependent, we may not be here at the right time to catch her act."

"Okay." She pulled out her phone and looked at the time. "It's 5:20 p.m. now. Carol should be here to pick up Jack any minute. I need to get back upstairs." She looked around skittishly. "If I had to guess, I'd say I saw the woman around eight o'clock one night. Jack told me he saw her late one evening as well. Maybe we're too early."

"Do you want to scan the floor and shelves in the cave area tonight?" Lea asked Montgomery.

"Let's do it," he said. "By the time we finish, maybe it will be late enough for our ghostly woman to appear."

"I've got extension cords if you need them," Ryan said.

"That's not necessary. We have cords in the van with the lights. I'll go check on Kamika. She had plans tonight, so I'll send her home before I bring the lights down," said Montgomery.

Lea wandered over to the door to the wine cellar and pulled. The door didn't open. "Do we need a key to this door?" she asked over her shoulder.

"That door sticks because of the natural humidity in the cave. Yank it hard, and it should open," said Ryan as he turned to go back up the stairs with Montgomery and his wife.

Lea left the door and followed the others, pausing at the bottom of the stairs to look back into what had once been a torture chamber. Her skin was crawling. Evil had left an indelible mark.

In a flash, she could see a man in a tattered shirt with both hands in manacles. The manacles were attached to chains that were bolted into the wall by his head. His face was streaked with dirt and dried blood. A wound on his temple was caked with dried blood and matted blonde hair. In spite of his condition, his eyes were bright blue and defiant. His jaw was set firmly.

Lea blinked, and the man's image was gone. She wondered if he had been a rival soldier captured in battle, or a marauding Viking. He seemed too self-assured and defiant to be a common criminal. Lea hastened up the stairs to help Montgomery get the equipment they would need to scan the wine cellar.

In the garage, Lea saw Wendy chatting with another woman. An indefinable air of similarity between them, something in the way they moved and stood, gave away their relationship. Lea thought this must be the sister, Carol.

Jack emerged from the stairs into the main level of the house. He carried a small backpack-style suitcase. "Hi, Aunt Carol!" he yelled, confirming Lea's assumption.

The woman turned with Wendy and answered him, "Hi, Jack. Are you ready to go?"

"Yes. Where's Kevin?"

"He's at Tae Kwon Do. He should get to my house at the same time we do."

"Oh, okay," said Jack with some disappointment in his voice.

His mother hugged him. "Be good for Aunt Carol. I'll see you tomorrow."

"Bye!" he said, pulling away from his mother and rushing to the waiting minivan.

Carol laughed. "He's ready, all right. I'll see you tomorrow," she said to her sister with a wave. Then she walked quickly down the drive after Jack.

Wendy saw Lea. "Ryan and Montgomery went to get lighting equipment. You can wait here if you want. I'm going back inside before our ghostly lady decides to show herself again."

Lea looked around at the large open space around her that was now only vaguely subdivided into garage, game area, and laundry space. Once, many people had labored here doing chores for the castle. The space would have been teeming with activity. The stairs to the space below seemed innocuous from a distance.

Lea sighed. She didn't want to go back into that fog of painful emotion, but she wanted to look at the wine cellar. She walked slowly across the garage, took a deep breath, and, ready to investigate, stepped into the tumultuous, emotional haze emanating from below.

CHAPTER 6

WALKING SWIFTLY DOWN THE STAIRS, STEELING her nerves against the painful atmosphere, Lea crossed the dungeon and found the door to the wine cellar. As before, it didn't open at her pull. Lea yanked the door hard. The hinges squealed slightly, and the door came open. Lea leaped through the door and pulled it sharply closed behind her to block out the horror of the dungeon.

She gulped a deep breath of moist cave air. She hadn't realized she was holding her breath in the dungeon area, as if not breathing the air might somehow limit her exposure to the pain seeping from the walls. Lea shuddered and shook off the sense of terror that was building in her stomach, trying to fight down the anxiety. She couldn't understand the strength of her response. Even the blood-soaked ground around the Alamo, where hundreds had died and then all surviving defenders were executed, didn't cause this severe a reaction. The horrors in the dungeon felt fresh, in spite of the passage of hundreds of years. Could that room have seen more recent horrors?

Using the flashlight, Lea found a wall switch. An obsolete incandescent bulb in the center of the ceiling flickered a moment before coming to life. Lea took a few steps forward into the room, taking deep breaths as her heart rate slowed. The atmosphere in the cave wasn't rife with horrors like the dungeon had been. This space exuded a sense of self-satisfaction. Lea wondered if she was feeling old Mr. Hanover's appreciation for his wine collection. Thanks to plentiful wood flooring and shelves, this room was much more likely to reveal a few of its secrets.

A decades-old, straight-backed wooden chair with a broken woven seat stood against the wall by the door. A dozen or so crumbling wine crates in a precariously stacked pile littered the corner opposite the door. Shelving, warped with age and moisture and covered with cobwebs, lined most of walls on either side of Lea. A rusty hammer head with a broken handle lay in the center of the wooden floor. A sconce, missing its candle, hung on one wall.

"Lea? Where are you?" Montgomery's muffled voice floated through the door from the dungeon room.

She walked to the door, jerked it open, and said, "I'm here."

Montgomery joined her, carrying two large directional lamps and an orange extension cord looped around his right shoulder. He paused to survey the space. "Look at this dust. This place hasn't seen much use since the 1950s. That will be good for sound-pattern analysis. Can you set up these lamps while I get the rest of the equipment?" He kept his voice low, trying not to contaminate the room.

"Sure." She took the lamps from him and relieved him of the extension cord. "Where is the closest outlet for this cord?"

63

"Probably back up the stairs to the laundry room. Sorry about that. I forgot to unroll it as I came down. Can you handle hooking things up on this end and unrolling the cord back to the laundry room while I get the last light?

"Sure." She accepted the looped roll of cord and threw it over her own shoulder.

Montgomery trotted back the way he'd come.

Lea plugged the lamps to the cord and then slowly unrolled the rest of the length back through the dungeon, up the stairs, and into the laundry room. The hairs on her arms stood on end, and her stomach was knotted again, but she tried to shake it off.

As she bent to plug the cord into the outlet, her peripheral vision caught movement outside the laundry room door. She turned, expecting to see Montgomery returning with the scanning equipment, but her greeting froze in her throat as she saw the figure of a woman running, and yet not running, toward the stairs.

The woman's skirts billowed as she spun, looking frantically around her, calling out. She was desperate to find someone. Panic turned to terror as she looked around and screamed at something she'd seen coming toward her. Her mouth was open wide. Her teeth were yellow, and two were missing on the bottom right side.

Her scream echoed off the stone walls and sent a chill down Lea's spine. The woman began to run again and reached the top of the stairs before Lea pulled herself together and jumped from her crouched position by the laundry room outlet.

"Wait! Please wait!"

The woman continued down the stairs, vanishing into the darkness below, showing no signs of having heard Lea.

Lea ran after her, sprinting through tingling air, which was so full of terror that cold enveloped her as she moved. Goose bumps rose on her skin, and her throat constricted with fear.

"Wait! Come back!" Lea called as she reached the stairs to the dungeon. She forced herself to plunge through the now painfully thick morass of emotion after the woman.

Lea stopped in the dungeon, engulfed in fear, and spun around searching, but the woman was gone. She tried to remember what the woman had been saying. Could it have been a name? Yes: It had been Angus. The woman was looking for someone named Angus. She'd descended the stairs of the dungeon still looking for him.

Suddenly, Lea's chest constricted, making her breathing shallow and more difficult. The feeling in the air changed from terror to something even worse. Lea felt malevolence swallow her as she backed against the stone wall and watched the stairs, afraid of what might be coming next.

A pair of brown-shod feet appeared, and Lea began to breathe again as the rest of Montgomery's bulky form clunked down the stairs.

"Kamika is leaving. She's upstairs if you want to say goodbye," he said, coming even with her and stopping.

Lea tried to speak but had to clear her throat before she could answer. "Kamika? Okay. I need a second." Her knees began to shake as the adrenaline coursing through her body took effect. She leaned heavily against the wall, trying not to collapse.

"What's wrong? Are you okay?" Montgomery dropped the equipment bags and lamp case and reached out to stabilize Lea as she began to sink to the stone floor.

"I'm okay. It's my fight-or-flight reflex in overdrive."

"What happened?"

"I saw the crying woman when I went to plug in the extension cord. She ran through the ground floor garage area searching for someone, calling the name Angus. She ran down the stairs, still looking for him but in complete terror of something that was coming after her. I followed her down here, but she vanished. Then I felt something evil coming after her. Whatever it was never appeared. The sensation vanished when you came down the stairs. I hope the feeling of the evil is all that remains and that nothing was actually coming."

"So there is a ghost?"

"There's something. We may be seeing an echo being reenacted over and over again. I tried to speak to the woman, but she gave no indication that she heard me at all. The souls in question may be long gone."

"That's good," said Montgomery with a grin. "Unless you speak ancient Irish, or Gaelic, or Celtic, or whatever it's called, we have no way to communicate with a trapped soul."

Lea laughed. Her heart was slowly returning to a normal rhythm, and the shaking in her knees had stopped.

Montgomery offered his mitt-like hand to help her to her feet. Lea took his hand and was lifted by Montgomery's powerful grip. "What time is it?"

Montgomery glanced at his wrist. "It's five-thirty. Let's go back to the ground level until you catch your breath." They began to ascend the stairs, Montgomery following Lea.

Lea took a shaky breath. "I wonder if this echo plays out all the time or only in the evenings, or only under certain conditions. Perhaps it's always here, but you have to be alone with your thoughts to catch it. I don't know how this works—if there's logic to it, if it's random. I can see why Wendy and Jack don't like to come down here. The experience was absolutely terrifying."

"I'm not sure how to eradicate an echo in space. We'll have to give it some thought," said Montgomery. They emerged at the top of the stairs.

"Lea! I saw her!" Kamika's voice, filled with horror and barely a whisper, floated to Lea's ears from the game room.

Lea turned to see Kamika trembling by the ping-pong table, one hand grasping the table for support, the other clutched to her chest. Lea ran to her.

Kamika grabbed Lea and held on tight.

"Are you okay?" asked Lea.

"That was the most horrifying thing I've ever felt in my life. You know those haunted houses that scare people at Halloween? They've got nothing on this woman and whatever is following her. And she was yelling. I could hear her. How can you see ghosts all the time and not have a heart attack? I thought I would die of fright. I never want to see anything like that again." Kamika's whole body was still shaking.

Montgomery asked eagerly, "Could you understand what she was saying?"

Kamika looked blank. "Understand her?" She paused. "I could repeat what she said, but I didn't understand her. I speak a few languages, but ancient Irish, or whatever that was, isn't one of them."

Montgomery smiled. "No. But you have a good ear for language, so you can repeat it. Lea, could you repeat what the woman said?"

"No, nothing but the name Angus. Everything else was gibberish to me." She could see Montgomery had an idea, but what it was she couldn't imagine. "What are you thinking?"

"If Kamika can repeat what she heard, I could record it," said Montgomery.

"How will that help?" asked Kamika.

Montgomery laughed. "We could get it translated by someone who does understand ancient Irish."

"The university might have someone," said Lea. "I'm not sure that will help us get rid of the ghost though. We still can't talk back to her."

"One step at a time," said Montgomery enigmatically.

Lea was sure he had a plan forming, but he apparently wasn't going to reveal it, not yet.

Montgomery pointed down the driveway out the open garage door. "Kamika, you're going to be late for your double date, and I see that the ride you ordered has arrived."

Kamika squealed. "I have to go now! I'm fine. I'll see you tomorrow." She raced out through the open garage, down the driveway to a waiting car.

"Don't forget what the woman said," Montgomery called after her.

"Forget? Are you kidding? I'll be hearing it in my sleep tonight," Kamika yelled over her shoulder, barely breaking her stride to answer.

Montgomery laughed and turned to Lea. "Let's get started on the wine cellar. We still have to finish searching the castle for Ryan and find out who has been breaking in. None of which concerns a medieval ghost story."

Lea looked toward the dungeon stairs. At least the analysis of the wine cellar would give her something else to think about so she could temporarily forget the crying woman. "The shelving is going to be a pain," she said, forcing herself to focus on the job at hand.

"Scan the back wall of the shelves. If we find something interesting there, we can go back and do the top and bottom surfaces of each individual shelf," said Montgomery.

They walked single file back down the stairs. Lea shuddered as the pain-filled, violent atmosphere engulfed her. At least now she knew why the terror still felt so fresh.

She moved through the dungeon space at a trot and yanked hard to open the recalcitrant wine cellar door. The damp wine cellar lay before her, her own footprints mixed with the other sets on the floor. "Hang on," she said and paused in the doorway.

Montgomery stopped behind her.

"What is it?" he asked.

She pointed down to the plank flooring. "The floor is the largest wooden surface in here."

Montgomery nodded. "We can start with it instead of the shelves. You prep the analysis programs, and I'll scan." Montgomery handed her his tablet.

"Got it."

He turned on the scanner. "Sound first, then emotional energy."

Lea launched the necessary programs. "Ready when you are."

Montgomery began to walk the room from side to side at a slow, steady pace, carefully scanning the floor, moving the broken chair and other small objects out of his way as he came to them. After ten minutes, he'd completed a scanning pass over the entire floor.

Lea watched the data compile, looking for likely spots to examine more closely. Montgomery joined her.

Lea pointed to the scan results. "This corner looks promising."

"Yep. Let's see what we have."

The program went to work comparing the patterns left in the wood to known words.

"Yes!" said Montgomery, as the words began to appear. "Two voices. Very loud discussion." He read the pieces of conversation as the program found them. "The first voice said, 'Pay up what you owe. Phil . . . patience,' and 'Use poison. Put . . . in his drink . . . old lady will inherit . . . softer touch . . . One month . . . Do it or B . . . removing fingers one by one!' The second voice said, 'Can't. Don't have it! Won't give . . . more . . . suspects I took . . .'" Montgomery smiled. "That's an interesting conversation to have in the basement."

"Mr. Hanover was probably helped to his heart attack with poison. Someone, probably that nephew of Mae's, hoped to talk Mae out of the money," said Lea. "If no one suspected poison, the signs of murder may have been missed."

"While disturbing, this is ancient history. It doesn't tell us anything about what's going on right now. Nothing hints at a hidden treasure to be found. Instead, it looks like someone in the house other than old Hanover and his wife took the money. That suggests no hidden hoard of cash will be in the house." Montgomery clicked to expand an area for closer analysis.

"Yeah, but whoever's searching the house doesn't know that. The owners don't even know that yet." Lea watched him examine the data. "That area might have a word or two," she said as he paused over a spot.

"I'm checking it now," he said.

The program completed its task, and Montgomery and Lea gaped at the words that appeared.

"Valuables hidden . . . somewhere."

Lea looked around and correlated the data points to the room around them. "That's by that shelf against the wall."

"Let's scan the shelf for sounds to see if we get any more words in that area. Then we can do the emotional energy reading. We'll look for voids in the walls as we go." Montgomery lifted his equipment and moved across the room as the door squealed open. Ryan and his wife appeared.

Montgomery nodded to the couple. "Perfect timing. We might have something new for you. I'm going to scan that shelf. Lea, show them what we found while I do the scan."

Lea explained the findings quickly, then turned to watch Montgomery finish his sound scan of the back wall of the shelf. He switched scanners and did the emotional energy reading, skipping the surfaces of the shelves themselves.

"I'll do the shelves if we think it will add to what we've got, but we may not need to do them," Montgomery told the Hanovers.

"It's compiling now, and I do see a void," said Lea, excitement creeping into her voice.

"Where?" asked Montgomery, examining the shelves closely.

"Down at the bottom."

Montgomery got on his hands and knees to examine the bottom shelf. "I don't see anything." He ran his fingers over the shelf, feeling for a button or catch. "Nothing yet. How large is the void?"

Lea looked at the data, "A lot bigger than the one upstairs: three feet square easily. It may cover most of the bottom half of the central shelf unit."

Montgomery glanced up at her. "Any more dialogue?"

She clicked back to the other program. "I'll check."

Ryan moved over beside Montgomery and began examining the shelf with him. "Let's try to shift this whole shelf," Ryan said.

Lea interrupted, "I don't see anything on the sound scan, but be careful. The emotional energy scan is showing guilt there."

"Whatever they were doing almost a hundred years ago is unlikely to hurt us today," said Montgomery.

The men each grabbed a side of the shelf, which was made of heavy oak boards.

"Ready? On three. One, two, three," Ryan said.

Both men grunted as they tried to pull the shelf away from the wall. It refused to budge.

"Wait a minute, Ryan. I have an idea. Lea, could you move that lamp over here?" Montgomery said, directing her to one side of the shelf.

Lea repositioned the lamp. Montgomery ran his fingers along the back where the shelf met the wall of the cave.

"This side may be a hinge," he continued. "It's attached to the wall. The whole shelf may be a door. If this is the hinge side, it may have a release somewhere near you, Ryan."

Wendy and her husband both began a careful inspection of the shelf.

Lea, standing across the room and looking at the whole wall, considered the problem. "Check the inside corners of the shelves."

Ryan crouched by the bottom shelf. "There's something in this corner. It doesn't slide. Oh, it's a button. I pushed it in."

"That did it," Montgomery said. He and Ryan grabbed the shelf, which now swung open like a door, revealing a natural opening in the limestone wall behind it. The opening was only hip high to Montgomery.

CHAPTER 7

Lea pulled the lamp closer to the opening.
Montgomery and Ryan crouched to look into the
darkness beyond.

"It's another room to the cave, smaller, like a storage
closet. Lea, hand me the flashlight," Montgomery said.

Lea passed the flashlight over quickly. Montgomery
aimed the light into the interior of the newly
discovered space.

Ryan peered over Montgomery's shoulder. "Is that
a trunk?"

"Yep," Montgomery said.

Ryan dropped to his knees and scooted into the
void. "The space is tall enough for me to stand, barely.
The floor is natural stone, but it's been hewn out. The
whole area is only a little bigger than a coat closet. Oh,
it's not one trunk, but two. There's a second behind
the first."

Montgomery remained crouched by the opening in
the wall. "There isn't enough room in there for me to
join you. Are the trunks locked?"

Ryan's muffled voice answered, "Yes. I'm going to try to push one out to you."

Lea could hear a scraping noise. The rasping of metal against stone made her skin crawl.

Montgomery reached forward and pulled an old travel trunk out of the space and pushed it in front of Wendy.

Wendy ran her hand over the grimy lid, exposing the initials *R. O. H.* intertwined in ornate black calligraphy on a copper or brass plate that had turned green. She knelt to examine the lock.

Following more scraping noises, Ryan edged a second chest matching the first into the mouth of the opening. Montgomery pulled the second trunk out as well. Then Ryan reappeared, duck-walking out of the low space.

Montgomery examined the lock on the second trunk. "Did they give you any odd keys when you inherited the castle?" he asked the Hanovers.

"The lawyer in charge of the estate gave me a key ring with an assortment of keys. It's upstairs. I'll get it." Ryan trotted out the door. The sounds of his feet pounding on the old stone stairs echoed back to those who remained in the room.

Wendy gave Montgomery a triumphant smile. "Maybe we've found the treasure, whatever it is that someone has been trying to find. If we announce it to the neighborhood, post it online, maybe the person who has been breaking in will give up."

"I hope you're right," said Montgomery as he examined the sides and bottoms of the trunks, "but whoever was searching the house never came down here. The grime on the shelves hadn't even been disturbed. I'd have thought someone looking for treasure would start down here, rather than risking the inside of the castle first. Here, under the garage, in an area that's accessible from the outside via the garage door, would have been the first place to search."

Wendy frowned. "You have a point, but maybe our searcher isn't the most logical person."

Ryan returned with a ring of keys jingling in his hand. "I know which ones go to doors around the house, since I tried them all and labeled them. That only leaves us five to try on the trunks. Hopefully, one or two will work for us."

Montgomery stood aside as Ryan began fitting keys into one of the trunks.

Lea, Montgomery, and Wendy stood over him and watched as he inserted key after key until at last one clicked into place and turned.

"Open sesame," said Ryan with a laugh as he tugged the trunk lid open. The hinges were green and encrusted with oxidation and refused to give easily.

Montgomery plucked the broken hammer head from the floor and banged on the hinges a few times. Finally, the hinges moved. Ryan pushed the trunk open.

Large, graying linen clothes were wrapped carefully around several small items in the bottom of the trunk. Wendy lifted one bundle and unwrapped it, revealing a tarnished silver tea pot. Ryan switched his attention to the next trunk.

Montgomery and Lea stood back watching.

Wendy gestured for them to come closer. "Help me unwrap this stuff."

Lea reached into the trunk and came out with a silver creamer.

Montgomery found a sugar bowl.

Wendy unwrapped a large oval tray. "We have a silver tea service in here." She set the pieces on the tray on the floor.

Lea selected another bundle. "These are silver serving forks and spoons."

Montgomery held up a decorative glass box. "This one isn't silver. It's a jewelry box." He flicked open the tiny hasp and raised the lid. "It's got three rings inside. If the stones are real, they look to be sapphire, emerald, and the last has multiple smaller stones, possibly diamonds."

Ryan had been laboring over the second trunk. "I've got this next trunk lid loose." He pushed it open.

Three oblong packages wrapped in brown paper leaned against each other, filling the trunk.

Ryan pulled the brown paper loose from one package, revealing an oil painting in a heavy, oak frame, roughly eighteen inches long by twelve inches high. The canvas depicted a pointillist landscape. The other two packages were unwrapped to reveal neo-impressionist paintings.

Ryan squinted to read the nameplate on the frame. "I don't recognize the name on this one. It says *Lemmen*."

"I've heard that name," said Lea. "We can do some quick Internet research."

"Let's take this stuff upstairs to the kitchen," Wendy said as she shifted her feet toward the door. "I want to get out of here."

Lea heard her anxiety and looked at the time on her phone—almost seven p.m. "Wendy, relax. Kamika and I saw the crying woman earlier this evening. Maybe she's done for the day."

Fear flashed across the woman's face as she looked at Lea. "You saw her, too?"

Lea could sympathize with her fear. "She was running for her life from some terrible evil that was following her. It scared me to death. I tried to speak to her, but she didn't respond."

"Can we discuss this upstairs?" Wendy said. "I don't want to be down here if she decides to put on an encore."

Lea glanced nervously toward the dungeon. "Has she ever appeared twice in one day?"

Wendy stooped to gather several silver pieces into her arms. "I haven't stuck around to find out."

"Good plan," said Lea, stooping to retrieve a painting.

Leaving the trunks in place, they collected the rest of the "treasure" into their arms and took it to the kitchen for closer examination. Over coffee and cookies, they discussed the sound results from the cellar.

"Old Mr. Hanover wasn't willing to give someone any more money to pay debts. This person thought getting it out of your great-grandmother Mae might be easier. This person may have poisoned Mr. Hanover. If this person was Mae's nephew, maybe he was the embezzler as well."

Ryan pursed his lips together in thought. "Should we go to the police? What can we do?"

Montgomery sipped his drink and thought for a moment before he answered. "At this point, we *could* exhume your great-grandfather's body for testing. We might find evidence of poisoning. However, that would be an expensive project on a cold case in which all the suspects died ages ago. What would you hope to achieve by it?"

Ryan frowned in thought. "I suppose I want to iden-tify the person who killed him. Then I could research that person to see if he was in a position to embezzle from the company. Exhuming the body would be a possibility, but I don't know if I want to do that."

"Those diaries may have additional information on what was going on at the time of your ancestor's death," Lea said. "Mae Hanover might have written down her nephew's name.

"I'll read the diaries," Wendy said.

Montgomery gestured to the paintings and tea service. "You'll need to put the things we found today in a safe place. We still don't know who has been searching this place or how they are getting inside. All this could be what someone is trying to find. Along with the ring we found this morning, we discovered a pretty tidy little treasure. But we have no way of knowing if this is what the person wants. Did you complete the security upgrades that you mentioned to me?"

"I'm still working on the whole system, but I've added cameras and motion sensors. We'll know if anyone comes around," said Ryan.

"That's a relief. The idea of someone sneaking through the house, searching it, has been keeping me awake at night," Wendy said. A surprised look crossed her face. "Or, could I be feeling the emotional atmosphere in the castle? We should reset this whole place." She looked at her husband with consternation.

"You may be right," he said. "I want you and Jack to be comfortable here." He reached one hand out and covered his wife's hand, squeezing it gently.

After some discussion, Ryan decided to lock the smaller articles away in a safe in the master bedroom. The paintings and tea tray were too large to fit in the safe. Wendy suggested locking them in a storage closet.

Kamika had completed her recommendations for the "lady's chamber" bedroom before she left for her date. Wendy began reading them and asking questions.

Soon, glancing at the time, Montgomery decided to call it a night. The Hanovers agreed that Lea and Montgomery would return in the morning to continue the analysis of the house.

"I've got some reading to do tonight. If Mae wrote who wanted money, we may have a murder suspect," Wendy said.

CHAPTER 8

THE NEXT MORNING, LEA SAT SIPPING a double espresso with four packets of sugar in the break room at the Bad Vibes Removal Services office while Montgomery told Kamika about all the things they'd found at the castle after she'd left.

Kamika sipped her own coffee. "Glad you enjoyed your work, but I had more fun dancing."

"Now," said Montgomery, "can either of you repeat what the ghost said?"

Lea shook her head no.

Kamika nodded, causing her curls to jump. "No problem!"

Montgomery took out his phone, and Kamika spoke as he recorded.

Montgomery looked doubtful as Kamika repeated what she'd heard twice for him to record.

"I can hear breaks between the words," said Kamika, "but I can't understand the words."

Lea looked at Kamika with amazement. "All I hear is a series of noises that I could never reproduce. Still, even if we find out what she's saying, how is that going to help?"

"It's an avenue to explore," Montgomery said.

"Lea, you yelled back at our ghostie. What if she didn't respond to you because she didn't understand you?" asked Kamika.

"She gave no hint that she heard me at all."

"What if she was deaf?" Kamika said impatiently.

"Kamika, enough already," said Lea with a laugh. "An echo from the past is hard enough to deal with. Don't get me started on deaf ghosts."

"Okay. No deaf ghosts. I've got bigger problems to solve." Kamika flared her nostrils and huffed in annoyance.

"What's up?" asked Montgomery.

"I got a call last night from my credit card company. They caught a suspicious charge."

"Oh, did your card number get stolen?" Lea asked with sympathy.

"Looks like it. Usually when that happens, the charges are on the other side of the country or on some Internet site I've never used. This time the charge was local. Could someone I know have used my card?"

"It's more likely some waiter at a restaurant scanned it and used it," Montgomery said, gulping his coffee.

"I s'pose," said Kamika, with uncharacteristic worry lines forming between her eyebrows. She shifted restlessly in her chair and nervously straightened her tailored, bright-green blouse, a favorite top that brought out the color of her eyes.

Lea noted that although Kamika was dressed with her typical flair, her confident air seemed missing. Her hunched posture gave her a look of dejection. Even her curls seemed less bouncy than usual.

Montgomery patted Kamika's shoulder, "Don't worry about it. The credit card company will cancel the charges. You won't be held responsible."

Lea had a flash of insight. Something else was wrong. "Why do you think someone you know could have used the card?"

"Well, I hate to accuse family, but . . ." Kamika stopped and sighed. "Remember, my cousin Lusa Maeko is staying with me for a few days while she visits UT in Austin?"

"Lusa Maeko. That sounds like the Finnish/Japanese side of the family not the Finnish/Nigerian side of the family, right?" Lea knew all about Kamika's interesting ancestry: how her Japanese and Finnish mother and Nigerian and Finnish father had met at a Scandinavian students' group in college. They'd come together because they had been the only ones who didn't look like everyone else in the room. They'd married and produced Kamika, a multilingual, exotic-looking beauty with mocha skin; bronze, shoulder-length corkscrew curls; and wide, green eyes.

"Yeah, my mom's sister's daughter. She is so sweet, polite. She makes her bed, wipes the bathroom sink, and washes her dishes without me asking. I wouldn't be as good a houseguest as she is."

Montgomery elevated an eyebrow, "Then why do you suspect her?"

"She arrived Thursday night, right? I got that call yesterday while I was out to dinner with Lusa and her boyfriend. Lusa got in late last night because she stayed out dancing after I called it quits and went home. Here it is Saturday morning. As I was getting ready to come here this morning, I pulled open my drawers in my dresser to get clothes out, and I noticed things looked odd. Somebody went through my dresser drawers. Lusa was supposed to be touring the university yesterday before dinner, but she still could have gone through my things. Lusa is the only one with a key to my place besides my parents."

"Anything missing?" asked Montgomery.

"I don't think so, but I didn't take inventory before I came in this morning," Kamika said with annoyance.

"Check your house when you get home. Make sure nothing is missing. Is your cousin at your apartment today?" Montgomery asked.

Kamika shook her head. "No, she's attending a program at the university. She left when I did."

"Then get home before she does and look around your apartment. If anything is missing, call me. I take it you don't want to involve the police at this point?" he asked.

"Oh, no. No police. I'd like a chance to talk to Lusa, and maybe my mom, and my Aunt Hana to see what they have to say."

"I can investigate this for you," Montgomery said. "Happy to help."

"If anything is missing, I'll call you," said Kamika. "Although, I don't want you investigating my clothing drawers." She grimaced at him and then changed the subject. "Lea, how's Patrick?"

Lea blushed slightly and pushed strands of black hair out of her face back into the cloth around her head. "He's fine."

Kamika leaned sideways and nudged Lea with her shoulder. "Uh-huh. Come on. You've got to give me more than that."

Lea considered the matter before surrendering. Kamika could be almost as persistent as Montgomery when she wanted information. "He'll be formally discharged from the Army next week. He's not having short-term memory loss from his head injury anymore, but he's still being treated for post-traumatic stress. He's put out his resume and had a few interviews. He says some of the companies may do two or three interviews before making a decision." Patrick Garcia was a previous client of Montgomery's. He and Lea had started dating soon after his case was resolved.

"He's smart and good-looking. I bet he's snapped up so fast it'll make your head spin. No one could resist that face and that body, all wrapped in a war hero," Kamika said.

"He doesn't like to be called that. He says having his vehicle hit an IED doesn't make him a hero," Lea admonished lightly.

"Being willing to join the Army and go where he might get blown up makes him brave," Montgomery said. "He'll find a position soon." He smiled at Lea and Kamika. He grinned and his eyebrows bounced up and down—he looked as mischievous as ever. "Maybe I should find somebody to date. Based on watching you two, I might enjoy having a private life. Now, time's a-wasting. We have a castle to investigate. We could find more treasure today." He rubbed his hands together joyfully, heaved himself up from his chair, and bounded out the door.

Kamika followed him, calling out, "Just as long as I don't see any more ghosts! That's Lea's department. I don't want any part of it ever again. Seeing one ghost will last me a lifetime."

Lea laughed, took her last sip of espresso, and went to the sink to wash her mug. She thought the likelihood of

Montgomery taking time to date was about as likely as a cold day in July in Texas. Montgomery worked all the time. Even when he was supposedly taking time off, he was courting clients or working angles to get his equipment used by law enforcement agencies. She couldn't imagine a scenario in which he took time off for himself. He was the quintessential workaholic, all consumed by his inventions and his companies. She dried her mug and put it away, then left the breakroom to join the others.

A few minutes later, they all piled into one of the company vans for the trip from Georgetown, just north of Austin, to the Hanovers' castle outside Cedar Park.

✂

Wendy was waiting for them by the front door with several of Mae's diaries in her hands. She waved the books at them as they emerged from the van. "I found some interesting things in the diary that may have something to do with the crying woman in the basement. Mae writes that she and her husband took a vacation to Boston in 1920 and heard a man speak at a rally about the ongoing oppression of the Irish by the English. In May 1921, Mae and Ryan traveled to Ireland to see the situation for themselves and to visit places that their ancestors were born. Their son, Ryan, Jr., was away, newly graduated from college and working as a vice president for his father's company."

"They went to Ireland in 1921. That was dangerous," said Lea.

"Why was it dangerous?" Kamika asked.

"They arrived in the middle of the Irish War of Independence," Wendy explained, smiling at Kamika. "I researched it all last night, or I wouldn't know anything about it either. Northern Ireland had just been created, and battles were being fought for Irish independence from British rule. So Mae and Ryan, being wealthy and inspired to help the Irish people, bought the castle. The town didn't own the castle. The land it sat on had been purchased by an Englishman with a big mansion near the town. The Englishman fled to London with his family when the fighting began several years earlier. The money for the purchase of the castle went straight into Irish Republican Army coffers."

"What does that have to do with the crying woman?" Kamika asked.

"I'm getting to that. Mae recorded the folklore associated with the castle from tales that the local residents told her while she was in Ireland. One of the stories dates back to the 1100s. Here, I'll read you the passage." She opened the slim diary volume to a bookmark she'd placed in it and began reading.

"'The innkeeper's wife was full of local lore about the castle we toured yesterday. She says that many people in town have seen a ghostly woman running through the ruins at night. After much roundaboutation and a few difficulties understanding her Irish way of speaking, I gathered that in medieval times, the castle once had a Lord Cormac and a Lady Aillenn O'Dwyer, who ruled over the area under allegiance to a king named O'Brien.'"

Wendy paused in her reading and added, "I researched Irish history. A King O'Brien was powerful in Ireland in the 1100s, and a King O'Neill came to be more powerful soon after him. Anyway, I'll continue.

"'A rival, King O'Neill, wanted to gain control of the area and made overtures to the O'Dwyers, who turned him down. A steward of the O'Dwyers' was bribed by the O'Neill faction to win the castle for O'Neill. The steward charmed a lady's maid to put something in Lady Aillenn's nighttime drink, telling the maid that it was merely a sleeping potion when, in truth, it was poison. The lady was found dead in her chamber later that night by her husband. Lord Cormac called the maid and his steward to issue instructions regarding the lady's funeral, thinking the death a natural one. In his grief, he didn't pay attention to his steward, but turned his back. The steward then stabbed Lord Cormac, hitting his heart and killing him instantly.'

"Then, we get to the part about the ghost," Wendy said.

"'The ghostly woman is said to be the maid, who ran away grief-stricken and horrified. Some say she tripped and fell all the way down the circular stairs, landing with a broken neck. Others say she threw herself down the well in the basement. Still another version says that the steward chased her through the castle with his gory knife in hand, dripping with the blood of Lord Cormac, and murdered her in the dungeon. The townsfolk say the ghost was seen for centuries, especially when greedy or traitorous people plagued the owners. Now that the building is falling to ruins, the ghost is still seen, but her visitations are linked to the current troubles. People think she walks to warn of traitors to Ireland, those loyal to the British, who turn in their neighbors for money. As we will be taking the castle with us, I sincerely pray that the ghost stays in this tumultuous and blood-bathed land.'"

"I like the version with the bloody knife," Ryan said as he walked out to join them from inside the castle. "It makes a great Halloween story."

His wife gave him a look that launched annoyance and disapproval at him with both barrels. She turned pointedly back to Montgomery. "Back to the diary. At the end of the Ireland trip, Mae describes packing two trunks and having them hauled to the ship for the trip home. She describes carefully packing away a solid silver tea set that she'd bought at auction. A lot of old English families were forced to sell prized possessions and long-held family homes because of higher taxes and failed financial speculations after World War I. Mae wrote that she thought the tea set was several hundred years old and quite valuable. She was pleased to get it so cheaply at the auction. I'll bet that's the tea set we found in the trunk."

"That makes sense," Ryan said. "We'll have it appraised and insured along with the paintings and jewelry. Hopefully, the ghost won't think we're robbing the place and haunt us forever."

"Ryan, that's not funny!" Wendy faced her husband with one hand on her hip and exasperation in her voice.

He held his hands out in surrender. "I'm sorry. It's a sad tale, and I'm insensitive in more ways than one. I haven't seen her. She isn't bothering me."

"Well, I saw her. She's a walking nightmare. You haven't got any greedy or traitorous people hanging around, have you?" Kamika asked, only half-jokingly.

"No, no. No traitors under the roof," said Ryan with a laugh.

Wendy's head popped up from the diary again. "Ryan, is your old business partner Owen Keller coming today?" she asked, tossing a challenging look at her husband.

He looked at her face, and his laugh died away. "Yes, but he's not traitorous . . . he wouldn't . . ." His words died on his lips and he gave a sheepish look.

His wife's lips were parted, waiting to spill out a contradiction to whatever he might utter in defense of his former partner. "He'd sell his own mother for a dollar," she said.

"I'll grant that Owen can be ambitious, but he isn't traitorous. Besides, he doesn't want anything from us."

"How do you know he doesn't? Why is he coming? You haven't been in contact in five years. Why is he reconnecting now?" Creases dug in around Wendy's mouth, giving it a downward turn.

"I can handle Owen. If I couldn't, I wouldn't have gone into business with him all those years ago." He dismissed her concerns with an airy wave and a shrug of his wiry shoulders.

Montgomery stepped between them. "Is Owen Keller someone who might have reason to be searching the house? You didn't mention him to me when we were discussing people who might want to break into the house."

Ryan paused with one hand on his chin in thought. "Well, he knows the rumors associated with this place. He was one of my college roommates. We used to joke that we could use the hidden treasure to start our company. We started a small business together right out of college. The venture failed spectacularly in about nine months. We didn't know what we were doing, and our idea wasn't quite as easy to market as we had hoped. We parted amicably. He had another venture he'd been invited to join, and I decided not to go with him."

"Your next venture eventually sold for enormous amounts of money, didn't it?" Montgomery asked.

"Yes," Ryan nodded with a satisfied smile playing on his lips.

"How did Owen's next business do?" Montgomery asked.

"I heard it crashed and failed badly. A backer pulled funding unexpectedly. They had to lay off people, and even that wasn't enough to save them. It ended in bankruptcy. However, that can happen to anyone. Most start-ups don't last five years. My company could easily have gone the way his did. If our capital had been pulled at the wrong time, we would have been in the same position he was." His voice was sympathetic. "I know several people who found themselves in similar situations. Mostly they bounce back and try again, or they quit the start-up world and go to work for established companies. Which choice they make usually depends on whether or not they have a family to support. Owen doesn't have anyone dependent on him. He'll try again."

Montgomery turned to Ryan with a serious expression. "All the same, please let me know how your meeting today terminates."

Ryan stared at Montgomery for a moment before nodding his agreement. "Where do we start today? I realize we've found quite a lot of valuable items, but there may still be more. And we can't be sure if we've found what our intruder was looking for. We need to be thorough."

Chapter 9

Montgomery's characteristic good humor returned, and he nodded. "I agree completely. We have to be thorough, or we might miss something important. We can continue our analysis of the house while Kamika resets your son's room, if you approve the suggestions she gave you yesterday." He glanced from Ryan to Wendy.

Wendy nodded vigorously. "Yes, Jack will be home after his baseball game. Do you think you can finish before he gets here?" She looked at Kamika with raised brows.

Kamika flashed Wendy a winning smile "Yep. A few hours and I'll be done with the basic reset. Some of the interior design suggestions may take longer if you want to add paint, but I can handle sound, smell, reorganization of furniture, and the wall infusions this morning."

Wendy turned to her husband. "Should we tell Jack what we're doing?"

"Yes. He'll notice the changes, and we need him to give the room a second chance. If he doesn't know we're working on the way the room feels, he may not be willing to try sleeping in there again," her husband pointed out. "We don't necessarily need to tell him the whole history of the room."

Wendy touched Ryan's arm. "I have an idea. We could let him help with the redecoration. Of course, if we do, the whole place will be plastered with pictures of characters from that computer game he's always playing with his friends."

Ryan laughed and shrugged. "That would be better than being pushed out of the room by its bad emotional history." He led the whole group off the porch and into the castle.

"Kamika, if you need help with any of the furniture, come get us. We'll be doing more scans on the floor below you," Montgomery said.

"I'll be fine so long as that ghost stays down in the garage and basement. I never want to see her again." Kamika shuddered dramatically.

Wendy nodded vehemently. "While it's nice to know other people can see her too, I don't want to see her again either."

Montgomery turned to Ryan and said, "Remind me again what's on that floor below the top floor?"

"If you count the garage level with the laundry room and game area as the ground floor, and the main level with the great hall, living area, and kitchen as the second floor, then that's the third floor. It has the two guest rooms, my office, my wife's office, another bathroom, and a large living room lined with shelves that will eventually hold my wife's book collection," Ryan said. "I can't get her to entirely convert to digital, so boxes of books are stacked all over that room waiting to be unpacked."

Wendy gave a derisive snort. "A few of those boxes are *your* books. And I already reduced my collection to my absolute favorites." Her tone indicated they'd been over this topic before and her opinion wasn't changing.

While they lightheartedly debated the matter, Lea thought back to the plans she'd seen the day before. Originally, that third floor had been the children's suite: a nursery, a schoolroom, and space for the servants who had tended the children. Also, if memory served, the family chapel was on that floor. "What did you decide to do with the old chapel?" she asked, interrupting what was evidently an ongoing disagreement between the Hanovers.

Ryan glanced at her, disconcerted momentarily. "Oh, I forgot about the chapel. My great-grandfather decided it should remain a chapel, and so it is. We could hold tiny weddings in there if we wanted. It's a lovely space but only designed for religious purposes. Using it for something else would take quite a bit of remodeling. And that would feel wrong."

Lea gave him a look of surprise. "You've noticed that the chapel has a particular feeling to it?"

His wife interjected in a teasing tone, "Maybe you're not totally insensitive after all."

Ryan rolled his head on his shoulders. "Fine, you got me. Yes. The chapel feels like a church to me, as if I'm supposed to pray in there. It's solemn somehow."

Lea gave him a smile. "It's got history, too. If that space has always been treated with reverence, it should feel solemn." Lea looked forward to seeing the chapel. If it hadn't been modernized, it might be the best-preserved, most original room in the castle.

Kamika touched Wendy's shoulder. "I'll get started on your son's room."

"Can I help you for a while?" asked Wendy. "I'll have to leave at ten-thirty to get Jack from Carol and take him to baseball, but I have some free time now. Will an extra hand make the work go faster?"

"You're welcome to join me," Kamika said with a welcoming grin. "I love company."

Wendy smiled back at her. "Wonderful!"

Kamika and Wendy walked away together to start the process of redesigning the emotional environment of the boy's bedroom. Lea and Montgomery left to scan the guest rooms and offices. Ryan excused himself to his office.

✄

Four hours later, Montgomery groaned and stretched his arms. "I don't know about you, Lea, but this bulk of mine requires sustenance to maintain it, and my arms are tired from holding this scanner. Let's see if Kamika is ready to break for lunch."

Lea placed her scanner by her feet and tucked an escaped strand of black hair into the Roman-style hairdo she'd achieved for the day. "Sounds great. I need a caffeine kick. We haven't exactly made any earth-shattering discoveries today. We can do the chapel after lunch."

They found Kamika putting the finishing touches in place, including a small fountain that she'd placed on the dresser in Jack's bedroom. The water was trickling down a tiny incline forming a miniature waterfall. A sweet scent that reminded Lea of childhood made the room feel happy and invited them to step inside to enjoy the tantalizing smell.

Lea stepped into the room. The overwhelming sense of sorrow, grief, and death she'd felt before was no longer the primary presence in the room. She could vaguely sense unease in the walls, but it wasn't the most prominent sensation. Instead, the room smelled, sounded, and felt like innocent, unfettered childhood, before the worries of adolescence. It had a sweet guilelessness, like looking in a newborn's face. Kamika had done a great job with the infusions.

"Lunch break?" Montgomery asked.

"Sure. I'm starved," said Kamika. She looked at Lea. "How's this room feel now? Better?"

Lea looked around and let the room talk to her before answering. "I'm impressed. I've seen you work on spaces hundreds of times, but this may be the most profound change I've ever felt in a room."

"Thanks," Kamika grinned. "I hope the little guy likes it too."

After checking in with Ryan, the trio set out for lunch in Montgomery's car, deciding on Italian-style fast food. Montgomery updated Kamika on their lack of progress as they drove. The guest rooms, offices, and soon-to-be library had revealed no hidden compartments and only the humdrum conversations and jumbled emotions of routine lives. The bathroom revealed that someone had enjoyed singing in the shower. Montgomery thought the cadence and the few words they found looked like something out of a Gershwin musical comedy. The only third floor room that they hadn't scanned was the family chapel.

Kamika's phone rang in her back pocket as they crossed the parking lot to enter the little restaurant. She paused to answer. "Go on in. I'll be right there," she said, waving them ahead of her.

Lea wondered about the puzzled look on Kamika's face when she saw the caller identification, but then she turned and followed Montgomery inside the pizza and pasta joint they'd selected for lunch. Kamika would tell her soon enough if something was wrong. Kamika wasn't one to keep her thoughts or feelings internalized.

As Lea was deciding on a pepperoni and mushroom calzone, Kamika appeared and slammed down into the chair across from her. She banged her phone onto the table with unnecessary force.

"Problem?" asked Montgomery, with an irrepressible twinkle in his eye.

Kamika slitted her eyes half shut and gave him an irritated look. "Some *bastard* tried to open a credit card in my name!"

The twinkle vanished, and Montgomery rearranged his features into a look of concern. "Well, at least they didn't succeed."

"Yeah, the—" She spouted something unintelligible to Lea, who was sure it was a curse word or an insult but wasn't sure what language it was in, "applied for credit at my bank. I have a freeze placed on credit applications, so they called me about it."

Montgomery blinked twice and then said, "Good for you for protecting yourself."

Lea could see the surprise Montgomery was fighting to hide. She knew Kamika better than he did. Kamika may know little of history or literature, but she was sharper than many when it came to personal finance. "First your credit card is stolen, then someone tries to open an account in your name. Do you think someone is trying to steal your identity?"

Kamika gritted her teeth viciously. "They can try, but they're going to fail. I have every protection possible. The alarms are ringing, so they won't be able to touch any of my accounts or open any new ones. I wish I could unleash the hounds and chase this person."

Montgomery laid a hand over Kamika's clenched fist on the table. "Would you like me to look into it?" Though he asked the question in an offhanded tone, his posture was intent.

Lea thought he looked like a bloodhound that'd caught a whiff of a scent to track. He was the hound waiting for Kamika to unleash him.

Kamika twisted her napkin in her hands. "What would you do?"

"I could request video surveillance recordings from whatever store your credit card was used in. A pal in the police could run facial recognition software for us. We might be able to identify the thief."

Kamika stared into blank space. "S'pose it's someone I know. Would I *have* to press charges?" she asked at last.

Montgomery's mouth twisted in both sympathy and distaste. "No, you don't *have* to do anything. But people who do this kind of thing will likely do it again, and may have already done it before." He paused, letting the implications of doing nothing sink in.

At last, Kamika nodded her understanding. "Let's try and identify the thief."

They placed their orders on the touch pad screen on the table. A few minutes later, a waiter appeared with their drinks, silverware, and a bowl of garden salad. Soon, their entrees arrived, and they began to eat silently, each lost in thought.

A comment Montgomery had made the day before came to Lea's mind. "Montgomery, what did you mean when you asked Ryan about helping you to upgrade the software to make it easier for others to use? Are you thinking of expanding the business?"

He paused before biting into his pizza with everything on it and gave her a sly smile. "Yes. I'm thinking about opening more branches of the company in different cities."

"Wow!" Lea said. "So there'd be other branches of Bad Vibes Removal Services?"

"Eventually all around the country," Montgomery said. "I intend to expand Montgomery Investigations as well."

Kamika giggled. "That idea of taking more personal time flew out the window."

"Not necessarily," he said, stopping abruptly with a quickly veiled look.

Lea knew he had something else up his sleeve. Something he wasn't telling them yet. She decided not to press him. As stubborn as he was, getting information out of him before he was ready was impossible. She'd learned to wait. He'd share whatever was going on when he was ready and not a moment sooner.

They finished eating. Lea sipped her iced tea as Montgomery sent out a request to the store where Kamika's credit card had been used. He'd most likely receive the video of the credit card thief before the end of the day unless the manager was unavailable. She glanced at Kamika, who looked worried but resolved to proceed.

Then they hopped back in the van for the return trip to the Hanovers' castle.

Kamika, Lea, and Montgomery arrived to find Wendy sitting on the stone steps up to the front door with one of Mae's diaries in her hand. She was engrossed in the book. Her son, Jack, and another little boy, both in baseball uniforms, were playing tag in the green grass of the front yard. Both boys stopped running to watch as Kamika, Lea, and Montgomery got out of their van.

Wendy looked up and waved them over as the boys returned to their game. "I've been reading more of Mae's diary. She wrote a lot about the details of making the castle livable and comfortable—delays with the workers, the whole process taking more money and time than she expected—which I can relate to completely right now. This place may turn out to be a money pit. But Ryan loves it." Wendy sighed and looked up at the stone edifice looming behind her, mystified but resigned, before she continued. "Anyway, in the late 1920s—August 1927—Mae's nephew Harry Sutton became a prominent fixture in her life. Her son Ryan, Jr., was away, working as a vice president of his father's company with a family of his own. Her husband was always working. She was lonely. She talked her husband into giving Harry a job at her brother's request. That got Harry out of big city life and into Texas and hard work. She wrote that Harry needed steady work and a change of scenery to keep him out of trouble: drink, chorus girls, and jazz being his primary temptations. She hoped to help him see the error of his ways. He was a project for her to focus her attention on."

Lea glanced at Montgomery. "We found evidence of someone singing late 1920s-era show tunes in the guest bathroom," she said.

Montgomery mounted the first step up to the massive front door and paused there. "Harry must be the one in the basement being threatened for owing money, too. Moving him to Texas wouldn't prevent people from following him here to collect debts."

Wendy tapped the diary cover. "That makes him the prime suspect in the mystery of the missing company money. He could have taken it to pay off his debts and have more to spend. Although I doubt we'll ever have enough evidence to prove it conclusively."

"Maybe not," Montgomery said, "but we may have enough to prove it to your husband's satisfaction. Right now, he's the only one who matters."

Wendy stood with the diary in her hand. "That's true. All the players in our murder mystery are long dead. Speaking of dead, I found our crying woman ghost." She grinned, then laughed out loud at the stunned look on Kamika's, Lea's, and Montgomery's faces. "I didn't speak to her or anything. I found her again in Mae's diary." She waved the slim, leather-covered volume in her hand.

Lea's lips parted in surprise. "Mae saw her too?"

"Yes. In September 1927, after Harry arrived. Mae writes about going to retrieve a handbag that she'd accidentally left in the car which was parked in front of the castle. She walked down the interior stairs to the ground level and exited the castle through the area that we use as a garage. After she closed the car door and turned to go back inside, she saw the woman. Here, I'll read you the section." Wendy opened the diary to a slip of paper she'd used to mark a page in the middle of the book.

"I was about to go up the stairs when a woman, dressed in heavy brown skirts with a creamy white apron, came from nowhere, sobbing hysterically," Wendy began reading. "Her brown hair was coming loose in long strands from under the kerchief on her head. I started to open my mouth to say something to her when I was overcome with terror. I felt paralyzed where I stood, unable to move or speak. The woman passed through the room coming from the corner stairwell and then descended the stairs to the cellar area. She seemed to be calling a name and looking about her for someone she needed desperately to find. As she vanished down the stairs, an even more horrible sensation filled me. Evil entered the room. I heard a scream rise and thought it was from the woman before I realized that my mouth was open and the sound was me. Darkness like the devil himself passed through in a wave that caused my body to tremble and left me feeling faint. I had to grasp the wall to keep from collapsing to the floor. Thankfully, Ryan called to me then, and I rushed up the stairs and into the castle. I shall never enter the ground floor storage area alone again!"

She stopped reading and looked up with a thrilled expression. "I've read to mid-1929, and Mae reported seeing the woman three more times between September 1927 and Christmas 1928. Every time she convinced herself to go into the garage again, she regretted it. Nephew Harry never saw the woman. I'll bet he was too self-absorbed to notice someone else in pain. Mae's husband never saw or felt anything in the garage. He was always too focused on his company. From her description, his mind was never entirely on where he was. He had too much going on in his head to pay attention to his surroundings. Old Hanover sounds a lot like my husband. The intense focus on ideas for business must run in the family."

Montgomery pointed at the diary. "Have you read about old Hanover's death yet?"

"I'm almost there. I'm going to keep reading to see if I can find anything that might implicate Harry in the old man's death. Who knows, maybe the old man did have a heart attack when he found out his wife's nephew was robbing him blind. Or maybe Harry did poison him. I'll let you know what I find." Her face glowed with anticipation, as if she were reading an exciting novel instead of a long-dead in-law's diary.

Kamika gestured toward Jack as he ran across the lawn, "Has your son seen the changes to his room?"

Wendy turned to Kamika, "Yes! He likes the new furniture arrangement. I've shown him the paint colors you recommended for the wall that isn't bare stone. He chose an orange that reminds me of sunsets and summer flowers. It's a wonderful, bright color."

Kamika grinned enthusiastically. "Did he like the fountain? It puts out a scent we call cookie dough. It's sweet and happy. The sound of the water flowing should be soothing at night as well."

Wendy gestured toward the fountain. "Jack had a question about the fountain. His friend Wyatt got a fish tank in his room with a filter that has flowing water. He wants to know if he can have a fish tank instead of the fountain."

Kamika nodded. "Fish are calming and add a sense of serenity to a room that complements the sounds of water flowing. That's why you see so many tanks in dentists' and doctors' offices. If you prefer a tank and don't mind the work they require, I highly recommend getting one. I typically put in fountains because a lot of people don't like the hassle involved in the upkeep of a fish tank. The infused scents can be added to the air with a simple plug-in device instead of through the fountain."

"Jack will be delighted to hear that. Ryan and I need to discuss setting up a fish tank," said Wendy. "It will be worth the trouble if Jack is finally comfortable in his room. I asked him how the room felt after I showed it to him, and he said that it didn't make him feel funny anymore. I asked him what he meant by 'funny,' and he said that the room made his tummy feel tight and scared before. I told him that tonight should be better."

Kamika, pleased that her efforts were appreciated, bounced joyfully on her toes, making her curls jump on her shoulders. "Since you've chosen the paint color, I can start the color scheme redesign with painting that one wall. If you don't like the color after you see the whole room put together, we can change it. I've got throw pillow covers, a lamp shade, and cut-to-fit window treatments to bring the room together. That orange is a very happy and healthy color, so we keep it in stock. I've put it in several children's-themed hotel rooms, physical therapy and rehabilitation facilities, and even in treatment rooms for people with mental health issues like depression. It's a winner when it comes to cheering people up. Ooh, and fancy goldfish match that color too!"

"I'll let Jack know. He and Wyatt are going to play in the yard until Wyatt's mom comes to pick him up in . . ." she glanced at her watch, "about half an hour." Wendy sat on the stone steps with Mae's diary in hand. "Jack and I will be in to see how the room is coming along after Wyatt leaves."

"See you then," Kamika said with a pleased nod. She bounded up the stone stairs to the massive wooden entry doors.

Lea and Montgomery followed Kamika more slowly but stopped when Wendy suddenly said, "Oh, heck. He's here."

Lea turned to see a sleek, cherry-red Mustang stop by the curb. As the driver got out of the car, Lea noted his thick brown hair was perfectly styled and gelled into place, and his suit fit him like it had been tailor-made. He looked like the quintessential, successful businessman. First impressions clearly mattered to Owen Keller. Lea wondered if there was any substance under the glossy exterior. She'd long since learned never to judge a book by its cover. Well-made clothes could disguise all sorts of personality flaws and failings. She watched as Wendy walked over to greet the new arrival.

Wendy reached out her hand to shake Owen Keller's, but her voice held only politeness, not warmth, when she greeted him. The two little boys ran over and stood just behind Wendy to admire the red car.

Lea hustled into the castle to catch up with Montgomery. Wendy could handle her husband's business partner.

CHAPTER 10

WHEN SHE ARRIVED AT THE CHAPEL doors, Lea stood back to study the entrance.

"What?" asked Montgomery, pausing next to her.

"This space was originally open to the hall. These big doors were added at some point in the building's history. That's typical. New owners would have modified different areas over the centuries." She reached forward and pulled the heavy door open.

Inside, Lea scanned a space large enough for only for about twenty people to stand—not a large room by any measure. The ceiling was vaulted, but not higher than the surrounding rooms on the floor. A narrow window let in light through stained-glass panes depicting the Holy Family. Blue and red rays fell in shafts from the window onto a heavy altar table topped in pink Texas granite that clearly wasn't original to the building but which fit the space well.

Lea's eyes were drawn to two niches carved into the stone walls, one on the right and the other on the left side of the room. One niche held an expensive, bronze, miniature reproduction of Michelangelo's *Pieta*. The other held a ceramic statue of St. Patrick. The statues were covered with dust and cobwebbed into the surrounding space. Neither piece was particularly old, but they were appropriate and fit the spaces well. Perhaps, Lea thought, Mae Hanover had chosen them. A red Persian rug, approximately four feet wide by six feet long, covered the floor in front of the altar. The rest of the room was bare.

To Lea's relief, the chapel hadn't been modernized. Minus the few decorations, the chapel looked almost exactly as it had looked for the previous eight or nine centuries.

Montgomery stood with his hands on his hips looking around the room. "We won't be able to get any readings in here."

"Not unless you want to read the door," said Lea.

He considered it speculatively. "We could. It wouldn't take long. The scanners are in the office next door. I'll grab them." Montgomery walked out of the room.

Lea took in the atmosphere of solemnity around her before wandering over to the statue of St. Patrick. The statue hadn't been touched in decades, like Mae's dusty, hidden diaries. On a whim, Lea decided to free the statue from its cobwebbing and dust. She ran her hand around the niche, collecting a handful of cobwebs, and then slid her fingers behind the figure to clear the back side of it. Her hand met an object. She was lifting the statue from its niche to see what was behind it when Montgomery reappeared in the doorway.

"What are you doing?"

"There's something hidden behind this statue," Lea said as she carefully lifted the St. Patrick figure and placed it behind her on the granite altar.

Montgomery looked into the niche. "It's an envelope." He dusted off the remaining cobwebs and wiped at the decades of dust until words appeared beneath the grime. He held the envelope out so that Lea could read it, too. On it, someone had written the words "my confession" and the date May 28, 1954.

Lea's eyebrows went up. "I'll call Ryan. The handwriting looks like a woman's, probably Mae Hanover. She seems to have hidden things all over the place."

"Wait." Montgomery laid the envelope on the altar and turned toward the other statue niche. "He's talking to his old partner. Whatever is in that envelope is over half a century old. There's no rush. Plus, we may as well check the whole room while we're at it." He brushed the webbing and dust from the bronze *Pieta* and lifted it with both hands.

The bronze piece made a substantial-sounding thud as he set it on the altar. Montgomery and Lea examined the niche. A small rectangle of cloth, discolored by time, retained the outline of the base of the bronze that had rested on it. Lea picked it up and found it to be a plain piece of flannel. The surprise was beneath the cloth.

"Look at this!" Montgomery said.

The cloth had hidden a carved-out, four-inch-square opening in the stone bottom of the space.

Montgomery leaned his head into the niche to look into the hole. "I can't see anything inside." He stuck two chubby fingers into the space. A look of disappointment crossed his face. "Darn. It's empty."

Lea ran her fingers around the edges of the cutout space. "Look at this . . . the way the edges are worn, the way it's shaped. That cut was done a long, long time ago.

It's an original feature of the castle. Family valuables, even a reliquary, could have been kept in there. The Irish had a tradition of placing relics into decorated containers. The reliquary would have been passed through the family. The last family member to leave the castle would have taken it with them."

Montgomery frowned. "Mae put things all over the house. Why didn't she put something in here, too?"

"Because too many people knew that the space was there. When this place was dismantled and rebuilt, all kinds of masons and stone workers would have been involved in the process. It would have been common knowledge."

Montgomery gave Lea a perplexed look. "So she put the envelope in the other niche, knowing everyone knew not to bother looking there? That makes no sense. Why leave it at all if she didn't want it found?"

"Given that the envelope is labeled as a confession, maybe she wanted the right person to find it: someone who was clearing out the room or cleaning it, not someone doing a cursory check."

Montgomery shook his head. "That could have been anyone. Who knows what she was thinking. Let's scan that door."

The door was a modern oak reproduction meant to look older than it was. The sound readings revealed no gunshots, no loud yelling of curse words, no interesting conversations. The emotional energy scan was more interesting.

"I see grief," Lea said.

Montgomery's eyes traveled over the data. "And lots of it. Not surprising. She lost her husband. She may have come in here to pray."

Lea searched the results. "Guilt, too, but not as much as the grief."

"You'd think there'd be more since she left a confession behind," Montgomery said.

Lea tilted her head, considering the matter. "It depends on what she was confessing."

"True. Well, we've stalled long enough. Let's go find out if Ryan is free." Montgomery closed the program.

Lea gave him a surprised look. "I thought you didn't want to interrupt them."

"I don't want Mr. Keller to ask who I am, so I'm not going with you. In case he is involved in the break-ins, I'd rather he not know we're here investigating. You're going to tell Ryan you found something *while cleaning the chapel*. Owen Keller will think you're a maid from a cleaning service." Montgomery grinned. "I'm going to check on Kamika."

"You think I look like a maid?" asked Lea, glancing at her jeans and t-shirt.

"You're young enough to look like you might be working your way through school, which, as it happens, you are. You're fit enough to look like you can handle physical labor. I'm an overweight, middle-aged man. How many people who look like me would have the energy and stamina to work for a cleaning service?"

She glanced at his bulging waistline. "Okay, I look more like a maid than you do."

Lea trotted down the stone stairs, envelope in hand, with Montgomery's heavy footsteps fading behind her. As she reached the great hall living area, she paused to listen before entering the room. She couldn't hear voices. Perhaps Ryan's guest had left already. She stepped into the room to see the two men seated at the dining table.

Ryan was engrossed in something on the laptop screen in front of him. The other man was watching him earnestly and somewhat impatiently. Lea took another step forward, and the visitor turned his attention to her.

She could see him trying to decide if he knew her. A puzzled look came into his eyes.

Lea continued forward into the room, "Excuse me, Mr. Hanover, but we found this envelope while we were cleaning the chapel."

Ryan's head jerked up, startled. He looked at Lea and reached out to take the envelope from her hand. His eyebrows shot up as he read the words on the exterior of the envelope, and a smile spread across his face. "Curious. Thanks, Lea. I'm almost done here. I'll be there in a few minutes."

Lea took his words as a dismissal, nodded, and turned to go back up the stairs. She found Kamika and Montgomery in Jack's room. Three-quarters of the only wall with wallboard over the stone had been painted a bright goldfish orange. Kamika held the no-spatter paint applicator that she used for quick wall color changes. On the other side of the room, Montgomery was stuffing a pillow into a brightly covered sham to go with the new throw pillows. The place was well on the way to being a brilliantly lit, color-coordinated, playful space. Lea found a smile glued to her face as she stood in the doorway and admired the changes. "The infusions you did this morning really helped cover the emotional history in here," she said to Kamika.

Jack raced past Lea into the room and stopped short at finding so many people around him.

Montgomery held out his large hand and invited the boy to look around. "What do you think? Do you like your room better now?" The boy smiled shyly and shrank away, bumping into this mother, who had followed him in.

Wendy tousled her son's hair. "Wyatt left, so we decided to see how the room was coming along." She looked around at the nearly painted wall. "This color is fabulous. It almost sings in here."

Kamika mock-curtseyed to the boy, making him laugh. He came out from behind his mother. "This is my specialty. Nothin' makes me happier than when I can make a room fit the needs of the owners. If you stand back, I'll be done in a few minutes."

In a short time, Kamika had finished painting the accent wall. While she painted, Lea and Montgomery added self-adhesive geometric patterns in coordinating colors to the stone walls that wouldn't be painted with input from Wyatt and Wendy.

As they applied the finishing touches of color, and replaced the furniture near, but not touching, the still damp wall, Ryan entered the room and stopped short to view the changes. "This place is bright now! Do you like it, Jack?"

"Yes!" The little boy jumped on his bed to touch the new orange throw pillows.

Montgomery turned to Ryan. "Did you have a chance to read Mae's letter?" he asked.

Wendy's head popped up from examining the fountain. "What letter?"

"Mae left a letter in the chapel behind the statue of St. Patrick. We gave it to your husband to read," Montgomery replied.

Ryan glanced at his son. "Little pitchers," he said to his wife over the boy's head. He turned to his son.

"Hey, Jack. We have work to do. Why don't you play in your room for a little while? We'll be down the hall. Remember not to touch the wet paint."

Jack was sticking his fingers in the water flowing from the fountain. "Okay." The boy didn't even look up.

Ryan Hanover led his wife, Kamika, Montgomery, and Lea to the media room and closed the door. He handed Mae's letter to Wendy and said, "In a nutshell, Mae confesses to helping her nephew Harry drink himself to death. After her husband's death, Harry began coming to her regularly, begging for money. Eventually, she decided that she was enabling him to make poor choices by saving him from the consequences of his actions, so she cut him off. She stopped giving him cash. Then she noticed that small, portable trinkets were missing from the house: expensive pieces of jewelry, a small drawing or two, an ancient Egyptian alabaster vase that her husband had purchased from an antiquities dealer."

Montgomery crossed his arms over his chest and nodded understandingly. "Harry started stealing. He must have been addicted to something or deeply in debt. No wonder Mae hid things from him."

"You got it. According to the letter, Mae tried to stop him from driving drunk. She cut off Harry's supply of alcohol in the house, locking the liquor up or hiding it. Then, to make sure he couldn't buy more, she hid the remaining portable valuables. Harry responded by becoming withdrawn and angry, prone to outbursts. Mae hired a detective to follow him. The detective reported back that Harry was heavily in debt from gambling and using heroin and alcohol. The detective discovered that Harry had purchased poison from someone the detective described as an undesirable contact."

Kamika shivered and glanced at Lea. "Poison!"

Montgomery nodded. "He'd only have bought poison to kill himself or someone else. If he did poison the old man, he may have decided to use it on his aunt as well."

"Mae wrote that she feared for her life and her son's life. Her son, Ryan Jr., was around more after his father's death, and he was constantly arguing with his cousin Harry. I gather from her letter that the cousins were about the same age, but Mae's son was responsible and settled in his life. They didn't agree on anything. Mae's son condemned his cousin's hedonistic lifestyle and hated the idea of his mother bankrolling Harry. However, Mae decided to placate Harry after the detective told her about the poison. She unlocked the liquor cabinet. Harry drank himself into a stupor. When he couldn't pour his own drink because his hands were too unsteady, he asked her to pour him one more. She complied, filling his glass to the brim. Then, leaving him alone, she went to bed."

Lea shook her head sadly. "He died, and she blamed herself?"

Ryan nodded. "Yep. It's all in the letter. He was found unconscious on the floor of the garage the next morning, August 23, 1930, less than a year after the old man died. Mae and her son guessed that he'd tried to leave but passed out next to the car. He died of alcohol poisoning in the hospital later that day."

Wendy offered the letter to Montgomery, who took it and began to skim it.

Kamika waved her hands for attention. "Hang on a minute. Why did the old lady leave everything in hiding? Once her nephew was dead, couldn't she have taken the things back out again?"

Ryan shrugged. "Who knows? That might be something we need to search for in her diary. She didn't put that in the letter."

"I'll read more of the diaries," Wendy said. "That does seem odd, given that she was clearly proud of the tea set in the entry I found. I wonder if someone tried to collect on Harry's debts after his death and threatened her."

Montgomery handed the letter back to Wendy. "If she didn't write it down, we may never know." He turned to Ryan Hanover. "What did your friend Keller want?"

"He wanted my opinion on the viability of a project he's considering. I looked it over for him. He also had heard that I had a new venture forming, and he wants in on it. In fact, I suspect asking me about my projects was more the object of his visit than asking me about his project. He knew all the faults I saw in the plan before I pointed them out. I think he was hoping I'd invite him to join me in a new business.

Montgomery looked at Ryan. "Do you have a new venture forming?"

Ryan shifted his feet restlessly. "I always have ideas, but I'm not planning on developing any of them right now. Should certain market factors change, something might work out. I keep them filed away, on the back burner, so to speak. The best thing I've seen lately would be to go into business with you, improving your software user interface. If we come to an agreement on that, you could use Keller. He's got a great mind for marketing new concepts, bringing in funding if needed, and making companies a household name."

Montgomery gave Ryan an appraising glance. "Did you tell him that?"

"I told him I was evaluating someone else's venture. We both learned the hard way not to jump too soon into something without evaluating it first."

"Was he satisfied with that?"

"Yes," Ryan said, his tone decisive.

Montgomery persisted. "Did you tell Keller about your treasure findings here in the castle?"

"I mentioned that my great-grandmother had hidden things around the house."

"How did he take that?"

"From his reaction, I don't think he'd thought about the rumors surrounding the castle for years. I had to remind him about the tales associated with this place. He was surprised. He congratulated me on my good fortune, but didn't seem envious, jealous, or otherwise annoyed by it. He fights for what he wants as hard as I do. He doesn't begrudge people luck. He knows sometimes things go his way, sometimes they don't. He's ambitious and driven but, in spite of what my wife thinks, not unethical. As an employee, he can be a great asset."

Montgomery pursed his lips together in a flat line. "If he was desperate and knew you were sitting on ideas, would he break in to try and find them?"

Ryan threw his hands up. "He'd do what he did today first. He'd approach me, sound me out, and try to get in on the ground floor. Who knows what anyone will do if they are desperate? Under certain circumstances, maybe he'd be pushed to break in, maybe if he was being blackmailed or owed the wrong people, but nothing I've got would lead to instant money," he paused, thinking out loud, "except maybe if he was committing industrial espionage. But nothing of mine would draw that kind of interest. I would rule him out as a suspect in the break-ins for the time being."

Lea was skeptical of Ryan's assessment. His old friend might still be involved. She knew Montgomery wouldn't rule him out as a suspect either.

The door flew open, and Jack rushed in to the room. "Mom! Mom! Now that my room is fixed, can Wyatt sleep over? He wants to help me search for the missing treasure!"

They all turned to look at the boy.

"What?" Ryan asked with a surprised look on his face.

His wife bent to look her small son in the face. "I'll have to call Wyatt's mom and see if we can schedule a time." She glanced up at her husband.

Ryan knelt down in front of his son. "Jack, why does Wyatt want to go treasure hunting?"

"His big brother told him that our castle has treasure in it. Wyatt says all of his brother's friends want to come inside and look for it." Jack stood balancing on one foot. "Oh, and Wyatt's brother wants to see the ghost," the boy said, switching to the other foot.

Ryan blinked rapidly but stayed focused on his son. "How does Wyatt's brother know about the ghost?"

"I told Wyatt, and Wyatt told his brother."

Ryan looked at Wendy. "How old is Wyatt's brother?"

"I'm not sure. He looks sixteen or seventeen." Wendy looked at her son. "Jack, does Wyatt's brother ever drive him anywhere?"

Jack looked from one parent to the other. "He can only drive Wyatt if his mom or dad goes too. They practice driving. Wyatt says he can't go on the freeway yet."

Ryan looked away from his son and met Montgomery's eyes. "All of the teenagers in the neighborhood think we have hidden treasure."

Lea could see both men processing the possibility that teenagers had been trying to get into the house.

Wendy chuckled softly and then grinned at her husband. "We could have a party, a housewarming, and invite the whole neighborhood. We can tell them about the renovations and make sure they all know that this place was reconstructed brick by brick in the 1920s. If we give them a look inside, we can convince them not to try to break in. We need to let people know that there isn't any hidden treasure. That we found it all."

"Let's get the word out now," Ryan said. He turned to his son. "Hey, Jack! You and Wyatt don't need to go treasure hunting after all. We already found the hidden treasure. Look here." Ryan walked over to the shelving on the wall by the wet bar where the first hidden compartment had been found. "See this? There's a hidden compartment here." He popped open the compartment. "We found your great-great grandmother's ring and her diaries in it. We found another hidden space in the basement under the garage. It had two trunks of stuff in it. Great-grandmother Mae did leave things here for us, but we think we've found everything. We've searched most of the castle and scanned most of the walls. We're going to finish scanning the walls this weekend."

Jack jumped up and down. "Can I see the ring? Can I see the place in the basement? Can I see what you found?" The little boy wriggled with energy.

"Yes, you can. We'll show you," Ryan said, smiling at his son's enthusiasm.

"However, you aren't allowed to play in the basement. You can only go there if one of us is with you," his mother said. "We have a lot of work to do down there still."

"Okay." Jack grabbed his mom's arm. "Can you call Wyatt's mom now? I want to show him the treasure and the hiding places."

"Yes, come on." Wendy turned to the door. "I'll catch up with y'all after I make that phone call," she said over her shoulder before following her son, who trotted out of the room ahead of her. "Oh! I had an idea about the other thing. Remind me to tell you later." Then she vanished down the stairs.

"Let's scan the main floor: kitchen, living, dining areas, the ground floor garage, laundry room, and storage rooms, and all the exterior walls, windows, and doors. We need to find out how your nighttime visitor is getting into the castle. If we can find that, we might find evidence of who it is," Montgomery said. "I don't think our problem is neighborhood teenagers. I'd have found how they were breaking in. They aren't exactly master criminals."

They worked solidly through the afternoon with little to show for the effort. They had finished the scanning in the main level of the house and were almost done with the ground floor.

Kamika helped with the scanning until five-thirty, when she left to check her place for missing items and then meet her cousin for dinner.

As they finished the laundry room scans, Lea placed the tablet showing no results of any merit on the washing machine and sighed. "Are you ready for a break?" she asked Montgomery.

He glanced at the time. "Are you about to collapse from hunger and thirst?"

"Yes!"

�֎

Later, over fajitas, Lea asked Montgomery for the details of items that the intruder had moved. Montgomery described how the kitchen cabinets and various closets had been rifled, but nothing was missing. "Wendy's phone vanished from where she'd left it charging, only to reappear later in the living room. Wendy's tablet vanished from the kitchen and reappeared in her car in the garage where Ashley found it. If Ryan hadn't seen her leave her phone charging and then go to bed, he'd think she'd moved it and forgotten. Similarly, he'd seen her working on her tablet the evening before it was found in her car, although she hadn't gone out that evening. Ryan insisted that he'd gone to bed after she had, and he'd passed by the phone on his way to bed. The items had to have been moved overnight."

"What about Jack?" Lea asked.

"They say he's been too anxious to wander around alone at night. I wouldn't call that definitive proof, but he denied touching the items." Montgomery popped a chip coated with salsa into his mouth.

"Who else has access to the house? A ton of workmen must have gone through with all the upgrades being done. Was anyone else given a key?"

"Ryan says he and his wife have taken turns meeting the workmen. None have been given keys to the castle. Ryan's still upgrading the electrical systems and wiring, so remote access and keyless entry aren't available yet. Even if the whole system were running, he says he can make it hack proof." Montgomery laughed and shook his head. "I've never seen a system that couldn't be hacked by someone determined to get inside, but that's not a factor yet."

"I'm sure the Hanovers checked her out before they hired her, but what about Ashley Olafsen, Wendy's assistant? Does she have a key?"

Montgomery nodded. "She does. I ran a background check on her. She has no criminal record."

"That doesn't mean someone didn't copy her key," Lea said.

"I've questioned her. Ashley doesn't think anyone could have taken it, but all it takes is a second to make an impression of a key."

Lea didn't comment but continued munching on tortilla chips and salsa. She switched subjects. Kamika needed their help, too. "Did you get anything back from the store where someone used Kamika's credit card?"

Montgomery took a gulp of iced tea. "Not yet. The head of security is at a training seminar this weekend. I won't hear anything back until Monday. I hope Kamika did a thorough check at her apartment and made sure nothing else is missing."

"She'll call if she finds something wrong," Lea said. At that moment, Lea's phone rang. "It's Kamika." She tossed Montgomery a look of concern as she answered. "Kamika?"

"Lea, someone went through my jewelry, and my passport is missing!" Kamika sounded near tears.

"Oh, no! Did they take anything else?" Lea paid her bill hastily on the table checkout screen.

"I don't think so. But Lea, my passport! I've looked everywhere. I keep it in the nightstand by my bed. It's not there. I took everything out and even looked under the drawers to see if it fell out. It's gone!" She sobbed and took a gasping breath.

Lea moved the phone away from her mouth and said to Montgomery, "Her passport is missing!"

"Tell her I'm coming over. Does she want to call the police?" Montgomery asked.

Lea moved the phone back to her mouth. "Kamika, are you going to call the police?"

"No! Oh, I don't know! What should I do? It's not as if anyone broke in. What does Montgomery say?"

Montgomery reached over for the phone to answer the question himself, since he could hear her voice clearly despite Lea holding the phone. "I'll be there soon." He gave the phone back to Lea.

Lea put the phone back to her ear. "Are you okay until we get there?"

"I'm fine. I'm going to call and tell my cousin I don't feel well. I won't even be lying. My stomach is tied in knots right now. I'll tell her to go to dinner without coming back here." Kamika's voice was steadier but still shaky.

"Call your mom and your aunt. Ask if your cousin has any kind of history with this sort of thing," Lea said. "Sit tight. I'll come with Montgomery."

"Yes. Please come."

"Okay, we'll see you soon."

CHAPTER 11

"HOW OLD IS THIS COMPLEX THAT it doesn't have better security?" Montgomery asked when Kamika opened the door.

Kamika grimaced. "Old! Thirty years at least. Upgrades are scheduled for next year. I don't have any of the residential system controls for remotely checking the property, locks, windows, or doors. I never needed a nanny cam since I don't have pets or kids to spy on. It never occurred to me to get cameras to monitor an empty apartment. I'm not living uptown and paying for views and lifestyle."

Montgomery examined the door. "Your front door looks clean: no obvious signs of tampering or being forced. Let me see the back door."

Kamika pointed to a door leading to a small patio as Lea gave her a hug.

Montgomery spent a few minutes examining the door, the locks, and the door frame. Then he went from window to window checking them before rejoining Kamika and Lea.

"Well, I don't see any evidence of a break-in. Chances are someone used your key. That could be someone from the complex, or your cousin. Does anyone else have access?"

Kamika started to shake her head no and then stopped. "Umm. My parents, but they haven't been over in a while."

Montgomery surveyed the room around him before saying, "Show me where your passport was."

Kamika walked down a short hall, past the bathroom and into the larger of two bedrooms.

"Did you check for fingerprints?" asked Montgomery, taking in the layout of the room and checking the window by the bed.

"I used the fingerprint scanner from the office. The drawer was wiped clean. Not even my prints were on it." Kamika's dejected eyes met hers. "That means someone covered their tracks. They've done this before, haven't they?"

Montgomery nodded and patted her on the shoulder sympathetically before he silently returned to the living room.

Lea and Kamika followed. Lea put her arm around Kamika's shoulders as Montgomery asked, "Do you want me to do a reading?"

"A reading? Here? In my apartment?" Kamika looked horrified.

"You reset the place when you moved in," Lea said. "If the thief was talking, we might get more details."

"Or you might get me singing, talking on the phone, or who knows what else. No way. This is my space, my private life. I don't want anybody doing a reading in here!" Her voice rose in volume and pitch with each word.

"Think it over, please," Montgomery said in a gentle voice. "In the meantime, I'll get the video from the store where your card was used."

"Did you talk to your mother or your aunt?" Lea asked.

"Mom says she hasn't heard anything negative about Lusa from my Aunt Hana. My aunt is a complainer, too, so if my cousins did anything, Mom would have heard about it. I'm still trying to decide if I should talk to my cousin or Aunt Hana first. I shouldn't assume Lusa did it. She may have had a friend over while I was at work. On the other hand, maybe she left the door unlocked and is afraid to tell me since she doesn't know if anything is missing. I should give her a chance to answer some questions at least." Kamika crossed her arms and slouched onto her couch with a pained, miserable expression.

"When do you expect her back?" Montgomery asked.

"Who knows? It's Saturday night. She's out with friends. She's underage, but they could still go to a midnight movie." Kamika blinked back tears.

"I'm going to run a background check on her," Montgomery said decisively. "Give me her full name and date of birth."

"Good idea," Lea said. "We need to know if she's ever been in any kind of trouble before."

"Any juvenile records might be sealed, but I might be able to find out if any records even exist if I reach the right contact. You two take tomorrow off and rest. I'll see you Monday. Lea, do you need a ride?"

Lea glanced at Kamika. "No, I'll stay here for a while. Okay, Kamika?"

Kamika gave her a weak smile. "I'll give you a ride home later. We could watch a movie and have some popcorn. Then, if Lusa comes back, you could help me figure out how to question her."

❀

Montgomery poked his head into the break room at Bad Vibes Removal Services on Monday morning, where Kamika and Lea sat chatting "Well, ladies, what's up?"

Lea put her coffee on the table and glanced at Kamika.

"Oh, we have a lot to tell you!" said Kamika, jumping from her chair and bumping the table, causing Lea's coffee to slosh in her cup. Anger reddened her cheeks. Kamika began stalking back and forth. "That girl! Lusa! She took my passport to use as fake identification to get into a club Saturday night! She attached a picture of her over my picture. She was hoping to put the passport back before I noticed that it was gone. She admitted going through my drawers looking for it. She said it was her boyfriend's idea, but I told her it's her fault for going along with him. What a ninny! What a stupid teenager!"

Lea wiped up her spilled coffee. When Kamika paused for a breath, Lea continued the summary of events. "We waited for her to come in Saturday night. At two in the morning, she finally returned. She reeked of alcohol, but she wasn't drunk."

"She handed over my passport and started crying. Can you believe her?" Kamika's green eyes blazed and her curls trembled on her head. To Lea, Kamika looked like a Fury from Greek mythology, one of the Erinyes, a beautiful goddess of vengeance ready to unleash her wrath. Although, Lea reflected, those goddesses were sometimes depicted as ugly; she preferred the later, beautiful versions, which were more in line with Kamika's appearance.

Montgomery interrupted the tag team explanation. "Did she say anything about the credit card?"

"She denied taking it! She said she didn't know a thing about it. Then she got upset that I would accuse her of stealing right after she admitted to stealing my passport. I told her I was having it investigated, and she went all pale and ran out of the room. I didn't see her again until Sunday afternoon when she packed her stuff and went home. She barely made eye contact as she thanked me for letting her stay with me. Good riddance!"

Montgomery threw a comforting arm around Kamika's shoulders and pulled her to his side. "Well, I got the results of her background check. She came back clean, so there's no record of her having done anything like this before. Did you tell her mother what happened?"

"No, not yet. I want to see the video of who used my card first. Did you get that back yet?" Kamika stopped pacing and gesticulating for a moment to eye Montgomery, her chest heaving and her hands perched on her hips defiantly.

Montgomery laughed. "It's barely eight-thirty on Monday morning! If I haven't heard from him by noon, I'll contact the store security officer again. In the meantime, you two are helping me at the castle again today. You're going to try a reset on the basement and garage while I help Ryan review his options for security. The electrician thinks the upgrades to the electrical lines and breakers will be done shortly, so Ryan can install a more complete system than just the cameras we added to try to catch his intruder. The Hanovers haven't had anything moved or taken in two weeks, and no one has shown up on the cameras skulking around, so they're hoping whoever the intruder was has given up. Ryan even rekeyed all the locks yesterday in case someone had somehow gotten hold of a key. Since we never found any point of forced entry, someone using a key was the most likely option."

"Why didn't he change the locks when he first moved in?" asked Lea.

"He did," Montgomery said. "Which is what makes this even stranger, because he only got four keys. The people with the keys have no reason to break in since they are there all the time anyway."

Lea's eyebrows went up with curiosity. "Who has keys?"

"Ryan, Wendy, Wendy's sister, and Wendy's assistant, Ashley." Montgomery clapped his hands together loudly. "Let's go. And Lea, let me know if you have any thoughts on ghost removal while you're resetting the basement." He gave Lea a grin and walked out the door.

Kamika turned to Lea and shook her head. "In the dark with a crying ghost! Wonderful. That's exactly what I need today!"

❦

Lea, Kamika, and Montgomery arrived at the Hanovers' castle to find Jack running across the front yard with Wyatt. Wendy stood on the high stone porch chatting with another woman, who wore jeans, a casual blouse, and white canvas tennis shoes—what Lea thought of as mom-style. Her bobbed, mahogany hair matched Wyatt's in color. Lea guessed she was the boy's mother.

As they exited Montgomery's van, Wendy looked over and waved at them. "Hello, come on up!" she called. "All the locks have been rekeyed. The motion detectors and remote monitoring for the security system have been installed. I feel more secure in the house already. Meet Wyatt's mother, Desty Miller. I was telling her about the troubles we've been having. She thinks curious teenagers, like her older son, are the most likely suspects."

They all nodded to Mrs. Miller, who smiled at them politely. "We haven't had any crime to speak of in this area. No break-ins or even vandalism, unless you count the teenagers papering each other's houses. Since nothing has been taken, rampant curiosity about this place is most likely to blame. Wendy was telling me that she might host an open house. That would go a long way to alleviate the problem."

"Desty is taking Jack and Wyatt to a trampoline play place," said Wendy, "so you won't have to worry about answering a billion questions from small boys while you work, and I get to finish preparing my presentation."

"I'll round them up and get going," said Desty. "Wendy, let me know if I can help with the open house. I'm happy to bring cookies or drinks, or help set up. See you around three o'clock." She nodded to everyone and descended the stairs, calling to the two boys as she went.

"It's good to have friendly neighbors," Kamika said, watching the woman usher the boys into a minivan.

Wendy waved to the van as it pulled away from the curb. "Yes, she was the neighborhood welcome wagon when we arrived. She brought cookies and a bottle of wine over the week we moved into this place."

"Is Desty short for something? It's an unusual name," said Lea.

"It's short for Modesty, which she hates. She's named after her great-aunt, who is apparently a wonderful old gal at ninety-five years old. So rather than risk insulting her great-aunt by changing her name, she shortened it to Desty."

"That's what I'd do if someone named me Modesty," Kamika said.

"What does she do?" asked Montgomery.

Wendy thought for a moment. "She has a home-based business. She said it was IT work for a small company." Then, shifting her attention, she said, "What's the plan for the basement? Ryan tells me we're going to try to reset the atmosphere like we did in Jack's room."

Montgomery gave her a half shrug. "That's the plan. I'm not sure how successful we'll be with all that stone, but it's a place to start."

Montgomery, Lea, and Kamika hauled three sets of infusing equipment to the garage.

Kamika's curls trembled and her eyes darted sharply from side to side. "I'm nervous. Usually Lea's the only one to see ghosts. I don't want to see her again."

Lea clapped Kamika's back encouragingly. "So far, she's only appeared in the evening. It's midmorning. We should be too early to see her."

They stood in a garage with one parking space empty and the other occupied by a minivan. Ryan was apparently out. Beyond the car area was the ping-pong table, and beyond that, the stair to the basement with its new surrounding bannister, and, at the far end of the room, stood the doors to the laundry room and several other smaller storage areas. Off to the right, Lea located the door that closed off the spiral stair to the main level of the house. The space was more than quadruple the size of any average two-car garage. The floor had been redone in some places, with sealed concrete in the car area. The ping-pong area and the laundry room floors were covered with ceramic tile.

Kamika sighed heavily and began to survey the walls. "We'd better infuse with something powerful. Forget serenity or calm. This place could use a dose of all-out joy. Anything less wouldn't last for a week. Neutral white noise might only last ten minutes."

"I concur," Montgomery said, then turned to Wendy. "More than that, you should break up the space. Separate the garage from the game area with framed sheetrock walls. Then, Kamika, you could do a redesign on the game area like any other room. Add color, throw rugs, scent, sound, the works."

Kamika brightened, nodding her head. "Absolutely. That's something I could sink my teeth into."

"Are we resetting the wine cellar, too?" asked Lea. "The cave isn't adding to the atmosphere problems, but it could help add to the sensory load below stairs to cancel out the death and despair."

"Please, do anything you think will help," Wendy said. Her arms were crossed over her chest, hugging herself, and she rubbed her hands up and down on her upper arms. "I'd love to be able to come down here without getting freaked out. Good luck. I have a ton of work to do that Mae's diary has been distracting me from doing. The presentation of my work to a potential buyer is next week. Come get me if you need me. I'll be in my office."

"All right," Montgomery said.

Wendy hurried over to the door to the spiral staircase leading to the main floor and jerked it open. She vanished up the stairs even before the door had swung closed.

Montgomery walked toward the stairs to the former dungeon. "I'll start the infusions below. Lea, you start this big open space. Kamika, you infuse the laundry room and the other storage rooms. Let's do a minimum of three coats. Okay?"

"Okay," Lea said.

"You're the boss," Kamika said.

They picked up the equipment and began the slow process of infusing white noise followed by essence of joy into the unyielding stone, the doors, and the small amount of drywall that had been added to cover piping and electrical wires in the laundry room.

�֍

Three hours later, Montgomery emerged from below to find Kamika and Lea still working on the large, open room. Kamika had finished the side rooms and moved on to help Lea. Montgomery waved his arms to get their attention over the noise of the infusers.

Lea saw and turned off her machine, leading Kamika to turn hers off as well.

"I've finished two full coats on every surface below, including the ceiling. My arms are about to fall off from carrying the equipment and directing the infusion nozzle. Are y'all ready for a lunch break?" he asked.

Thirty minutes later, all three sat down to sliced brisket sandwiches at a local barbecue joint.

Montgomery consumed his sandwich in three large bites and pulled out his phone to work on something while he munched more slowly on his chips.

"Kamika," he said, "the video from the store came in."

She almost choked on her iced tea. "What! Can I see? Who used my credit card?"

"My guess is that it's not your cousin—unless I misheard you, and your cousin is male."

"A guy used my card? No way! Let me see the video."

"You can see it more clearly on the tablet. Let me pull it up." He paused. "There. It's loading." He handed the tablet across the table to Kamika.

Lea peered over her shoulder, and they both watched a sales transaction take place on the screen. A man with short, dark hair and the sparse facial hair of youth on his upper lip and chin swiped a card at a self-checkout register in a clothing store. He glanced around furtively as he bagged his items, collected the receipt, and then walked slowly out of the camera's view.

"Wait. Let me see that again. Can I zoom in on his face?" Kamika asked.

"Sure," Lea said, pointing out the buttons to press. Kamika hit replay and zoomed in on the young man's face.

"Oh!" she gasped angrily and stomped her foot. "I know that guy! That's Lusa's boyfriend—the one who suggested that she take my passport for fake identification to get into clubs. We had dinner the night she arrived."

"Do you think Lusa gave him your credit card?" Montgomery asked.

"I don't know! Maybe he took it himself! He stayed at the table to guard our purses while we went for drink refills."

"How do you want to proceed?" Montgomery asked. "People who do this sort of thing will keep going until they are caught."

"Can you check him out?" Lea asked. "If he has been caught before, he'll have a record.

"Do you know his name?" he asked Kamika.

"No, but I can find out!" Anguished tears filled her eyes. "What if this guy is pulling Lusa into a life of crime?"

"She makes her own choices, just like the rest of us," Lea said, but with sympathy. "If she's helped him commit fraud or identify theft, she's going to get caught, too."

Kamika took a napkin from the table and dabbed gently at her eyes. "My mother is going to be upset. I hope Lusa isn't involved, but I can't protect her if she is. I'll get that guy's name tonight. After that, can you prepare the case for the police?"

"Yes," Montgomery said, accepting his tablet back from Kamika.

Lea finished eating quickly, noting the miserable look on Kamika's face. Kamika nibbled at her chips and sipped her tea but otherwise ate little, her appetite impaired by anxiety.

They returned to the castle to finish resetting the basement and ground floor levels. As they parked in front, Ashley Olafsen emerged from the front doors at the top of the stone stairwell entry. She looked around frantically, spotted them arriving, and began to wave her arms at them.

Ashley yelled, "Hurry! Hurry! Come help me! Someone attacked Wendy!"

CHAPTER 12

A SECOND LATER, SIRENS SOUNDED IN THE distance. Ashley stood in the open doorway at the top of the stone stairs. "I called 911. An ambulance is coming. She's on the floor to her office. Her head is bleeding!"

Montgomery bounded up the steps and pushed past Ashley. "Stay here and direct the medics to her. I'm going in," he said as he went by her.

Kamika stayed with Ashley. Lea raced behind Montgomery to the third floor.

They found Wendy groaning and curled on the floor, with one hand on her head. Her hand and her head were sticky with blood. The carpet under her was smudged red.

Montgomery knelt beside her. "Lie still. Help is coming."

Wendy opened her eyes and blinked at him. "What happened?"

"I was hoping you could tell me," Montgomery said with a grim smile.

She rolled over on her back and blinked a few times. "I was sitting at the desk, working on my presentation slides. Then, the next thing I remember, Ashley was here shaking me awake on the floor. Ohh, my head hurts." She closed her eyes again.

Lea retrieved a clean hand towel from the bathroom in the hall and gave it to Montgomery, who held it over the two-inch gash on the crown of Wendy's head.

Lea looked around the room. Papers from the desk had been scattered on the floor. Wendy's laptop sat open with a bubbly fish tank screen saver on the screen. A tablet and phone sat on the desktop, too. Whatever the motive for the attack had been, it wasn't theft of electronics.

Voices came from the hallway. A moment later, Ashley led a police officer and two emergency medical technicians into the room. Kamika started to follow them, but the police officer blocked the door.

"Stay outside, please," he said, using his back and shoulders to block Kamika's way. "Everyone out of the room so that the EMTs can work! Now! Everyone out now!"

Lea and Ashley jumped at the barked order and slid out of the room past the officer. Montgomery glanced up, but didn't move until an EMT had taken his place by Wendy and placed a pad of gauze where he had been holding the towel over the cut on her head.

As he exited the room, Montgomery began dialing on his phone.

"Ryan, this is Montgomery. Listen, your wife was attacked at your house. EMTs are with her. She was hit over the head, but she's conscious. They'll have to take her to the hospital for stitches and to check her for concussion."

As he talked, Montgomery began to shepherd Lea, Kamika, and Ashley back down the stairs. "Okay, see you in fifteen minutes," he said, then returned his phone to his pocket. "Let's meet Ryan on the porch. The police aren't going to want us in the house contaminating their crime scene any more than we already have."

"Do you think the cameras Ryan installed will show who attacked Wendy?" Lea asked.

"I'm hoping they will," Montgomery said.

More police arrived. Curious neighbors began to cluster on lawns near the castle, as Montgomery, Lea, Kamika, and Ashley waited on the great stone porch for Ryan Hanover.

Montgomery studied Ashley's worried face before he asked, "When I spoke to you previously about why someone might want to search the castle, you didn't really think they were looking for treasure, did you?"

Ashley glanced up at him but didn't answer.

Montgomery asked, "What did you think, Ashley?"

The woman shuffled her feet nervously. "I thought someone might be trying to steal Wendy's work. Her things and places where she spent time were searched."

Montgomery tilted his head, considering her answer. "Why didn't you say so, then?"

"Because it seemed so unlikely," she said. "I had no proof."

"Corporate espionage," Lea said to Montgomery. "Wendy must have had the same thought. She started to say something after you suggested that someone like Mr. Keller might be trying to steal Ryan's work. But Ryan doesn't have anything worth stealing right now. Wendy does."

Montgomery nodded, then turned suddenly and began examining the front door. "Hmm. Ashley, how did you get into the house today? You didn't have the new key yet, did you?"

Ashley shook her head. "No. Wendy called me yesterday to tell me that they'd changed the locks, so my key wouldn't work. She said that she would leave this door unlocked for me." Ashley's eyes opened wide in dismay. "Is that how her attacker got inside? Because the door was unlocked for me?"

Montgomery smacked his hand against his forehead. "That means the attacker could have walked right into the castle. He didn't even have to break a window or force a lock."

Ryan arrived as the EMTs were bringing Wendy across the lawn to an ambulance. He ran to her side, kissed her forehead, and held her hand.

As she was loaded into the ambulance, Ryan looked frantically around. He ran over to Montgomery. "Have you seen Jack?"

"He went with his friend Wyatt for a playdate earlier today. They're not due back until three o'clock."

"Thank God! I'm going with Wendy. I'll call you later." He sprinted back to his car and followed the ambulance as it pulled away from the curb.

Moments later, police officers separated Montgomery, Lea, Kamika, and Ashley to interview them individually. Lea and Kamika were soon finished giving their statements. They watched as two plainclothes detectives arrived. The uniformed officer who had interviewed Lea walked over to meet the detectives. They talked for a moment before one of the detectives turned and located Montgomery, caught his eye, and gave a nod of recognition. Montgomery returned the acknowledgment.

Lea and Kamika joined Montgomery as the detective who had nodded walked toward him. The other detective, a black-haired man with a large Roman nose, walked over to the officer questioning Ashley.

"Montgomery, what brought you into this case?" the detective asked, his eyes rapidly noting Lea's tunic and Kamika's well-fitting clothes before darting back to Montgomery.

"It's a long story, Schmitt," Montgomery frowned. "And I need permission to tell all of it."

Schmitt shook his head in resignation. "Then get permission quickly!"

"I'll tell you all about my movements here today and anything that might help identify Wendy's attacker. To start with, Ryan Hanover had all the locks rekeyed or replaced a few days ago. He had new security cameras installed as well. Whoever attacked Wendy may not know about all the new cameras."

A voice behind him spoke, "Where can we find the recording of the security camera feed?"

Montgomery whipped around to see the dark-haired detective standing behind him. "Oh. Hi, Marco. I can show you. I helped set some of it up."

Marco shook Montgomery's hand. "So this family put in a new security system and changed all their locks this weekend. And they have you, an investigator, working for them. Yet the lady left the door unlocked so that anyone could walk inside. It doesn't make sense."

"She must have felt safe during the day. Up to this point, all of their problems have been at night," Montgomery said.

"What problems might those be?" asked Schmitt, his hand poised to take notes.

Montgomery ignored him. "We should get a look at the security cameras." He pulled his phone from his pocket and dialed. "Ryan, can I show the police the security video here at the castle?" He paused, listening. "Okay. Update us on Wendy's condition when you can. We'll let you know what we find." Montgomery stuck the phone back into his pocket. "Let's go."

Marco moved to follow Montgomery, but Schmitt planted himself in front of them. "Wait a minute. We aren't all tromping through the building. It's a crime scene," said Schmitt, holding up his hand to stop Montgomery.

Montgomery gave him an exasperated look. "Do you want the security video or not? Also, my team and I have already been all over the building."

"Okay. Only you, but suited properly. Your team stays here. Show me the security video," Schmitt said.

"Lea, Kamika, wait here. I'll be back," Montgomery said with an apologetic look.

The women watched as the detectives and Montgomery put on shoe covers and gloves.

Kamika bumped Lea with her elbow. "Do you think Montgomery knows the entire police force for every town around here?"

"Yes," Lea said. "He's tried to get all of them to use his equipment, and he's conducted informational presentations explaining how the scanners work that have drawn all sorts of law enforcement personnel. As a private detective, he needs all kinds of contacts, and networking comes naturally to him."

"Think the cameras will show anything?"

"It depends on how careful the intruder was and what they wanted," Lea said. Giving Kamika a sidelong glance, she asked, "How are you going to find out Lusa's boyfriend's full name?"

"I'm going to ask my aunt first. If she doesn't know, I'm going to tell Lusa about the video of him using my credit card and make her tell me," she said decisively. A serious look settled over Kamika's lovely face, and she crossed her arms over her chest in a determined way.

"What if she won't tell you?"

"She will, or I'll tell her mother about the video. Her mother will get the information out of her. No one could withstand that nagging for long. Aunt Hana is the queen of nagging. Lusa will tell me, or she'll have her mother on her case. I'm betting, given the options, she'll tell me."

A moment later, Montgomery returned alone. The two detectives remained inside the castle.

"Was the attacker on camera?" Lea asked.

"Yes and no," said Montgomery. "We see a man in some sort of work coverall enter the house without even pausing at the door. It's as if he knew the door would be unlocked. Unfortunately, he's wearing a ski mask and gloves, so we don't know what he looks like, and we can't get fingerprints. He moved quickly. He's about six feet tall, and about a hundred seventy pounds. We know what he wanted. After he bashed Wendy on the head with a small blackjack or sap he carried in with him, he inserted a flash drive into her laptop and copied the hard drive."

"Oh!" Kamika gasped. "Then it's Wendy's work he's after. Not treasure or anything of Ryan's."

"Given that her phone and tablet were already targeted, that makes sense. The attacker didn't even try to get Ryan's data from his computer in his office." Montgomery pulled out his phone. "I need to let Ryan know what we found. He'll have some insight into who might be after his wife's work." Again, he reached for his phone.

Lea looked around the neighborhood at the few neighbors standing outside, still watching the activity in front of the castle. "How did the attacker know she was home alone? He had to have been watching the castle to know that Jack had left with Wyatt, that Ryan's car wasn't here, that we had left for lunch, and that Ashley hadn't arrived yet. Also, the attacker would have had to know Ashley's schedule and that the door was unlocked for her."

Kamika eyed the surrounding neighborhood. "Where would someone hide? Wouldn't we have noticed someone sitting in a parked car, watching the castle? Or wouldn't the neighbors have seen someone?"

"Maybe someone did see something but didn't know it was important. Do we need to ask them?" Lea asked.

"Don't worry about it," said Montgomery, finished now with his phone, rejoining the conversation. "The police will take care of canvassing the neighborhood for information on our attacker. In the meantime, this place is going to be a crime scene for a while. I'm going to the hospital to see Ryan and Wendy. I can drop you off at the office on my way to the hospital. Let's go."

Lea and Kamika sat at the table in the kitchen break room after Montgomery dropped them at the office. Kamika had a vegetable and fruit juice drink while Lea had her second caffeinated soda. It was midafternoon, and the Bad Vibes Removal Services office was humming with activity. Miguel had rushed in for a drink and glared at them before stalking back to his desk. If Kamika and Lea weren't working atmosphere resets, Miguel had to schedule fewer clients for the day.

Consequently, he couldn't always send a technician when a client requested. That made clients grumpy, which made Miguel grumpy.

Kamika stuck her tongue out at his back as he left. Lea admonished her for it. "We're making his job harder. You can't blame him for being annoyed."

"He makes a habit out of being perpetually annoyed. I think he likes to be annoyed. If he wasn't irritated at us, he would find something else. He'd be aggravated because the network was slow, or the phones were out, or his computer was down. He needs to be less negative all the time."

"Yep," Lea said agreeably, sipping her Dr. Pepper. "Or you need to accept that his outlook on life is different from yours and not let it bother you."

"You mean since I can't change him, I should change my response to him? How does that help morale in the rest of the office? Speaking of changing, when are you going to break that caffeine habit?" Kamika asked with a hint of mischief.

Lea rolled her eyes. "If you respond to him cheerfully, others might copy you. We might kill his bad mood with kindness. As for the caffeine, I'll quit when I'm ready. When are you going to confront your cousin?"

Kamika sighed. "You *would* mention that. I'd put it to the back of my mind, and you had to go reminding me."

"That's not an answer."

"Soon. In a while. *Later.*"

"Still not an answer."

Kamika's face drooped, her lips pouting. "This is such a mess. Can you help me?"

"Yes. Start by calling your aunt. We need that guy's name."

"Okay." Kamika picked up her phone from the table and called her aunt. "Hi, Aunt Hana. It's Kamika." She paused. "No, nothing's wrong. Mom's fine. . . . I'm fine. I called because had a question for you. When Lusa was here, we went to dinner with a friend of hers, and I can't remember his name. Do you happen to know who he is?" She paused again, listening. "No, I haven't asked Lusa yet. Is something wrong? . . . What? . . . Oh, she didn't seem happy when she got home? I see. Hmmmm. I might have an idea. I'll get back to you soon . . . Thanks . . . Bye . . . Bye . . . I really have to go . . . Bye, Auntie." She stabbed at the button to end the call.

"Now my aunt's gonna be on my case," Kamika frowned. "That woman has a sixth sense for trouble."

"That's good," Lea said. "She should be paying more attention to Lusa's activities and friends."

"She didn't know the guy's name. I'm going to have to talk to Lusa. I wish she lived in town. This would be easier face to face."

"So do a video call."

"It's not the same."

"It's better than nothing."

Kamika placed her phone on the table and turned off the screen. She turned away from the phone and looked at Lea. "How's Patrick's job search going?"

"Don't change the subject," Lea said. "We're talking about you."

"My troubles can wait." She brushed the subject firmly aside with a wave of her hands. "Tell me about Patrick."

Lea considered ignoring the question, but the stubborn set of Kamika's jaw line changed her mind. "I'm a little worried. I talked to him last night. When I asked him if he'd applied to any new jobs this week, he said no.

I asked him if he'd had any interviews, and he changed the subject. What if the job search is depressing him? It's hard to interview repeatedly and not be hired. I'm getting a little worried."

"A hot man like that will find a job," Kamika said. "That is a fact."

"Not if he loses confidence in himself. And I felt like he wasn't telling me something. Like he was holding back and feeling guilty about it."

"You read him too well. Give him a break. He'll tell you what's on his mind when he's ready. He knows how well you sense his moods."

"You're right. I'm overprotective of him because he's still recovering from his brain injury. He hates when I fuss over him. He hates feeling vulnerable."

"What do you expect? No one likes to feel like that."

"I'm praying he finds a job that he finds satisfying, something that uses his skills and makes him feel like he's contributing to the world. He wouldn't be happy with anything less. At the same time, he knows he has to start at the bottom and work his way up. I wish I could give him a morale boost."

Kamika grinned wickedly. "You want to boost that man's morale; I can give you some tips."

Lea pushed Kamika sideways in her chair but didn't push her quite out of it.

Kamika giggled. "Don't worry, hon. He'll get the right position. Give it time. He hasn't been looking very long." She reinforced her statement with a positive nod.

"Enough about Patrick." Lea slid Kamika's phone into Kamika's hand. "Call Lusa. We need to get on with this before that jerk steals someone else's credit card or identity. He could be at it again *right now.*"

A look of distress crossed Kamika's face. "You're right. He'll move on to someone else now. He's probably done this to dozens of people. If Lusa gets stuck in his criminal activities, she'll go to jail! I'm calling her."

Kamika dialed, but Lusa didn't answer. Kamika slammed the phone onto the table. "This is frustrating!" She ran her hand from her forehead onto her scalp, making her corkscrew curls stand on top of her head.

Lea had to press her lips together to keep from laughing.

"What?" asked Kamika, glaring at Lea.

"You look like you stuck your finger in an outlet with your hair sticking up like that," Lea said with a giggle.

Kamika stared at her, crossed her eyes, and stuck her tongue out, wagging it back and forth. "Blahhh! This is making me crazy!"

Lea laughed aloud. "Try not to worry about Lusa. She's probably still in school for the day. Call her again this evening."

Kamika dropped her hands from her head. "Okay, let's worry about something else. When do you think we'll hear something about Wendy's condition? Montgomery was supposed to call us with an update and instructions on what to do next."

Lea glanced at the clock on the wall. "We could call Montgomery for an update. He should have arrived at the hospital a while ago."

"I'll do it. That's a call I'm happy to make," Kamika said and grabbed her phone again.

"Hey, Montgomery, it's Kamika. Lea and I were wondering how Wendy is." Kamika listened. "Okay. So, they'll keep her for observation. Uh-huh . . . What?! . . . That's great! . . . Okay. See you in the morning. Bye."

"What's up?" asked Lea, her eyebrows lifted with curiosity.

Kamika turned to her with a big smile. "Wendy has a concussion. They did a brain scan, and it looks good. No permanent damage, but they're keeping her overnight. And there's some good news! She's pregnant!"

"Really? Jack gets a sibling," Lea said.

"Montgomery said Ryan is ecstatic. He also said he'd see us here tomorrow morning. So we are off the clock, lady."

"Movie time? I don't have a class tonight."

"I'll get the pizza," Kamika said.

"Your place or mine?"

"Mine. I had an idea." Kamika glanced at the doorway, then leaned in closer to Lea and lowered her voice to a whisper. "Listen; let's do a reading on my place. I don't want Montgomery there, but I don't mind you. We might find out what went on when my cousin was there."

"Okay. I'm going to have to check out the equipment."

"That's fine. Don't tell them it's for my place. Tell them you're demonstrating for a friend. Please?" Kamika gave her best puppy dog eyes as she spoke, making Lea laugh again.

"Okay, okay. Save that look for someone more gullible. You aren't fooling me," Lea said.

Kamika laughed, her wide mouth open exposing all of her small, even teeth. "Thanks."

❧

A while later, Lea finished her slow walk around Kamika's bedroom with the sound scanner. Kamika began the analysis program.

"It looks like someone had an argument in here recently, and I know it wasn't me," Kamika said, frowning over the tablet.

"Let's see," Lea said, joining her by the brightly blanketed double bed. Lea watched the results data tabulate. "That's by the dresser," she said, pointing to her right.

"A lower voice, likely male, said 'Keep looking!' and a higher-pitched voice, a female said, '. . . bad idea.'"

Kamika's shoulders slumped, and Lea felt a wave of sympathy for her. "At least it sounds like your cousin didn't want to take your passport. That's probably what they were doing."

"Yeah. Still, she let him push her into doing something stupid. Why couldn't she have been strong enough to tell him to go to hell?"

"Some people let others walk all over them for what they think is love. She's too young to realize that someone who loves her wouldn't do this to her." Lea looked over the data as Kamika wiped a tear from the corner of her eye. "Do you want to try this area for analysis? The program thinks there might be something there, and it looks recent."

Kamika refocused on the tablet. "It's probably only me cursing Lusa for taking my passport. Where is that?"

Lea rapidly coordinated the data to the layout of the room. "By the door."

"Huh? Okay, that's not me. Let's give it to the analyzer." Kamika jabbed a few buttons to zoom in on the area in question.

Words began to appear.

Lea felt her eyes grow wider, and Kamika stiffened next to her.

"Oh, no. That's not good. I've got to call Lusa and Aunt Hana right now." Kamika handed Lea the tablet and pulled out her phone.

Lea reread the words the analysis program had found. A deep voice had said, "Get me (indistinguishable) card or forget college! I fixed that grade, you owe me."

The female voice had screamed "No! . . . didn't ask for your help."

The male voice had said, " . . . make you regret it!"

A shrieking, high-pitched cry had followed, most likely female.

Lea shuddered. He had hit Lusa. She was being abused and blackmailed. She was in deep trouble and didn't know how to ask for help. Kamika was right; Lusa's mother needed to know. They needed to get Lusa as far away from that man as possible. Lea's heart sank. Would Montgomery be able to get the police onto the man without arresting Lusa, too? If Lusa went to the police and gave information about him, would they give her immunity in exchange for testimony?

Lea could hear Kamika talking rapidly on the phone, explaining the results they'd found. She must have gotten her aunt on the phone. Lea debated calling Montgomery to update him but decided to wait for Kamika. She looked over the results still collating on the tablet. Everything else looked older, less recent. She didn't need to run more data analyses. They hadn't done the embedded emotions scan. Lea decided to scan the area by the door while Kamika was on the phone.

A few minutes later, Lea watched the results appear. Rage and terror appeared. The man was probably the one releasing the rage, and the woman, Lusa, emitting the terror as he threatened and hit her.

Kamika came back in the room with a grim look on her face.

Lea said, "I did the emotions scan by the door. Rage, most likely from him. Terror, most likely from her. Lusa must be scared to death of him. How did your aunt take it?"

Kamika choked back tears. "Aunt Hana was horrified. She says Lusa is late coming home. She doesn't know where Lusa is. I'm worried that jerk will hurt her badly."

"So am I. All you can do is keep calling her. Let her know that you want to help."

"I wish I hadn't yelled at her," Kamika said. "She might have confided in me if I'd shown some sympathy."

"You didn't know. It's not your fault. We should call Montgomery. He may have some suggestions."

"All right. I'll do it." Her phone was still in her hand, but before she could dial, it began to ring. She glanced at it, and rushed to answer. "Lusa!"

"Help me!" cried the voice on the phone so loudly that Lea could hear it too.

CHAPTER 13

Lea listened to Kamika's end of the conversation and watched as Kamika fought to stay calm. Kamika was becoming more and more agitated, pacing, searching frantically for a pen until Lea tossed her one, and scribbling a note on her hand as she kept her ear glued to the phone. Finally, she said, "We'll pick you up. We're on our way."

Kamika looked around for her keys, but Lea said, "Uh-uh. You're too upset. I'm driving. Come on. You can tell me about it on the way."

They ran out the door to Lea's car, with Kamika talking and running at the same time.

"Go to Highway 29; I'll give you directions as we go. She's outside a nail salon. We have to get her before he finds her."

Lea slid into her car. "What do you mean, before he finds her? What is Lusa doing in town? She doesn't even live here." She started the car, barely waiting for Kamika to buckle her seatbelt before shifting into gear.

"Lusa came to break up with the jerk, whose name is Cody. He told her she wasn't allowed to break up with him. He hit her. He said that he would make her regret leaving him. Then he locked her in a closet and left her there. She thinks he was going to kill her. She's not sure. As soon as she heard him leave, she used a mailbox key to unscrew the screws on the doorknob and take it apart. She got out and drove to a shopping center. She didn't know anyone else to call around here, so she called me."

"She needs to call the police."

"She's afraid."

Lea glanced at Kamika. "We can't take her back to your place. This guy knows where you live. He might think to look for her there. We need Montgomery's help."

"Go faster." Kamika's eyes were glued to the road ahead. Traffic was heavy as the evening rush hour began.

"I could, but we'd get pulled over for speeding."

Kamika gave her an anguished look. "This is an emergency!"

"I'm going as fast as I can. Take a deep breath. She's safe. She got away. She's not still in that closet. The emergency is over."

"Just get there!" Kamika stamped her foot on the floorboard as if she had her own gas pedal.

Five minutes later, they pulled into the shopping center and located the nail salon. A dark-haired young woman paced nervously outside the doors.

Kamika pointed. "Stop! There she is." She was out the door almost before the vehicle had stopped moving.

Lea watched Kamika sprint across the pavement to grab her cousin in a hug. Kamika spoke rapidly, pointing to Lea's car, and began to lead her cousin by the hand.

In a moment, Kamika and her cousin settled into the back seat of the car.

Lea turned to look at them. Lusa's basic features were classically symmetrical and Japanese, but distorted at that moment by a blooming bruise on her right cheekbone, a bloody nose, and a busted lip.

"We should take her to an emergency room or clinic," Lea said, noting not only the beaten face but the bruises on Lusa's arms and the way she clutched tightly at her ribs.

"No!" Lusa said with fear and desperation in her voice.

"If your ribs are broken, one of them could puncture your lungs. We don't want that to happen. We should get you to a doctor," Lea urged gently.

Kamika put an arm around her cousin's shoulders. "Please, Lusa. Let us help you. We know he forced you to help him. We know he was blackmailing you over grades that he'd fixed for you."

Lusa's lips parted in surprise. "How did you know?"

"You know what work I do? How I reset and redesign places? We can cover up sound and emotional residue left in walls. Or we can read them. We can recover what was said. You argued with Cody in my house. We found that argument," Kamika said. "We want to help you. Your mother is worried about you. Please, I don't want things to get any worse. Let's go to a doctor and make sure you don't get a punctured lung." Kamika stroked her cousin's long, dark hair, tucking it behind an ear and out of Lusa's face, where it had been hanging like a long veil.

Tears dribbled down Lusa's bloodied face. "Okay. Can you call my mom for me, too?"

"Of course, honey." Kamika looked at Lea. "Nearest ER?"

Lea nodded. "On our way."

Two hours later, as the sun was setting, Lea was still waiting in a hospital lobby. She had updated Montgomery by phone. He said he was on the case. He'd reassured her that he would deal with the police. The police had come, determined Lea only knew hearsay, and left her alone, vanishing into the treatment area to photograph Lusa's injuries and take statements. Kamika had come out of the treatment area only briefly to update Lea on Lusa's condition. She had two broken ribs, internal bleeding, and a mild concussion. Kamika had called Lusa's mother, who was on her way.

Lea sat slumped in an uncomfortable, metal-framed chair. In one hand was a cup of hospital cafeteria coffee; she sat reading an archeology article on the geoglyphs in Kazakhstan on her phone with the other hand. A large, brown-shod foot nudged her shoe.

She glanced up to find Montgomery standing in front of her.

"Hi," she said, sitting straighter and closing the article.

Montgomery lowered himself into the chair next to her. "If Lusa can be convinced to avoid incriminating herself, all should be well. I explained to my contact that we had a kidnapping, possibly with intent to commit murder. The police went to Cody's house, found it open, and found the closet door exactly as Lusa described. Along with her injuries and statement, that was enough for them to put a BOLO out on Cody Presonet. A patrol unit spotted his car and tried to pull him over. He refused to stop and took them on a high-speed chase north on I-35 before he crashed and rolled near Salado."

Lea gasped. "Did he survive?"

Montgomery nodded. "He's injured, but alive. But given what they found in the car, it's a good thing Lusa was able to escape. My contact tells me the police found plastic tarps, duct tape, and saws in his trunk, all newly purchased, as well as ten credit cards that didn't belong to him. They have him for aggravated kidnapping with assault, speeding, resisting arrest, and reckless driving, plus the charges stemming from the credit card thefts. I'll give them the video of him using Kamika's card. He's going to prison no matter what."

"And Lusa?"

"She'll have to testify against him for the kidnapping at least. A good lawyer will have to help her make decisions on the credit card case. If she can testify against him, it would help the police, but they may have enough evidence without her. If he tries to blame it all on her, she'll have some explaining to do, but given the current circumstances, she should be fine. Cody's credibility is nonexistent at the moment."

"We've got the sound analysis from Kamika's house. If they'd admit it as evidence, it would help Lusa's case," Lea said.

"If they admit that as evidence, it would set a fabulous precedent. I would be thrilled. Business would boom. I'd be able to market the equipment to law enforcement agencies all over the world."

"What do you think are the odds of that?" Lea asked.

"Slim, but I can hope." Montgomery flashed a grin. "Come on. It's after seven. Let's find Kamika and get some food." He heaved himself from the chair.

Lea stood and looked around the lobby in time to see Kamika come out of the treatment area doors. "Look, there she is."

Kamika joined her colleagues.

Montgomery put his big arm around her shoulder and squeezed her against him in a side hug. "How's she doing?"

Kamika sighed loudly. "Lots of bruises, but only her ribs are broken. Aunt Hana arrived about twenty minutes ago, so she isn't alone. She gave the police an initial statement about the kidnapping, but that's all. They took pictures of her injuries. Mostly, Lusa's scared he's going to find her again and hurt her."

"She doesn't have to worry anymore. He's been arrested. With luck, the arraigning judge will set the bail too high for him to pay or will deny bail. Lusa needs to get a good lawyer though to help her through the process," Montgomery said. He explained how Cody had been arrested and what was found in the car.

"Maybe Lusa will relax if I tell her," Kamika said, turning to go back to the treatment area.

"Do you want to come to dinner with us?" Lea called after her. "We can wait for you, if you want."

Kamika turned around, "I'm starving. Let me update Lusa and Aunt Hana, and I'll be right back." She trotted back across the lobby and through the treatment area doors.

Lea's phone rang. "It's Patrick," she said to Montgomery, excusing herself to take the call. "Hi, Patrick, what's up?"

"Lea, I was wondering if you want to grab dinner."

"Montgomery, Kamika, and I were about to go to dinner. Join us. We've had a crazy day. A client was assaulted, and Kamika's cousin was beat up and kidnapped. I'll tell you all about it over dinner."

"What? Sure, I'll join you. Where are you going?"

"We hadn't discussed it yet. Let me ask Montgomery if he had an idea." Lea turned back to Montgomery, who was checking his email. "Did you have any place in mind for dinner? Patrick wants to join us."

"I was going to let y'all choose."

Patrick suggested Tony's Italian, and Montgomery and Lea agreed. As soon as Kamika returned, they all left for the restaurant.

Patrick Garcia, who'd been dating Lea since she had helped clear him of a murder charge, was a tall, clean-cut, young man, with a scar on his temple from an encounter with an IED.

Kamika liked to embarrass Patrick by telling him how handsome he was. It was a mark of how stressed out she was that she neglected to say anything to him when he joined them at the restaurant.

Patrick sat looking perplexedly at the tired faces around him. "Clearly you didn't have an average Monday of resetting atmospheres. Was the client who got attacked at one of your resets?"

"Nope. She was at an investigation of Montgomery's that also involves a reset. We were working on removing the overwhelming sensation of death from her garage and basement this morning—her basement used to be a dungeon. We left for lunch, and when we came back, we found the client had been hit over the head and knocked out. The police and EMS came. The client went to the hospital. The client's castle became a crime scene. We left," Lea said, watching Patrick's eyebrows inch higher as she spoke.

Kamika took over the story. "Yep. Then my cousin's credit-card-thief, abusive boyfriend beat her up and locked her in a closet while he went to get tools to murder her, but she escaped and called us. We picked her up and took her to the hospital."

Montgomery picked up where Kamika left off. "But the boyfriend has been arrested, and the cousin is going to be okay. Now we need to determine who knew that the castle was unlocked and that our client was alone this morning."

Patrick looked from face to face around him. "That's the second time someone has said castle. And you said *dungeon*? Your client has a castle around here?"

Lea grinned. "Yep. A genuine Irish castle, complete with a ghost or echo or something that we also need to figure out how to remove."

"I'll bet you love seeing the castle!" Patrick said to Lea. "Though not the ghost." He winked at her.

Kamika shuddered. "I saw the ghost, too. I hope I never see another one again."

Patrick's eyes popped open wide in surprise. "Kamika saw it, too? How about you?" he asked Montgomery.

Montgomery shook his balding head. "Nope. I didn't see her. I guess I'm still not sensitive enough. Our client who was attacked saw the ghost, though."

"So lots of people can see this ghost. That's new. Usually it's only Lea." He looked at her. "What do you think are my chances of seeing her?"

"I don't know. I'm less worried about the ghost right now than I am about solving the break-ins at the castle before someone gets killed," Lea said.

Patrick turned to Montgomery. "Can you tell me about it?"

To Lea's surprise, Montgomery summarized the case for Patrick. He went over what he had done to try to identify the break-in point, the background information he had found on the family, the treasure hunt, and the things they had found using the sound and emotional residue reading equipment. He even detailed investigative programs he used that Lea had never heard him mention before. She had never heard him give a full rundown on a case to anyone. Montgomery concluded with a piece of information that she hadn't known—that the attacker who had copied the hard drive might not be able to break Wendy's encryption protecting her files.

A waitress came with drinks and took their orders for dinner.

When the waitress left, Patrick asked Montgomery, "What do you know about the assistant, Ashley?"

"She's deeply in debt from school loans, but, otherwise, nothing stands out on her record."

"Someone could have offered her money to let them know when they could get into the castle. You know she didn't attack Wendy herself since it's a man on the security video, but that doesn't mean she wasn't paid to leak information," Patrick said.

Montgomery sipped his iced tea and nodded. "I've considered that. And she did have a key before, so she could have been the one breaking in at night. Still, her statements so far ring true. Besides, she already had access to everything, so why would she break in or help someone else break in?"

Kamika interrupted with a worried look on her face. "I don't want to think it's possible, having met him, but could Ryan have hit her? I don't trust my judgment of men too much right now."

Montgomery patted her hand. "Your judgment is fine. Ryan was in a technology conference this afternoon as the guest speaker. He couldn't have done it.

He knew she was alone with the door unlocked but swears he didn't tell anyone about it. I don't think he's involved, or he wouldn't have called me in to investigate the break-ins."

Lea had an idea. "Did Wendy tell anyone other than Ashley that the door was unlocked?"

"I don't know; I haven't had a chance to question her," Montgomery said. "But we can search the castle for electronic bugs. If someone has been getting inside the house, they could have planted bugs, or even cloned her phone. Someone could be listening to her conversations."

"Will we be able to get inside tomorrow, or is it still a crime scene?" Lea asked.

"They'll release it tomorrow. But I'm not sure when. Ryan sent Jack to Wendy's sister Carol's for the night, since Ryan is staying with Wendy at the hospital. I'll have to ask the detectives on the case when we can get inside."

The food was delivered, and they all began to eat.

Patrick took a swallow of his Dos Equis and frowned thoughtfully. "Is anyone watching the castle tonight? If it's unoccupied, someone might take another shot at breaking in."

"If all he wanted was on the laptop, the man won't be back," Lea said.

Montgomery shrugged. "You never know. Ashley's arrival could have interrupted him. He might not have had a chance to get everything he wanted. I'll put one of my guys on surveillance."

The conversation became more general as the waitress appeared with their plates of food. Kamika asked Patrick about his job hunt, but he parried the question and turned the subject back to her cousin. Lea noticed and was troubled. She glanced at Montgomery, who was eating a large serving of lasagna with gusto. He didn't seem to have noticed Patrick's lack of answer.

The meal ended with everyone agreeing that they were much too full for dessert. They split the bill and went their separate ways for the night.

Lea went home to copious amounts of reading and an analysis paper on the home life habits of various groups of ancient Roman noncitizens. Her mind kept wandering back to Kamika's cousin and the Hanovers. She finished the paper much later than she had planned but submitted it online before the midnight deadline.

She went to bed, her mind still turning over how to deal with the ghost in the castle. She'd never encountered anything like it and wasn't sure if she could devise a solution. As she drifted off, she realized that the Hanover men, and men in general, never saw the ghost—only women. Mae had seen the ghost when her nephew was plotting against her husband and trying to get money from her. Wendy had seen the ghost and, subsequently, been attacked for her work. According to Mae's diary, a woman in Ireland had told Mae that the ghost walked to warn of betrayal and traitors. The ghost maid in the legend had betrayed her own mistress. The ghost might warn women of betrayal. Kamika had seen the ghost, and her cousin had betrayed her by stealing her passport and credit card. Who was betraying Wendy Hanover? Would the ghost leave if they caught the traitor?

Lea drifted off to a restless sleep after jotting down her thoughts, knowing from experience that she would never remember her thought process in the morning unless she wrote it down. The last note she wrote said, "I saw the ghost, too. Who's betraying me?"

CHAPTER 14

T UESDAY MORNING, LEA WAS FINISHING HER second large mug of black coffee by the time Kamika and Montgomery appeared in the break room of the Bad Vibes office.

"Hon, you look awful," Kamika said with characteristic candor. "What's wrong? Are you sick?"

"I didn't sleep well last night."

"The bags under your eyes already told me that. When you don't sleep, it's because something is bugging you. You weren't worrying about this mess with my cousin, were you?"

"No, I had an idea about the ghost in the castle. If her appearances warn of betrayal like Mae wrote in her diary, why do the men not see her? Remember the legend in Mae's diary? Suppose whenever betrayal threatens the women in the castle, the ghost appears and replays the sequence of movements she went through after her own betrayal and leading up to her own murder. Someone who knows Wendy betrayed her, and she was attacked."

"That sounds possible," Montgomery said as he made himself a cup of coffee. "Did that prevent you from sleeping?"

"Kamika saw the ghost, and her cousin was betraying her. I saw the ghost, too. Does that mean I'm in danger of betrayal, too? Or does the ghost see me as an extension of the family since I'm working there?"

Montgomery laughed. "You're probably overthinking this. You're already sensitive to this kind of thing. You're probably one of the few people who can see the crying woman no matter what. You see ghosts all the time."

"Not all the time!" said Lea, defensively.

Montgomery sipped his hot coffee carefully. "Well, compared to the two of us, you do."

Kamika nodded. "He's got a point. Don't worry about it. This is about the Hanovers. You're detecting signals meant for them."

Lea shrugged noncommittally and sipped her coffee. "What's the plan for today?" she asked Montgomery.

"We'll be allowed back into the castle at noon. But before that, how would you like to join me on a callback on one of your resets?" Montgomery asked with a sparkle in his eye.

Kamika's eyes popped open in surprise. "A callback on us! No way! You mean someone called in unsatisfied with a reset we did?"

Montgomery sat down at the table next to Lea. "Yes. That's generally what a callback means."

"That's never happened before," Lea said. She paused in thought. "Was it the house from last week that only wanted one room reset?"

Montgomery paused with his coffee cup halfway to his mouth and stared at her. "Yes. How did you know?"

"We couldn't get that room to be neutral no matter what we did," Lea said. "Either something is seeping through the walls because the whole place has been remodeled so many times that the problem is under the current surfaces, or the closet in that room contains a nasty history."

"I remember that place," Kamika said. "We couldn't get the place to a point where Lea was satisfied, and the troubled area was definitely near that locked closet."

"That explains it. Let's go take a look," said Montgomery. "I told Miguel I'd take you two there before we go to the castle so he doesn't have to send Keely and Jose."

Lea finished the last of her coffee, still tired but starting to feel the caffeine in her system. She rinsed her mug and set it out to dry. "I'm ready. Let's go."

They rode together in a Bad Vibes van, preprogrammed to take them to the correct address.

Kamika filled them in on her cousin Lusa's situation. "The hospital released her last night, and Aunt Hana took her home. She'll be sore until those ribs heal. They're getting a lawyer to help her through this mess. She's not a bad kid. How she fell in with a thug like that Cody, I don't know."

Montgomery sighed and shook his head. "She might have fallen for the idea of helping him or fixing him. She's eighteen years old and doesn't know the meaning of real love. She didn't have the experience to see the pitfalls in front of her. Hopefully, she'll learn from this and not repeat her mistake."

"Aunt Hana is going to send her to counseling. Lusa doesn't want to go, but I told her she should," Kamika said. "Is Wendy being released today?"

Montgomery nodded. "Yes, Ryan notified me that he expects to be able to take her home around noon, which is about the same time as the police will release the crime scene."

Lea found her next reading assignment on her tablet and opened it. "Good. She can tell us if she remembered anything about her attacker or if she told anyone that the door would be unlocked."

Montgomery worked on emails, Kamika reviewed social media, and Lea read research materials on geoglyphs in Kazakhstan for her masters' thesis for the rest of the trip.

They arrived at the house where Lea and Kamika had failed to reset one of its rooms. Montgomery met with the owners and explained that they needed to analyze why the reset hadn't worked. The owners allowed Lea and Montgomery to walk through the entire house while Kamika prepared the equipment.

"It's definitely not coming from a different area of the house," Lea said. "The rest of the house is basically a neutral mix. The kitchen even comes through as happy. The problem is in that one room."

"Okay, let's analyze the room." Montgomery grabbed the emotional energy scanner and began a slow circuit around the room.

Lea watched the data collate on the tablet as he worked. Most of the areas that they had previously treated were coming back neutral. Finally, an area came back with anger, turning to rage at the strongest point. The data was associated with the closet door. Montgomery finished and joined her.

"It's the closet," she said. "We treated the door, but not the inside."

Montgomery glanced at the owners. "Could you unlock the closet?"

The man stepped forward and complied.

Montgomery opened the closet door and surveyed the boxes, papers, crates, and plastic bins stacked to the ceiling. A rocking chair was wedged upside down over the pile. He turned to the owners: a balding, middle-aged man in a tweed jacket with leather patches at the elbows and a forty-something woman with carefully coiffed hair and botoxed eyes. "We can't neutralize the room because the emotional stamp from the closet is too strong. The problem is either in the boxes themselves or in the walls of the closet."

The balding man turned to the woman, whose eyes looked permanently surprised. "It's your brother's crap. We need to throw that stuff out. Donate it. Get it out of the house. Something."

"It's time," said his wife, looking as somber as her frozen face would allow.

"Are you sure it's the boxed items and not the closet walls?" Montgomery asked.

The couple exchanged wary glances. The woman shrugged and turned away to look out a window, leaving her husband to answer.

"My wife's brother was a very angry man—angry at humanity, the government, and his family to varying degrees. His coworkers were afraid of him. He'd been sent to anger management to no avail. His boss had to fire him or half the office would have quit because of the hostile environment he was creating. He tried to put a bomb in his boss's office after he was fired. When he was arrested, he asked my wife to keep his things for him until he got out. Only he never came back for his things since he died of a stroke in prison."

"I see," Montgomery said.

The woman continued to stare blindly out the window. "How could such a promising child turn so sour? We had such fun together as children. That rocking chair belonged to our parents." Her voice cracked, and a tear slid down one cheek.

Montgomery cleared his throat and spoke to her husband. "For now, we can't neutralize this room. Once you dispose of the items in the closet, we can come back and reset the room and the closet. Until then, this room will be uncomfortable, mostly because of your brother's things being here. You may not even need us to come back once you get rid of those things."

The couple escorted Lea, Kamika, and Montgomery back to the front door. Lea looked back as they walked to the van just in time to see the man put his arm around his wife to comfort her as he closed the door.

As they climbed into their vehicle, Montgomery's phone rang. Kamika and Lea waited for him in the van as he paced beside it, deeply immersed in his conversation.

Finally, he ended the call and climbed into his seat. "I have news," he said as he directed the van back to the Bad Vibes office. "One of my contacts called about your cousin's situation, Kamika."

Kamika gripped the armrest on her seat. "Tell me!"

"Lusa will get immunity if she'll testify against Cody. They recognize that she acted under duress and won't charge her with the theft of the credit card. With her testimony, the video I sent them of him using your card, and the stolen cards found in his possession, they have a very strong case against him. They intend to prosecute him twice: first for the credit card theft and fraud, and second for the assault, kidnapping, and plan to murder your cousin. The combined sentences for his offenses should keep him in prison for years."

"That's great to hear!" Kamika said with a smile. "I'm so relieved."

They rode for a few minutes in silence before Lea looked up from the selection of primary source documents she was reading for class and asked Montgomery, "Have you ever reset a piece of furniture?"

"No. Most furniture can be replaced easily enough."

"Suppose it was a family piece, something passed down for generations that the family didn't want to lose, like that rocking chair in the closet."

He nodded thoughtfully. "I see what you mean. Yes. We could do that. I'll let the last client know."

Lea smiled and went back to her reading as the van took them back to the office.

As Lea and Kamika entered the office, they were met by the smug face of Miguel.

"Did you take care of whatever you missed?" he asked with a taunting note in his voice.

Kamika bristled. "We didn't miss anything. We did everything properly!"

"If you'd done everything properly, you wouldn't have had a recall," he said, smirking at her. He pointed to a board on the wall where he kept statistics on how often each team had had to return to a call because a client was dissatisfied. Miguel used a red marker and put a vicious slash in the column next to their names.

"Recalls happen even when our employees do everything correctly," Montgomery said, strolling in behind Kamika and Lea.

The smug looked dropped off Miguel's face as he turned to see Montgomery entering the room.

Annoyance was still plastered all over Kamika's lovely features. Lea could see that she wanted to say more to Miguel. Lea grabbed Kamika's arm and dragged her toward the break room.

"Leave him to Montgomery," Lea whispered.

Kamika pulled her arm free from Lea's grasp. "Talk about hostile work environments. I'm going to file a complaint about him if he doesn't stop."

"He's good at his job," Lea said.

"I'll bet Montgomery could find someone as good but with a better personality." Kamika exhaled sharply, making the curls on her forehead jostle to the side.

"Come to the break room. Call Lusa. See how she's feeling," said Lea, trying to distract Kamika. "Then we can get an early lunch before we go back to the castle."

"Okay, okay. I know, I can't control him, but I can control my response to him. I shouldn't let him get under my skin. I'll ignore the mean-mouthed jerk."

❦

Later, as they approached the castle, its 1920s history ran through Lea's mind. "Montgomery," she began, "that house this morning gave me an idea."

"What?"

"We only scanned the walls and built-in shelving. We didn't scan the furniture. A lot of it is solid wood and dates back to before the first Ryan Hanover's murder. If we scan the furniture where Harry stayed, we might find evidence to tie him to the embezzlement or even further proof that he poisoned Ryan's great-grandfather. Finding whoever attacked Wendy obviously takes precedence, but it might be worth considering."

Montgomery looked up from his phone. "We could scan that wardrobe in the room nearest the bathroom where we found him singing and the massive headboard on that bed. I'll keep that in mind, Lea."

The van came to a stop in front of the castle, and they all climbed out.

Ryan appeared on the porch to greet them. "Hello, again," he called from above them.

Lea waved at him. "How's Wendy today?"

"She has a headache, but otherwise she's great. She's trying to decide where to put the nursery as we speak." Ryan's eyes glowed as he spoke before turning serious. "We need to find out who attacked her. The police are investigating, but anything you can suggest that would solve this sooner would be welcome."

"Can I talk to Wendy?" asked Montgomery.

Ryan led them inside the stone tower. "Sure, but she doesn't remember anything about who hit her."

"That's okay," Montgomery said. "I'm more concerned about who knew she had left the door unlocked. I assume the police are looking into her business competitors. What can you tell me about them?"

"Wendy is in competition to sell her company— that is, the software she designed plus the customers—to a large conglomerate. They are considering similar software companies and will only buy the one that best meets their needs. But I don't know how her competitors could be involved. The designers of the other two products aren't local. One's on the west coast in California. The other is in Minnesota." Ryan looked perplexed.

"That doesn't mean they couldn't hire someone to steal her work in an attempt to get a competitive edge," said Montgomery.

"True. Come on. She's upstairs." Ryan led them up the spiral stairs to the media room, where they found Wendy with Jack.

Wendy's greeting was unusually cheerful for a woman with stitches in her head. "Hi! The floor below this one was considered the nursery floor, but I want the kids on the same floor with us. I can't imagine going up and down those spiral stairs in the night to feed the baby. Ryan, do you think we could convert this room into a nursery?"

"Absolutely, but listen, Montgomery wants to ask you some questions."

The happy smile vanished from her face. She glanced significantly at her son, playing with an electronic game on the couch. Ryan followed her gaze and nodded.

"Hey, Jack, buddy. Come with me. You haven't had lunch yet. Let's go to the kitchen and get something to eat," Ryan said to his son.

The boy jumped up and ran out of the room. "I'll beat you to the kitchen, Dad!"

After Ryan and his son had vanished down the spiral stairs, Wendy turned to Montgomery. "Sorry," she said. "We told Jack I had an accident. I don't want him scared again when he's finally getting comfortable here."

Montgomery questioned her on the names of her competitors and took notes as she answered. "The police will dig into them, I'm sure. But it won't do any harm if I look into them, too. I have one last question. I know you told me that there were only four sets of keys to the castle originally. Did you give any keys to the castle to anyone other than Ashley? Anyone at all, for anything at all, even for a few minutes?"

"Well, my sister Carol has one for emergencies, but no, no one . . . oh, wait. I gave a copy to Wyatt's mom,

Desty, once. She was taking the boys to baseball one day when I had a meeting and Ryan was out of town. Jack forgot his shoes. She met me, got the key, and got Jack's shoes before the game. She gave the key back that evening."

Montgomery nodded. "Anyone else? Anyone at all, even for a minute? With that many people coming in and out for remodeling and electrical work, could any of them have even held a key, had a few seconds to make an impression that could be used to copy a key?"

"Ryan wouldn't have handed the keys to anyone, but he might have left them on a table. I'm not sure. He usually keeps them in his pocket. I keep mine in my purse. I keep my purse with me when we have people in the house. No one could have copied my key. Ask Ryan if he's ever left the keys lying around." A worried look filled her eyes. "Why does it matter if we changed the locks?"

"Someone must have used a key to get in and search this place at night. We found no other point of entry. Once you changed the locks, someone came in after we left, before Ashley arrived. That person had to know the door was unlocked. We need to find someone who had access to a key previously and who knew the door was unlocked yesterday, someone a competitor might pay to break in and steal from you. So far, it's a short list with only your husband, your sister, and Ashley on it." Montgomery spoke gently, but his tone was serious. "We know you didn't hit yourself, and your husband didn't do it either. Unless someone else is added to the list, we have to consider Ashley and your sister's family."

A tear tumbled down Wendy's cheek. "My sister Carol didn't do this! You can eliminate her. I don't believe Ashley would do this to me! She wouldn't. Besides, if

Ashley or Carol wanted to copy my hard drive, they could do it any time. Or my tablet or phone. Neither of them would have to break in since they are both here all the time. And the video shows it was a man who hit me."

"Whoever hit you went straight to your laptop. He didn't take your phone, which was on your desk, or look for your tablet. That suggests that he went for the one item he hadn't already searched," said Montgomery. "Someone told him when to get in here.

"Did anyone else know that the door was unlocked for Ashley?" asked Lea, wishing she could comfort the upset woman.

"No. Who else would need to know?" The tears were flowing in a steady stream on her cheeks as she spoke.

"It's okay," Montgomery said. "We didn't mean to upset you. We will solve this. I'm going to recheck the house for listening devices, too. Someone may be eavesdropping on your conversations. I'll do that while my colleagues here go back to resetting the basement and ground floor. After that, Lea had an idea where we might find more information on old Hanover's death and the embezzlement from his company. Can you tell me what furniture was in the guest room that Mae's nephew might have used? Is it all still in the room? Have you moved anything to other rooms? Did you get rid of anything? We might be able to do scans on the larger pieces of furniture."

"Ummm, let me think." Wendy wiped her eyes, making an effort to pull herself together. She frowned in thought. "The third floor guest room nearest the bathroom is intact. We didn't take anything out of it. We did move the bed and nightstand that were in the other room, which is now my office, but the wardrobe is still in there since the room doesn't have a closet. The bed and nightstand are with some other furniture that we were going to donate or sell, in one of the storage closets in the garage. You are welcome to scan whatever you want."

"Thank you, ma'am," said Montgomery. "We'll leave you to your work now."

As Lea and Kamika trudged down the spiral staircase to the garage level, Lea said, "Montgomery only did two coats of infusion on the basement last time we were here. You finished the side rooms, and we finished two coats in the garage area. Do you want to do another infusion layer in the garage while I do one in the basement?"

"Okay," Kamika said as they arrived in the garage. She glanced at the opening to the basement with apprehension. "I haven't been down there yet. I'd like to keep it that way."

Lea brushed her loose black hair back out of her face, regretting not having tied it up like a Roman house servant again, and glanced toward the basement stairs. "I'm hoping the layers Montgomery added had some effect; otherwise, I'll have trouble even going down the stairs. Wish me luck." She lifted her equipment, took a deep breath, and walked to the basement as Kamika watched. She hoped the ghostly woman would not be visiting today and that a listening device would be found. Otherwise, someone very close to the Hanovers was definitely betraying them.

Chapter 15

Lea's first step down the stairs was uncomfortable, but she didn't slam into the wall of emotional horrors that had met her before. She turned on her equipment and began infusing white noise and essence of joy into the stairs as she slowly backed down them. She heard Kamika's equipment running and knew that Kamika had begun her infusions as well.

Lea arrived at the bottom of the stairs. The hairs on the back of her neck prickled. She stood and looked at the room. The single bare bulb did little to illuminate the cavernous rectangle of stone around her. She found the directional lamps that she and Montgomery had used the night they had scanned the wine cellar and lit the room. The shadowy corners sprang into view, exposing dirt and stone but nothing scary. A sense of anguish and death seeped through. Lea took a deep breath to try to slow the increase in her heart rate.

She walked to the door leading to the wine cellar and yanked it open. The dank cave room was as they'd left it after finding the hidden trunks. The wine shelf door stood ajar. The deteriorating crates and broken chair remained in place. Lea walked to the center of the room trying to get a sense of the atmosphere. It felt neutral. The terror in the room beyond hadn't penetrated and bled through to this space.

Lea returned to the door and stepped back into the original dungeon area. A chill ran down her spine, and goose bumps covered her arms. The air tingled with emotion. The woman was coming. Lea could feel her horror, terror, and pain.

The sound of Kamika's equipment humming overhead faded from Lea's ears as the form of a woman materialized on the stairs. Her mouth was open. Her hair was slipping from under the covering she wore on her head. Her eyes were dark pits of fear. Lea could see the tears on the woman's cheeks and hear the words coming from her mouth, but she couldn't understand anything but the name Angus. The ghost reached the bottom of the stairs, paused, looked frantically around, and then ran to the middle of the room and crouched. Lea could see that she was next to where the well had once been.

A wave of sheer terror engulfed Lea as she felt the presence of something evil coming into the room. She couldn't see anything but felt as if a dark shadow had dimmed all the lights and sucked the air from her lungs. The evil moved toward the huddled form of the woman. An earsplitting scream reverberated around the room, echoing off the stone.

Lea closed her eyes, afraid she might see pure evil take on a solid form. The evil thing filled the room, pressing against her, forcing her back against the stone wall, suffocating her.

Something grabbed her arm. She pulled away, adrenaline flowing, ready to fight or flee. She opened her eyes to Kamika's worried face.

"It's me! It's me! What happened? I heard you scream!"

Lea clutched Kamika's arm for support. "The evil thing chased the crying woman down here again! Didn't you see her?"

"I didn't see anything. I had my back to the stairs. If I hadn't paused to move to a new section of wall and turned off the equipment, I wouldn't have heard you scream," Kamika said. "If you shake any harder, you're going to pull me over with you." Kamika nudged Lea gently toward the stairs. "Let's get you out of here."

They emerged and walked to the bright and open game area near the garage space.

Adrenaline was still coursing through Lea. She sank to the floor and sat with her head on her knees, waiting for the shaking in her limbs to stop and trying to banish the tightness in the pit of her stomach.

Kamika shoved a cool water bottle into Lea's hand. "Here. Drink this."

"I'm okay."

"No, you're not."

"I will be."

"Drink the water. I've never seen a ghost affect you like this before."

Lea opened the bottle and took a sip to appease her friend. "If we're right, and the crying woman is a warning of betrayal, why am I seeing her?" She closed the bottle and held it against the side of her face.

"I don't know. Maybe it's trying to warn Wendy through you." Kamika gently patted Lea's back.

"Why didn't you see her again? You were betrayed by your cousin."

"Yeah, but that's over. We put it behind us."

"But if the ghost, or echo, or whatever she is, was trying to warn Wendy, wouldn't you have seen her too?" Lea frowned, completely puzzled. The shaking was slowing, and her heart rate began to decrease.

Kamika shrugged her delicate shoulders. "I don't know. You're the sensitive one. Besides, who would betray you?"

Lea could see Kamika's wide green eyes were still assessing her. "I'm fine." She rose to her feet and took another swig of water from the bottle.

The garage and game space no longer felt neutral. A vague sense of fear hung in the air.

"Well, there's no sense in treating this space until we solve the problem of the woman. I hate to say it, but this space may never be comfortable for Wendy and Jack." Lea looked around and spotted the storage closet containing some of the furniture that had been in the guest room. "Kamika, let's scan the furniture in the closet. If we can't reset this space, maybe we can find something from the time of old man Hanover's death." She crossed the room and opened the door.

The closet contained stacks of labeled boxes. Some labels were marked "stemware," others as holiday decorations. A bed frame leaned against one wall. Several chairs were stacked on top of each other.

Lea spotted a nightstand behind the chairs and pulled a chair from the closet. "Kamika, help me get the nightstand out."

"Okay." Kamika removed another chair and set it aside.

Once the chairs were removed, Kamika and Lea carried the nightstand between them into the game space.

"Sound scan first?" Kamika asked.

"Let's take the drawers out and make sure it's empty," Lea said. She bent to pull out the top drawer.

Kamika reached for the second drawer, but it refused to move. "It's stuck." She bent down to tug on the drawer, wiggling it up and down in the frame of the nightstand. "Either it's not on the tracks, or something is in the way."

"Is something in the drawer?" asked Lea.

Kamika slid her hand into the slim opening she had managed to create. "No. I don't feel anything, and I can see the inside. Maybe the wood is warped. Hang on, it's starting to move." She yanked the drawer upwards at a sharp angle, finally pulling it free. Kamika bent to look into the interior of the nightstand. "I don't see anything in there."

"What's that on the bottom of the drawer you're holding?" Lea pointed to a file-sized manila envelope taped to the bottom of the drawer. The envelope was thick, lumpy, and spotted with age.

Kamika flipped the drawer around so that she could see the bottom. "No wonder the drawer wouldn't open. Whoever put this on here must have tipped up the night-stand and attached it from the bottom." Kamika put the drawer upside down on the floor and squatted next to it. Carefully, she detached yellowing tape from the edges of the envelope and began to pry it loose from the drawer. Some of the envelope itself had adhered to the drawer. Kamika used her beautifully manicured fingernails to scrape the paper loose.

"A chisel would come in handy right about now," Lea said, watching Kamika. The envelope was coming apart rather than detaching from the bottom of the drawer.

"I'm going to have to rip this thing off," Kamika said at last, giving it a sharp tug. The envelope ripped, leaving a portion of it attached to the drawer and the rest in Kamika's hand with the contents exposed.

Kamika gasped as she realized what was in her hand. A pile of one hundred dollar bills stuck out of the torn envelope. As Kamika tipped the envelope to take out the money, a brown glass bottle with a screw cap started to slide from the envelope. Lea reached out and caught it as it fell.

"Good catch," Kamika said. "What is it?"

A small amount of liquid sloshed inside the dark brown glass as Lea held it to the light. "It's not labeled, but something is inside it."

Kamika set the money aside and looked at the envelope. "There's a slip of paper in here." She pulled out the paper. "It says, 'Enough for two doses in drinks. Two more deaths that look like heart attacks will be suspicious. This better not come back to me.' And it's signed 'J. O.'"

Lea stared at the small brown bottle of death that fit easily into the palm of her hand. "It's poison. Harry was going to kill his aunt and maybe his cousin—if he hadn't died of alcohol poisoning first."

"And he did kill his uncle, too," Kamika said. "The note says 'two more deaths.' That implies that the first wasn't natural either."

Lea stared at the stack of money. "How much money is that?"

Kamika pulled the crumbling remains of a rubber band from around the stack and began to count the one hundred dollar bills into stacks of ten. She ended with ten piles. "Ten thousand dollars! I wonder if that's what's left of what he embezzled from the company."

"Or Harry's gambling paid off for once. Who knows? Maybe that's why he hadn't used the poison yet. He had some money, so he didn't have to resort to murdering more family members." Lea grabbed the scanner. "Let's do a quick sound scan."

She scanned the nightstand while Kamika watched the data compile on the tablet. They both reviewed the results.

"I don't see anything significant," Lea said.

"Me either," Kamika said. "Emotions scanner?"

Lea nodded and scanned the table again.

Kamika looked up from the results on the tablet. "Now we've got something."

"Let's see."

Kamika scrolled through the results. "I see desperation. I see guilt. Good! He should have a guilty conscience after what he did."

"Let's get this upstairs to Montgomery and Mrs. Hanover. Come on." Lea gathered the piles of hundred-dollar bills and the brown bottle and stuck them back into the remains of the envelope.

Kamika followed her through the garage to the spiral stairs leading back to the main floor of the castle. "Hey, Lea, didn't Wendy say that the furniture was from her office? That means Harry must have slept in that room. We should double check the wardrobe in there. He could have hidden things behind it."

Lea paused at the door in front of the stairs. "We scanned the wardrobe. We didn't find anything."

"Yes, but the scanners wouldn't show if something was taped to the back of it," Kamika said with mock exasperation. "Pick up the pace. Harry could have taped even more money to the back of that huge wardrobe."

She bounded up the stone stairs past Lea, vanishing around the spiraling space out of view.

When Lea emerged from the stairs into the main floor living area, she saw Kamika talking rapidly and gesticulating wildly. Montgomery stood listening intently in front of her. He glanced up and smiled at Lea over Kamika's head. Lea held the envelope for him to see.

"Ten thousand dollars!" he said. He looked back at Kamika. "Yes. We can check the back of the wardrobe. Let's find Wendy. Ryan ran an errand with Jack."

"You don't have to look far," Wendy said, exiting the kitchen. "I'm in here."

They all turned and saw her drying her hands on a towel.

"What's going on?" she asked.

"Lea and Kamika found poison and ten thousand dollars taped to the bottom of a drawer in a nightstand. Remember we were going to examine and scan the furniture from Harry's room? Well, they did and found evidence of murder. Based on a note found with the money, Harry had poison on hand for two more people. He must have drunk himself to death before he got the chance to kill his aunt and cousin."

"Oh!" Wendy's eyes opened wide in surprise. "Let me see!"

Lea held out the envelope. "Be careful. The bottle of poison is small. Don't let it slip out."

Wendy cautiously took the torn envelope and examined the contents. "So Mae saved her own life and her son's when she let Harry drink himself into a coma. Ryan's not going to believe this. Can we get the liquid in the bottle tested? I'd like to know for sure that it's poison."

Montgomery nodded. "I know a lab that will test it for me. I can take in it tomorrow."

Wendy handed the tiny brown bottle over to Montgomery. "Thank you. What should we do about the money? Could it be part of the embezzled company funds?"

"Kamika and I were discussing that," Lea said. "Given that Harry died a year after his uncle, the embezzled money was probably gone by then, since he was already trying to get more money out of his aunt. If he had a gambling problem, this money may be winnings from a run of luck. When this money ran out, though, he was ready to pull out the poison."

Wendy fingered the stack of bills. "Wow." She seemed at a loss for words.

Kamika shuffled her feet excitedly. "Can we check the wardrobe in your office? If that was Harry's room, he could have hidden other things. We scanned the room already, but we didn't move the wardrobe to look at the back of it."

"Let's go do that." Wendy led the way up the stairs, the torn packet of money still clutched in her hand. When they reached the next floor, she led them past the chapel to the room that served as her office. She set the packet of money on her desk.

"When we decided that this would be an office, we moved out the bed, nightstand, and a couple of cheap landscape prints from the walls. The prints didn't have anything on the backs. I know because I liked the frames, but the prints were yellowing with age. I took the prints out and kept the frames. We dismantled the bed and put the bed frame in the storage area in the garage with the nightstand. I sure hope he didn't have anything hidden in that ratty mattress. We threw it out!" She covered her mouth and nose with both hands. "It was a thin, ancient mattress. A couple of springs were poking out of the ticking. We would have noticed if it had a rip or opening where something could be hidden. Wouldn't we?" She opened her eyes and gave Montgomery an uncertain look.

"Most likely," he said with a reassuring smile. He put his large hand on her shoulder. "How did you get it out of here? Down the stairs?"

"Yes. It was a pain."

"If nothing fell out or clunked around as you were taking that mattress down the spiral staircase, I'd guarantee nothing was hidden in it."

She smiled thankfully back at him. "Thank goodness. I'd hate to think we threw out something important. Shall we check the wardrobe?"

Montgomery walked around the desk to the eight-foot-tall by five-foot-wide oak cabinet that had served as the room's closet. The front was bisected by two vertical doors with brass handles. Montgomery pulled the handles to open both doors at once. One door revealed shelving and small drawers. The other contained a rod and hooks for hanging clothing. Both halves appeared empty.

"This thing must weigh a ton. The cabinetmaker must have assembled it here. There's no way anyone brought this thing up those stairs. I may not be able to budge it." Montgomery put one shoulder into the side of the cabinet and heaved forcefully, attempting to move one end away from the wall.

The heavy oak creaked in protest but slid a fraction of an inch.

"It moved!" Montgomery said with amazement in his voice. He squatted to examine the feet. "Its legs are on small pieces of cloth! Somebody thought about how hard it is to move this thing and dealt with the problem for us. Lea, Kamika, come help me."

Wendy moved forward to help, but Montgomery stopped her.

"No! Absolutely not! Your husband would kill me if I let his pregnant wife move heavy furniture. I'm sure your doctor will tell you that you shouldn't be trying to move heavy objects."

Wendy froze in place, and her hand went protectively to her stomach. "You're right. I'll get out of the way then." She went to stand on the other side of her desk, well out of the way of the wardrobe.

With Lea helping push and Kamika stabilizing and directing the other end, Montgomery slowly maneuvered the heavy piece of furniture until it stood at a thirty-degree angle from the wall.

He stepped behind it and ran his hand over the back and bottom of the cabinet. Finally, he reached up and ran his hand along the dusty top edge that had been against the wall.

"What's this?" he asked, his dust-covered hand clutching a dark object.

He rubbed away the dust to reveal a silver flask, heavily tarnished with age.

"It's engraved," Lea said, pointing at a marking barely visible through the tarnish.

Montgomery rubbed the area with his thumb and traced the markings. "Looks like initials: HMS. Harry something Sutton, I imagine."

He shook the flask. "It feels empty." He passed the flask to Wendy.

"He must have been an awfully unhappy scoundrel," Wendy said, staring at the initials. "I'm surprised it's not his ghost that we have wandering this place."

Kamika had busied herself examining the drawers and shelving in the wardrobe, checking for false backs and loose boards. She stopped and glanced at Lea. "By the way, we forgot to mention that Lea saw the crying woman again in the basement."

Wendy turned to Lea with a sympathetic look. "I'm so sorry. Was it awful?"

"Every bit as terrible as before. No amount of resetting is going to clear the atmosphere down there as long as she's around," Lea said apologetically.

Wendy crossed her arms anxiously over her chest. "So I might as well get used to being scared out of my wits when I go to the laundry room?"

"Not necessarily. If she is a warning of betrayal, once we solve what's going on with you, maybe she'll go away. Kamika didn't see her this time. Her betrayal issue was resolved."

Wendy looked curiously at Kamika. "What happened to you?"

Kamika explained about Lusa and her credit card and passport.

Wendy listened intently to Kamika. "Well, let's hope resolving things here will make our ghost vanish for me, too."

Montgomery pushed the wardrobe back against the wall and dusted off his hands. "Next order of business: I screened the whole house for electronic listening devices but didn't find anything. Can I see your phone? I want to run a diagnostic program on it."

Wendy removed her phone from her pocket and gave it to Montgomery.

Montgomery pulled cables from his pocket and sat at the large desk. He attached the phone to his tablet.

Wendy watched over his shoulder as he quickly opened and executed programs. "You're checking to see if someone cloned it?"

"Yes." After a minute or two of typing and reading, Montgomery stood and detached the phone from the cables. "Your phone is fine."

Wendy threw her hands up in frustration. "Then how did someone know that the door was unlocked for Ashley? No one else knew, and I refuse to believe it was Ashley."

Lea had a sudden flash of insight. "Wait. Wendy, how did you tell Ashley that the door would be unlocked for her? Did you call her, email her, text message her, chat with her?"

Wendy gave Lea a perplexed look. "I called her. Normally, I would text or email, but I had something else to ask her and it was easier to say it than to type it all out. Why?"

Lea smiled at her. "Where were you standing when you called Ashley?"

Wendy pointed across the room. "In the kitchen."

"Near the intercom system for the house?" Lea asked.

Wendy looked stunned. "Yes. Are you saying someone tapped into the intercom system?"

"No. I'm saying someone else in the house could have heard your conversation."

Chapter 16

"Who else was in my house?" Wendy asked.

"Jack!" Kamika said with a gleeful look.

Wendy shook her head, still puzzled. "You're right. Jack could have heard me talking through the intercom. But who could he have told? Who does he know that's willing to come in here and attack me?"

"Children answer questions," Montgomery said. "If someone asked him about the locks being changed, he would tell them. Where has he been, who has he been with, and who approached him with questions? That's what we need to ask him."

"Ryan took him to the park to get him out of the house." Wendy got out her phone. "I'll call him and tell them to come home."

A few minutes later, Ryan and Jack entered the heavy front door of the castle into the main living area. Montgomery, Lea, Kamika, and Wendy were there to meet them.

Ryan looked at his wife's worried face and frowned. "What's up?"

"We need to talk to Jack," Wendy said. She turned to her small son and knelt in front of him. "Jack, did you tell any of your friends about how we changed the locks here?"

Jack looked from his mother to his father to Montgomery. A wary look appeared on his face.

His mother took his hand and patted it reassuringly. "You aren't in trouble. You can talk to people. I just want to know who you talked to."

"Why?" he asked with a cautious look still on his face.

Wendy looked to Ryan, who shrugged.

Montgomery stepped forward, and the boy looked up at him. "We need to know if anyone knew the door would be unlocked for Ashley on Monday."

"Why?" the boy asked again, a frown settling in on his brow as he stared at Montgomery.

His mother sighed and pulled him toward her. "Because someone came in the house."

"Oh." Jack paused, considering that. "When?"

Ryan answered his son in a calm, matter-of-fact voice. "On Monday, while you were with Wyatt. Someone took information from Mom's computer."

Jack's eyes widened, and he turned back to his mother. "I told Wyatt that we changed the locks. His mama asked how Ashley would get in, so I told her you would have to leave the door unlocked. Is that okay? She didn't come in and neither did Wyatt. They were with me."

Ryan walked over and tousled his son's hair. "Of course, Jack. It's okay. Did you tell anybody else? Did anyone else hear you tell Wyatt and his mom? Where were you when you told them?"

"We were in Wyatt's mom's car, driving to the trampoline place. No one else heard. I didn't tell anyone else."

Jack looked around the room, expecting more questions. His wrinkled forehead and downturned mouth made him look older and much too serious for a child of his age.

Ryan smiled at his son. "Thanks, Jack. That's all we need. Don't worry about it. You didn't do anything wrong. Can you go play upstairs for a while?"

Relief flooded the boy's face. Jack asked, "Can we go back to the park now?"

Ryan laughed. "Not yet. I need to talk to Mr. Montgomery and his friends."

"Can Mom take me?"

"Later, Jack," said his mother, turning him gently toward the stairs.

"When later?" he asked, still not moving.

His mother looked at the time and said, "It might be tomorrow. You have a birthday party to go to this evening. Can you make a birthday card for Zander right now?"

The boy's face lit up. "Yes! I can do that!" He bounded out of the room and up the stairs.

His mother watched the stairs until the echo of his footsteps faded. She turned to Montgomery.

"He told Wyatt and Desty. Wyatt's older brother may also know, but I don't think treasure-hunting teenagers would break in to steal my work."

"No," Montgomery said thoughtfully. "I'm going to run a background check on your neighbors the Millers." He crossed his arms on his wide chest and looked at Ryan and Wendy. "Were the Millers friendly from the moment you moved into the castle?"

"Yes. Wyatt and Jack spotted each other when we came to check the place out before we moved in. They bonded immediately. Jack begged us to move in as soon as possible because he wanted to see Wyatt again."

"How about Wyatt's parents? What does his father do? Was he as welcoming?"

Ryan ran one hand through his thinning hair. "We've only seen Hugh Miller a few times. He's a charter pilot, constantly flying somewhere. He came over and introduced himself one afternoon when we were having the landscaping redone. He said he was pleased to see the castle occupied and maintained. The regular mowing by the landscape company over the years only kept the grass from becoming overgrown. Dead trees and bushes hadn't been removed, and no flowers had been planted. The trees overhung the sidewalk and hit people in the face. He was happy we were fixing the place up."

"What about Desty?" Montgomery asked.

Wendy bit her lower lip. "Desty came with a welcome basket two days after we moved into the castle. She couldn't have known anything about us then, other than that Wyatt wanted to play with Jack." She sighed deeply. "I hate this! I hate suspecting people I like of trying to injure me and steal from me."

Lea sympathized. However, if the ghost was holding true to tradition, someone was betraying Wendy—maybe her friend, maybe her assistant. Either one of them could have told someone when to break into the house. Lea had another idea. "Wendy, did Ashley know that Jack wasn't here with you on Monday? Did she know that you were completely alone?"

"No. I don't generally apprise her of Jack's social schedule."

Lea looked hopefully at Montgomery, but he shook his head. "It doesn't make any difference if she knew or not. If someone was watching the castle, someone who already knew that the door was unlocked, that person would have watched for people to leave. The intruder might have seen Ryan leave and Jack leave with Wyatt, then watched us leave for lunch, and decided to take his chance to steal the files on the laptop with only Wendy in the castle," Montgomery said. "All someone needed to do was communicate the information that the door was unlocked."

Wendy threw up her hands in frustration. "But why would either of them do that to me?"

"People do all kinds of things for love or money, out of jealousy, envy, or greed. For some, it's merely business. I can't say what is motivating the person who told the intruder how to break in. However, the intruder went for your business software on your laptop. He could have killed you, but he didn't. The intruder was here to steal, not kill."

"That's not much comfort," Ryan said, pacing the room.

Wendy clasped her hands together nervously. "Now what? Ashley's due to arrive here any minute, and Jack will see Wyatt at that birthday party this evening. If Wyatt's there, Desty will be there. How do I face these people?"

Lea could sense Wendy's rising panic and dismay. She put one hand on the agitated woman's shoulder. "We have no proof that either of them meant you any harm. We may not have covered all the options. One of them might have told someone, not realizing how the information would be used. They could be innocent of intending to harm you."

Montgomery faced the Hanovers with both hands on his hips. "I want to talk to Ashley. Do you two want to be present when I talk to her?"

Ryan shifted uncomfortably and then nodded. "Yes."

Wendy set her jaw in a stubborn line. "Yes. I don't believe she would intentionally harm me. There has to be an explanation for this."

"Okay. Then we'll talk to her together." Montgomery smiled. "Lea and Kamika, did you check the bed frame from Harry's room? It's in the closet in the garage area, isn't it?"

"I saw it," Lea said. "It's a turned-wood decorative frame without any solid panels. I don't think we'd get any good, sound readings off it. We didn't check it to see if Harry hid anything on it, but there isn't much to it. The Hanovers would have noticed if he'd taped anything to it."

"Double check it anyway," Montgomery said. "We can't all question Ashley. She'd feel like she was facing some kind of tribunal."

Kamika grabbed Lea's arm. "We'll get out of the way! Come on, Lea. Let's go look at that bed frame."

As Lea and Kamika entered the garage area, Lea opened the garage door to allow for more light. Once the door was open, Lea saw Ashley walking from her car to the castle. Lea gave her a friendly wave. Ashley responded with a perky smile and a wave and then vanished up the stone steps to the front door.

"If she's guilty, she hides it well," Kamika said.

"Maybe she's innocent."

Kamika watched with one hand on her hip and a skeptical look on her face. "She's the only one with any motive, remember. She has debt."

"You never know. What if it's someone we didn't think of yet?"

Kamika gave her a searching look. "Like who? Who else could there be?"

"I'll let you know if I think of someone. Let's get this bed frame out of the closet." Lea opened the storage closet door and squeezed past the boxes. "I've got the back end. You get the front."

Together, they lifted the turned-wood frame to get it out into the garage next to the chairs and nightstand that they'd previously removed from the closet.

"I don't see how anything could be hidden on this," Kamika said doubtfully. "We're wasting our time."

"We're killing time while Montgomery questions Ashley. Come on, run your hands along all the curved sections. See if anything is loose. See if any of the sections pull apart."

"Okay. I'm going." Kamika sat and began to examine the footboard. "This feels solid enough to me."

Lea hunched over the headboard. "Nothing feels loose here, either. Check the side rails that supported the box spring."

After a careful examination, Lea and Kamika concluded the search and began to return the all of the furniture to the storage closet. As they were replacing the last chair, movement on the lawn caught Lea's eye. "Look, Kamika." She nodded toward the retreating form of Ashley, almost running back to her car.

Kamika watched Ashley climb into her car with a frown. "She looks upset."

The young woman hadn't started the car. Instead, she sat in the driver's seat with her hands over her face and her shoulders heaving.

"She's crying," Lea said. "Come on. Let's go talk to her. If she's innocent, she needs a sympathetic ear. If she found out that something she said aided in the attack, she's miserable." Lea brushed dust off her hands from the furniture and strode out of the garage toward Ashley's car.

Kamika held back. "You talk to her. I don't want her to feel like we're ganging up on her right after she faced Wendy, Ryan, and Montgomery."

Lea nodded and resumed her path toward the car. She tapped on the window.

Ashley's startled head swung around to Lea. The young woman's eyes were red. She looked distressed.

"Are you okay?" Lea asked. "Do you want to talk?"

"I'm okay." She moved to start the vehicle.

"Wait. Don't go. You're too upset to drive. I'm not here to accuse you of anything," said Lea. "You'll have a wreck if you try to drive like this."

Ashley dropped her hands to her lap. "They think I told someone how to break in! They think I helped someone steal from the Hanovers and hurt Wendy!" Tears leaked from the corners of her eyes.

"Montgomery considers everyone a suspect. It's his job. He has to ask questions. It wasn't a personal attack," Lea said gently. "Can I sit down?" Lea gestured toward the passenger seat.

Ashley unlocked the door. Lea took that for permission, walked around, and sat next to the tearful young woman.

"I would never hurt Wendy like that!" Ashley said.

"Someone did, though. Montgomery has to find out who."

"Not me!"

"No, a man in a mask is on the surveillance video," Lea said. "However, the only people outside of the family who knew the door was unlocked were women. Someone must have told the attacker when to come in."

"I didn't tell anyone!" Ashley hit the steering wheel with the palms of both hand, actively punctuating each word.

"Not anyone at all? Not your mom, not your boyfriend, not your roommate?"

"Not anyone! I had no reason to mention it. Besides, my roommate was out of town this weekend, and my boyfriend had to work on a project he has due this week. I didn't even see him."

"Did you tell that to Montgomery?"

"Yes!"

"Then relax. No one is mad at you."

"Wendy doesn't trust me!"

"Yes, she does. She insisted on being there while Montgomery questioned you. She told him that she refused to believe you were involved in any wrongdoing."

Ashley brushed the tears off her face. "She did?"

"Yes!" Lea gave her an encouraging smile.

A relieved look crossed Ashley's face, and then she turned to Lea. "Who else knew the door was unlocked?"

"Jack told Wyatt and his mom, Desty Miller."

"Oh." The crease between Ashley's eyes deepened. "That doesn't help either. Why would the Millers care if the door was unlocked?"

"We don't know that they would," Lea said. "Montgomery will investigate them, too."

Ashley looked shocked. "He has to investigate the Hanovers' friends. Wow. Poor Wendy. She doesn't know who she can trust, does she?"

"No. She doesn't want to believe anyone she knows would do this to her."

Ashley sniffed loudly and ran her hands through her hair to straighten it. "It was silly to run out like that.

Should I go back? Wendy needs me to help her finish her presentation today."

"Yes," said Lea, giving her a smile.

Ashley glanced in the mirror, grabbed her purse, and refreshed her makeup resolutely. Her eyes were still red, but they held resolve and were brighter than they had been. "Okay, I'm going back inside. Thanks."

"You're welcome," Lea said, sliding out of the car.

Lea trotted back to Kamika in the garage as Ashley straightened her shoulders and climbed the stairs to the castle doors.

Kamika and Montgomery stood together waiting for Lea.

Montgomery gave her a questioning look.

"I don't think she did it," Lea said as she joined them.

"No?" Kamika asked "Not even unintentionally?"

"No. The only people she might have mentioned the door locks to were her roommate and boyfriend. The roommate was out of town, and the boyfriend was preoccupied with a project that's due this week. She didn't even see him," Lea explained.

Montgomery smiled at Lea. "Nice work. She told me that she didn't tell anyone, but she didn't get that specific with me. She was too upset at being suspected of any involvement in the attack."

"She's calmed down now," Lea said. "She understands that it isn't personal, that you had to ask."

"Good," Montgomery said.

"Now what? She's the only one with anything even close to a motive," Kamika said. "Why would Desty Miller want Wendy's software?"

"I don't know if she would, but if someone could pay Ashley, they could pay Desty," said Montgomery. "I'm going to do a thorough background check on both of them. Let's go back to the office. We can't do anything else here."

"Okay." Lea paused in thought. "Did you ask Ryan if he told anyone about changing the locks?"

"Ryan?" Montgomery said, "Oh, yes, I did. He didn't mention it to anyone." Montgomery turned to get into their van but stopped as Kamika cleared her throat.

"Um, Montgomery? Wendy would never suspect her sister. Will you be running background checks on her and her husband, too?" Kamika's voice was sad but determined.

Montgomery nodded. "I've already instigated background checks on Carol and her husband, Louis. Their kids are four and nine years old. No other adults reside with them. I should get more back shortly." He gave a sympathetic shake of his head and then climbed into the vehicle.

Lea, Kamika, and Montgomery rode silently back to the Bad Vibes Removal Services office. Montgomery typed away on his tablet as they went, allowing the autopilot function to control the van. Lea tried to read an article for her upcoming class while Kamika played on her phone.

Lea's mind kept wandering away from her reading to the Hanovers' problem. Someone close to them was betraying them, probably for money. She wondered how she would feel in that position. She hoped she would never find herself similarly misused by someone she trusted. Lea remembered the crying woman and the terror she radiated. She had never before encountered a ghost that had inspired such intense fear. Lea couldn't escape the nagging feeling that the woman was warning her of something, too, something personal, but she couldn't imagine what.

CHAPTER 17

LATER THAT NIGHT, LEA SAT IN her living room with her tablet on her lap, procrastinating instead of working on her next essay. She clicked the link to read the history department newsletter. Most of it was for bragging about the various professors' upcoming publications in this or that journal, expounding a new view on old information. Sometimes Lea enjoyed the articles. Other times, the arguments set forth were too farfetched to suit her intellect. The pressure to publish could push people to invent more outlandish ideas. She rejoiced when an archeology dig discovered new material about a period or civilization. Good theories and new articles abounded for months after a discovery, before the wild ideas began to emerge. She scanned the article titles and saw one attributed to her thesis advisor.

Lea clicked the link and was suddenly jolted through her spine by the title of the article. The title of the article was almost the same as her thesis topic. Rapidly, her eyes skimmed the paragraphs. The idea set forth was hers. Even the words were hers. He'd copied sections of her thesis and published it under his own name. She wasn't mentioned at all.

Lea sat fighting back tears. The professor's name still would have been on the thesis, as an advisor. Why did he have to steal her work? How would this affect the completion of her degree?

She wiped her eyes and looked for her secondary advisor's contact information, suddenly very angry. Professor Zarolt would have a copy of her plan and rough draft. He would know what to do. She hadn't seen him since their last meeting two months ago. She was due to confer in a week or two. He would help her.

Lea typed furiously and fired off the email. She was satisfied only for a short moment. Then she noticed that the email had bounced back. The email address was no longer valid. Lea double checked to make certain that she'd typed it correctly.

The address was correct. What was going on?

Lea picked up her phone and called the professor's cell phone number. He'd given it to her to call with questions, but she'd never used it. She hadn't wanted to abuse the privilege of having the number. It was late to be calling, but this was an emergency.

After the third ring, a woman answered. Lea apologized for calling so late, explained that she was a master's thesis student, and asked for Dr. Zarolt.

"I was his assistant. His wife gave me his phone because she kept getting calls from students with questions at all hours of the day. He was always giving this number out. I would have canceled the phone plan, but his wife wanted to make sure everyone heard about Dr. Zarolt. Anyway, didn't you hear?" the woman asked. "Dr. Zarolt died suddenly of a heart attack five weeks ago.

All his master's students are being reassigned. Was he your advisor?"

"He was my secondary advisor."

"Oh, they didn't call you yet since he wasn't the primary. You'll have to find a new secondary advisor. Ask your primary advisor to help you," the woman offered helpfully.

Lea muttered thanks and ended the call. Now what? Whom should she consult? Her advisor was the head of the department. Who was his boss? Was it some department chairperson? Maybe a dean? She didn't know. She sighed and sat with one hand under her chin.

This was the betrayal the crying woman had been trying to warn her about. She'd worked for months on her thesis, researching pieces and putting them together into a cohesive theory. Her theory wasn't quite a breakthrough—rather a well-reasoned synthesis of the material already on hand plus one new finding from a recent archeology dig in Kazakhstan that, when put together, provided a brand-new picture of the early cultures who'd built geoglyphs and mounds in that country eight thousand years ago.

Lea stared at the phone in her hand. She wanted to scream. She wanted to yell. She wanted to act immediately. It was eleven at night. No one would give credence to an overwrought midnight phone call. She put the phone down. In the morning, she would type out an explanation of what her advisor had done and figure out where to direct it.

She forced herself to get ready for bed, vacillating mentally between anger and bewilderment over why he'd done it. Why did he need all the credit for himself? Why couldn't he have at least mentioned her?

Lea crawled into bed, her mind in turmoil; she was certain she'd never sleep. Not until three a.m. did she finally submerge into a deep, exhausted slumber, when the thought that she wouldn't have to see the crying woman anymore gave her a measure of relief.

�֎

The next morning, Montgomery popped his head into the breakroom, spotted Lea and Kamika, and trotted through the door. "Happy Wednesday, ladies. The background checks on Ashley and Wendy's sister and brother-in-law have arrived."

Lea stared at Montgomery, trying to read his face, but he revealed nothing. "What did you find out?" Lea sipped a large mug of espresso and forced herself to raise a tired eyebrow in query.

Montgomery dropped into a chair, his bulk causing it to creak in protest, and tapped busily on his tablet.

"Well?" Kamika tapped the table impatiently.

Montgomery, apparently engrossed, didn't look from his tablet.

Lea continued to sip her coffee, knowing that Montgomery enjoyed baiting Kamika like this.

"Montgomery! Come on! Tell us!" Kamika slapped one hand on the table, taking the bait.

"What?" Montgomery asked with mock innocence. "Oh, you wanted to hear the results? Fine. Here's what we got." He began to read from his tablet. "Carol and Louis Mertens have been married eleven years. They have a nine-year-old son and a four-year-old daughter. It's Carol's first marriage, but Louis's second. His first marriage was brief, only about a year and a half, and it ended fifteen years ago. He has no children by that marriage. Carol stages expensive houses for sale for a top-tier Austin realtor."

"How expensive?" Kamika asked.

"The houses sell in excess of ten million dollars."

Kamika whistled, and Montgomery continued.

"Louis works as a quality assurance manager for the local branch of a multinational tech conglomerate. They live barely within their means. Louis has debt—college loans from attending an exclusive, private college—but spends money very sparingly now. Carol holds the purse strings, handles their accounts, which are paid off monthly, and keeps them on a tight budget. They haven't opened an account for a big-ticket item like a car or new flooring in years. Other than two speeding tickets and a parking ticket between them, they are legally clean. However, their daughter has a medical condition that requires occupational therapy and ongoing treatments, which is expensive and is probably the reason they are on a tight budget. The computer flagged the treatment because it suggests the child may be in need of even more expensive treatments that they can't afford."

Here, Montgomery looked up. "That's a suggestion for further investigation. We can't know for certain without digging further into the little girl's medical history and treatment plan."

Lea shot Montgomery a concerned look. "Do you think you need to keep digging into that?"

Montgomery shook his head. "No. Nothing I've found suggests that we need to keep digging. In any case, Wendy and her sister are very close. If money for medical treatments were needed, I think Carol would just ask to borrow some from her." He glanced back at his tablet. "Both Carol and Louis and their son seem to be healthy and have the usual social affiliations: church, boy scouts, PTA."

Lea sipped some more espresso. "Anything new on Ashley?"

"I have a summary of her transcript from the university, the clubs she joined, her volunteer work with the local animal shelter, and all the basics. The only flag is her debt." He paused. "Her boyfriend is a computer science major. I may have to look into him, too."

Lea sighed. "Hundreds of people in the area are computer majors. And college debt for Louis and Ashley is all we have? Half the population has that. I have college debt! What about the Millers? Mr. Miller could have been the man who attacked Wendy."

"As we were told, Mr. Miller is a pilot who flies charter jets. I checked his schedule. He was on a flight to California at the time of the attack. Mrs. Miller's background check isn't back yet."

Kamika frowned and twisted one of her curls around her index finger. "We must be missing something. Maybe it's someone we haven't met, someone else betraying them."

Lea cleared her throat. "Speaking of betrayal, I think I know why I saw the ghostly woman at the castle." Lea explained about discovering that her professor had stolen her work and published it as his own.

"What will you do?" Kamika asked with empathetic tears in her green eyes.

"I'm not even sure whom to complain to yet," Lea said.

Montgomery's eyes flashed in an anger Lea had rarely seen him display. "I'll go with you to talk to this professor, or to his boss, whomever you prefer to approach."

"Thanks for the offer, but it's not necessary. I can handle this." She was grateful for his interest but a little alarmed by his intensity.

He looked skeptical. "No. A person like that only takes advantage of someone if he thinks he'll be able to get away with it. That means he thinks you can't challenge him. You need a demonstration of strength to prove that you aren't going to give up quietly. You should let me go with you." Montgomery held her gaze with his angry eyes.

Lea could feel the protective instinct behind that ferocious look. She sat back reflexively, waffling on her position. His visible support might be useful, but she wasn't sure she needed it yet.

"You could even say I'm your legal advisor. I have a law degree," Montgomery said with a ruthless smile.

Kamika thumped her glass of tea on the table, sloshing its contents. "What? You have a law degree! When did you find time to do that?"

"It's a long story," Montgomery waved her question aside, his tone suddenly light and his face returning to his typical, deceptively simple, jovial look. He winked at Kamika.

Lea reflected, not for the first time, that anyone who judged Montgomery only by that friendly, seemingly unconcerned expression on his face was severely underestimating the man. "Okay, you can come with me to talk to my professor." She threw him an appreciative look. "So, what is the schedule today? Are we returning to our regular routes or working at the castle again?"

Montgomery drummed both hands on the table happily. "You're coming with me to the castle. We're going to try one more thing to remove the ghost and reset the garage."

"What?" Lea was startled. "The ghost hasn't spoken to us and doesn't seem aware of us, so we can't talk her out of there." She stared at Montgomery, waiting for a response, wondering if he had discovered a new method of dealing with the crying woman.

"I found someone to help us speak to her." Montgomery's broad grin flashed.

"Who?" Kamika asked. "Someone else who sees ghosts?"

Lea's eyes rounded at the thought that Montgomery might have found someone else like her, and then she dismissed the idea. If Montgomery knew of someone like that, he'd have mentioned it already. She guessed again, "Did you find someone who speaks ancient Irish?"

"That's one of the benefits of having a huge university nearby in Austin. The ancient Celtic studies professor is coming to help."

"What are you suggesting? Waiting for the ghost to appear so that this professor can tell me what to say to her?" Lea swallowed the last of her espresso and looked at Montgomery in disbelief.

"That's one option. And we'll play the recording of what Kamika heard the ghost say so that the professor can translate it for us."

"You're kidding. We don't even know if the ghost will appear." Lea couldn't keep the doubt from her voice. "Besides, what if she only appears to forewarn of betrayal. I can't be warned anymore. The betrayal has been exposed. What if I can't see her?"

"We'll cross that bridge when we get there." He rose confidently from the table, tablet in hand, and left them in the breakroom.

Lea shook her head at Montgomery's audacity. She hoped this professor would be happy enough to see the castle that she wouldn't care about wasting a day waiting for a ghost who never materialized. Although, as the day wore on, Lea realized a ghost who doesn't appear might be the least of their worries.

CHAPTER 18

Montgomery, Lea, and Kamika were walking up the stone stairs to the massive wooden doors of the castle when the door in front of them flung open wide. Ryan stood framed in the doorway with a frantic look on his face. His wife was right behind him. Both appeared in distress.

"Ryan, what's wrong?" Montgomery's voice was tinged with alarm. He bounded up the stone stairs to the front door.

"It's Jack! He's been kidnapped!" Ryan exclaimed with anguish twisting his face.

"Have you called the police?" Montgomery asked.

Ryan shook his head. "No, the caller said not to involve the authorities."

"Okay, tell me what happened." Montgomery marched behind the distraught parents into the castle. Lea and Kamika rushed up the stone steps and followed them into the living room.

"Everyone, sit down," Montgomery said, then turned

to the Hanovers. "Now, start from the beginning. Tell me what happened."

Ryan took a deep breath. "Jack went to a teammate's birthday party at a skating rink two hours ago. We dropped Wyatt Miller and Jack off at the party together. Wendy was supposed to pick them both up. We just got a call from someone disguising his voice who said that he had the boys. He would let us know how much to pay to get our son back soon. He said that we'd better have the money ready. We called Desty Miller, but she didn't answer. We need to find her and let her know about Wyatt and Jack being kidnapped." His voice trailed off, and his wife's chest heaved as she fought to control the panic overtaking her.

"Can we verify that the boys have been taken? How do you know that they aren't at the party?" Montgomery asked.

"Wendy called the hostess." Ryan's voice cracked. "The hostess said she forgot to give the boys their gift bags when they left with their uncle."

Tears were flowing down Wendy's face. "I don't know how Jack could leave with a stranger like that! He wouldn't just go with someone he didn't know."

"Okay." Montgomery pulled out his tablet and began tapping away as he talked. "Let me explain how this has to work. We are going to need the police. I have contacts that I can call directly on personal phones. We can get a detective on this without sirens blaring all over the neighborhood. The kidnapper won't know. The police can start looking at the security video from the skating rink. They might be able to identify the kidnapper from the video. Give me a minute." Montgomery stepped to the side and began to dial.

"Let me get you a drink," Kamika said to Wendy. "You can't get upset like this. In a minute, you'll be hyperventilating. That can't be good for your baby."

Wendy struggled to take a deep breath, but it was broken by a gasping sob. Kamika hurried into the kitchen to get her a drink.

Ryan ran a hand through his thinning hair and jumped up from the couch. He paced toward the main door before turning around. He looked from his wife to Montgomery and back again. At last, he seemed to decide that his wife was okay with Lea. He followed Montgomery and hovered nearby trying to listen to his phone conversation.

"Wendy," Lea said, trying to think of a distraction, "when is your presentation on your software?"

Kamika returned and handed a box of tissues and a glass of water to Wendy.

Wendy sipped the water. "It's . . . it's supposed . . . to be this afternoon at two." She wiped her eyes with a wad of tissues and tried to breathe more calmly.

"If you don't go, will you lose the sale?" Lea asked.

"Yes, but it doesn't matter! We have to find Jack!" Wendy put the water glass on the coffee table.

Lea glanced over at Montgomery to make sure he'd heard. He nodded his understanding to Lea. Lea moved closer to Kamika and whispered, "Could someone have kidnaped the children to prevent Wendy from getting to a meeting?"

Kamika leaned toward Lea and spoke into her ear. "Probably not. Don't you think it's more likely someone wants ransom money? In any case, money's involved. When money is involved, people do stupid stuff."

Lea turned to Wendy. "If you sell your software and business to that conglomerate, how much money are you likely to make? Is it enough for a competitor to try to ruin your chances by any means necessary, including kidnapping?"

Wendy looked at Lea tearfully. "I'd expect to be offered at least ten million for the company. That's probably more than enough incentive for someone."

"That's a lot of money if you're desperate. What time do you need to leave?" Lea asked.

Wendy's mouth dropped open, and she gave Lea a look of consternation. "What do you mean, leave? I couldn't go while Jack is missing!"

"What if Jack was taken for the purpose of making you miss your meeting?" Lea asked.

"Then it worked! I won't go until we find Jack!" she surged to her feet with her fists in angry balls.

Lea recoiled away from the angry woman. "I'm not suggesting that you do." She looked to Kamika for help.

"Sit down, Wendy. We only want to help," Kamika said gently, patting the couch cushion next to her.

Wendy ignored her and stood staring at Montgomery's back, crushing and twisting the tissues in her hand, shredding them.

Finally, Montgomery ended his conversation. He and Ryan rejoined the group. "My friend is checking the surveillance video at the skating rink. We should hear back from him in the next twenty minutes." Montgomery sank his bulk into a chair by the couch.

Ryan wrapped his arms around his wife, who almost collapsed into his embrace with her face buried in his neck. They stood rocking slightly from side to side.

Silence settled over the group, broken only by Wendy's gasping sobs.

Lea tried to think of something to say, but every topic seemed too trivial for the occasion. She began bouncing her foot nervously on the floor, her whole leg moving more in a spasmodic tremor than a controlled tapping. Kamika reached out a hand and held Lea's knee to stop the tremor.

Finally, Montgomery's phone rang. Lea jumped to her feet. Wendy looked up from her husband's chest but continued to cling to him. They all stared expectantly at Montgomery. He looked at the Hanovers, begged pardon with a glance, and retreated to the kitchen, leaving them staring behind him.

Ryan looked as if he would follow Montgomery, but his wife still grasped him for support.

At last, Montgomery returned with his tablet in one hand and his phone in the other. "I know what's going on."

"You know where Jack is?" Wendy asked.

"What?" Kamika said, stunned.

Lea laughed in relief, afraid she might cry in a moment.

"Where is Jack? Is he safe?" Ryan asked and was soon followed by Wendy's, "Who did this?"

Montgomery looked at Wendy with sympathy. "I'm so sorry to have to tell you this." Then his flicked to Lea, and she knew instantly. Betrayal was the key. Betrayal by someone close.

She looked at Montgomery and threw out the name she thought he wanted to hear. "Desty Miller, Wyatt's mother?"

Montgomery nodded, watching the Hanovers.

Wendy gasped. "No! The kidnapper took her son Wyatt, too. Why would she do this? A man took the boys." Confusion filled her face, and she looked to her husband for answers. Ryan appeared to have been struck speechless, appalled by the situation.

"No way!" Kamika breathed, looking from Lea to Montgomery and back again. "No way! Really?"

Montgomery nodded. "My background check on Desty Miller arrived. Her so-called home-based information technology company isn't what you think. She calls herself an information retrieval specialist, which sounds better than hacker or thief. Desty Miller specializes in corporate espionage."

"But a *man* broke into the castle! He's on video!" Wendy repeated in disbelief.

"Yes, that was a man on the video, and it was a man who took the boys," Montgomery agreed. "Records show Desty Miller has one employee, Burke Scurzo, who's listed as a file clerk. He's never been any kind of clerk for her. I doubt she keeps paper files. He was hired for his experience in another area. Mr. Scurzo has a criminal record for breaking and entering that goes back fifteen years. Desty Miller commits electronic break-ins—hacks—to look for data. When she can't get what she wants that way, she has Mr. Scurzo as a secondary option. I had my contact compare the video of the man who took the boys with Mr. Scurzo's mug shot. They match. Wyatt knows Burke Scurzo well. He may even call him Uncle Burke. The boys went with him willingly when he said Desty had sent him to pick them up."

Anger blazed on Ryan's face. "You mean Jack might be at the Millers' house? Safe?" He hurried across the room toward the door with his wife close behind him.

He flung the door open and almost slammed into a fashionable woman in strappy sandals and a summer dress who was caught in the act of raising her hand to knock at the door.

Ryan stopped short and snapped, "Who are you?"

The woman looked shocked at his surly greeting. "I'm Dr. Jenny Tremayne. Montgomery asked me to come." She looked around Ryan and spotted Montgomery, giving him an uncertain look.

"Excuse me," Ryan said, racing out the door around her, with Wendy on his heels.

Dr. Tremayne stepped back and watched the pair race down the stairs, across the yard, and down the street.

"They should wait for the police," Montgomery said as he, Lea, and Kamika stood with the confused Dr. Tremayne on the stairs watching.

At that moment, two unmarked cars pulled silently onto the block and stopped. Men in khakis and white, button-down shirts emerged from one car as Ryan and Wendy ran by them. A woman and a man got out of the other car.

Montgomery trotted down the stone steps over to the arriving plainclothes men and spoke to them quickly. Lea recognized Marco and Schmitt, the detectives who had come when Wendy had been attacked.

All of the officers and Montgomery followed the Hanovers to the Millers' house.

Lea, Kamika, and Dr. Tremayne watched as the police led Ryan and Wendy away from the door. Two officers kept the Hanovers back by the street while Marco and Schmitt knocked on the door.

Ryan broke free and rushed toward the house, only to be stopped by Montgomery again. He gesticulated angrily toward the house. Desty Miller's car was parked in the driveway.

A sense of dread came over Lea. If the boys weren't at the house, where were they? What if the man, Scurzo, wasn't acting on Desty Miller's orders? Lea began walking toward the Millers' house with Kamika and Dr. Tremayne each a step behind her.

No one answered the door. The unknown male and female detectives stayed with the Hanovers while Marco and Schmitt began to walk around the house peering in the windows.

As Lea reached the Hanovers, she heard Marco shout from by a side window, "We've got a woman bound and gagged on the floor! She's not moving!" He rushed to the front door, broke the window inside it, and unlocked the door. He and Schmitt rushed into the house.

CHAPTER 19

THE HANOVERS TRIED TO FOLLOW THE police into the Millers' house but were quickly blocked again by Montgomery. They stood on the front porch watching through the open front door.

Marco knelt next to Desty Miller and checked for a pulse while Schmitt and the female officer vanished into the house to check the rooms. "Faint pulse," called Marco to the fourth officer, who was keeping the Hanovers outside the door. "Call an ambulance." He released her from her bindings, but she didn't move. He checked for breathing. "Not breathing." He checked her pulse again. "Lost the pulse. Starting compressions." He began CPR to try to revive Desty while the detective on the porch radioed for an ambulance.

Ryan pushed forward, again trying to enter the house. "We need to go in there! My son could be in there in another room!" Blazing anger and desperation commingled on Ryan's face. His hands were balled into fists, though he never raised them. His shoulders heaved as he fought for control of himself.

Montgomery stepped in front of Ryan and put one hand on the anguished man's chest and the other on his shoulder, ready to restrain Ryan bodily if necessary. "They'll let us know if they find the boys. They're looking now."

Lea watched the scene inside the house and the still-unmoving Desty Miller through the open front door.

"We don't have much time," Kamika said in Lea's ear. "Wendy's meeting is in two hours."

"She doesn't care about anything but Jack right now."

Schmitt, who had been searching the house, returned to the porch and said to Montgomery. "The house is clear. No one else is inside."

At that moment, the distinctive chirp of a mobile phone reached their ears.

Moving with impressive speed for a man his size, Montgomery leaped from the porch onto the nearby driveway and snatched a phone from the front seat of Desty's car via an open window. Schmitt watched in surprise before he asked, "Montgomery, what did you find?"

"A text came. It says, 'Think, or you won't see your boy again.'"

Montgomery handed the phone to one of the officers on the porch, "Schmitt, do you think you can trace the phone that sent this message? The person who sent this kidnapped two boys. Don't lecture me about search and seizure laws or tell me I stole this phone. Kids' lives are at stake."

"Okay, okay. Give it to me. We've got some great new software for tracking texts, even on cheap burner phones like this one." He trotted to his car and opened a laptop.

Ryan and Wendy followed him and stood uneasily by the car with Montgomery towering over them.

"The sender is using a burner phone, too. No owner registered to the number," Schmitt said to Montgomery. "The program is scanning now for the location of the phone. We might get lucky if the owner left the GPS on the phone activated. We used to have to get a tech to do this for us. And . . . we have a location. I'm calling it in to SWAT."

"Where?" asked Ryan, with desperation. "Can we go now?"

Detective Schmitt looked at the worried parents before him with sympathy. "Maybe after I have word that SWAT has arrived, assessed the situation, and has a plan, we can take you someplace nearby. We will not approach the actual location."

More police arrived. An ambulance rushed Desty Miller, still unconscious but breathing on her own, to the hospital. Montgomery had a long conversation with Marco and Schmitt. Crime scene technicians flooded into the house.

Wendy clung to her husband, who looked caught between supporting her and containing his own panic over his son.

Montgomery finally finished speaking to the police and rejoined Lea, Kamika, and Dr. Tremayne.

Montgomery smiled at Dr. Tremayne. Even in her heels, she only reached his chin. From her expression, Lea was sure she wasn't in the least intimidated by the size of the man in front of her.

"You arrived in the middle of a kidnapping and industrial espionage case, Jenny," Montgomery said, standing before her with his hands on his hips. "Sorry about this, but we had no idea this was going to happen."

Dr. Tremayne started to speak but was interrupted as a policeman called Montgomery's name. He turned to answer the summons.

Lea noticed that the police were directing the Hanovers into a car.

Montgomery started to jog away, calling over his shoulder, "Lea, go inside and show Jenny . . . er . . . Dr. Tremayne, the castle. I'm following Ryan and Wendy to see this thing resolved. I'll call when I have more information for you."

Dr. Tremayne laughed. "If you think we're waiting here while you go with them, you had better think again!" The professor gestured back at Lea and Kamika with her other hand as she continued, "I want to go with you, and I'm absolutely certain that these ladies do, too."

Kamika nodded emphatically.

Montgomery eyed Dr. Tremayne appreciatively. "Fine, you can come too. Let's go!"

They all piled into Montgomery's van and quickly followed the police car carrying the Hanovers.

Fifteen minutes later, they arrived at a light industrial complex composed of several blocks of nearly identical, aluminum-roofed buildings labeled for boat repair, tool rental, and car customizing. Police vehicles blocked the street.

The Hanovers were being kept behind the car barricade as an officer pointed to something off in the distance. Lea, Kamika, Montgomery, and Dr. Tremayne joined the Hanovers.

"Where are the boys being held?" Montgomery asked.

Ryan answered, his voice wavering with fear and frustration, "The officer says SWAT is set up about two blocks from here. We can't even see the building!"

Montgomery clapped one hand on the distraught man's shoulder. "We can't get in the way. If we're too close, we could complicate things for the SWAT team. You wouldn't want to do anything to interfere with the rescue operation."

"Can't we get a little closer? Please?" Wendy's voice trembled.

"Stay here. I'll find out." Montgomery stepped aside and pulled out his phone. He had a short and urgent conversation before returning to them. "I've got permission to move up to the staging area. I'll call and update you as soon as I know something."

He trotted to his car and opened the trunk, then pulled on a bulletproof vest and a lightweight jacket over it. A moment later, Montgomery nodded to the officer guarding the barricade, who allowed him through. He trotted up the sidewalk and vanished down a side street.

A few nervous moments later, Lea's phone rang. "It's Montgomery," she said, as she switched on the phone's speaker. "Hello? We're all here on speakerphone."

Montgomery's voice came over loud and clear. "I'm across from a storage facility two blocks north of you. It's all over. The boys are safe. Scurzo had them watching a movie while he worked on a laptop in the office area. SWAT arrested him without a shot behind fired."

"Thank God," Wendy said.

"Wendy?" Montgomery said. "Listen! Scurzo only wanted you distracted until you missed your meeting over the sale of your software. His goal was to make you miss it. Someone at the meeting was going to let him know if you came or not. We need to know who that accomplice is. We need you to go to that meeting. Don't let them win."

"Oh!" Wendy glanced at her watch. "My meeting is in thirty minutes. I can't go!"

"Yes, you can! If you don't, whoever did this succeeds!" he said.

"I won't go until I see Jack!" she said fiercely.

"Come to me, straight north two blocks. He's fine. I can see him from where I am."

Wendy took off with her husband close behind her.

"They're coming, Montgomery," Lea said.

"I'll get Marco to take her to her meeting," he replied through the phone. "He'll want to know who attends, in order to add names to our list of suspects and accomplices. Lea, listen. Marco received a report from the hospital. Desty Miller never regained consciousness. Her heart stopped again in the ambulance, and they weren't able to save her. She's dead. They haven't told Scurzo. He doesn't seem to know she died since he's telling the police that he doesn't know anything and to ask her. I'll tell the Hanovers. Her death may have been accidental, but, if Scurzo won't talk or doesn't know, we have no link to who hired her. I can see the Hanovers. Bye." He disconnected.

CHAPTER 20

Two days later, on Friday afternoon, Kamika, Lea, Montgomery, and the Hanovers stood in the castle living room as a knock sounded on the massive front door.

Wendy opened the door to admit Dr. Tremayne, whom Montgomery formally introduced to everyone. "Dr. Tremayne is a professor of Celtic studies. She can read ancient Celtic writings and might be able to decipher what our ghost is saying. We're going to tour the castle and then see what she can tell us about our crying lady."

The small woman shook hands with the Hanovers. "I'm so relieved that everything turned out well for your son."

"Thank you," Wendy said. "I'm sorry we weren't in any shape to welcome you the last time you came."

Dr. Tremayne laughed. "If I had been in your place, I would have told the arriving stranger to go to hell. You were beyond panicked."

Dr. Tremayne turned to Lea and Kamika, "I'm pleased to meet you both. Montgomery has told me so much about you." She gave them both a friendly smile, then turned back to Montgomery.

Lea shot Montgomery a puzzled look, but he didn't notice. He was too busy looking at Dr. Tremayne. Lea could sense a current of strong attraction flowing between the two and realized that Montgomery hadn't been kidding when he'd joked about getting a personal life. He was seeing someone, and she was a professor of ancient Celtic studies.

Lea glanced at Kamika, who wore a wide smile on her face—she had clearly noticed as well. Kamika was openly studying the tiny woman, evaluating her.

Lea guessed Dr. Tremayne was in her late thirties or early forties, with thick hair cut straight at her jaw line and curling under, with a heavy row of bangs on her forehead.

The group toured the castle from top to bottom, with Jack tagging along happily, chatting as if nothing had happened to him two days before. The professor exclaimed here and there over the rooms and provided interesting commentary on the history of Celtic castles as they walked.

When they reached the chapel, Dr. Tremayne spent a few minutes studying the small room. "I have a few students who would be thrilled to see this place," she told Wendy.

Wendy looked surprised but then smiled. "Maybe we can arrange a visit for a small group after we get the rest of the place in order."

"I would really appreciate that," Dr. Tremayne said.

As they completed the tour of the upper floors, Wendy sent Jack to his room to play, partly to stem the tide of comments from the boy and partly to keep him from joining them in the basement.

They all descended into the dungeon. Lea shivered on the stairs. The space still echoed with the horrors committed there. Dr. Tremayne took time examining the rusted iron remnants and holes in the walls of the dungeon. She concurred with Lea's assessment as to their probable usage for shackling prisoners. Lea's skin crawled the entire time they were below ground. Wendy hugged her arms around herself, nervously eyeing the stairs as if ready to bolt.

Once they were all safely back in the living room, Lea relaxed as she and the others sat down on the couches, relieved that the ghost of the crying woman hadn't made an appearance.

Wendy related her own encounters and Mae's meetings with the ghost that were mentioned in the diaries. "Oh, I finished reading Mae's diaries. It almost scared the life out of her to go into the cellar and hide those things from Harry that we found hidden in the trunks. The trunks were apparently always stored down there. All she had to do was carry the individual items that she wanted to hide and add them to the trunks. On her last trip down into the basement before Harry's death, she saw the ghost and felt the evil thing coming. She never went down into the basement again and didn't trust anyone else to get things out for her. Apparently, a housekeeper she trusted had stolen things from her in the late 1930s, and a gardener had walked off with items from the storage closet in the garage in the 1940s. She grew paranoid of betrayal toward the end, suspecting people of being either common thieves or mob members trying to collect on Harry's old debts. Poor old dear."

"You must have gotten a pretty good feel for Mae's character from her diaries," Lea said.

Wendy sat sipping from a glass of lemonade, one of several she'd brought for everyone on a tray. "Mae put a lot of herself into the pages. From what she wrote, she clearly had a good heart. She did her best, but I could see her mind beginning to deteriorate as she aged. It reminded me of my own grandmother's decline and death." Then Wendy turned suddenly to her husband. "See, Ryan! In a hundred years, will any of my great-grandchildren care to read my blog? Will they even be able to find it in a readable format? Moreover, even if they did, my blog doesn't contain the personal information and thoughts that Mae included in her diary. Nobody puts that stuff online!"

Her husband grinned at her and capitulated. "Then start hand writing a diary of your own. I'm not stopping you."

"I might," Wendy said thoughtfully. "Mae wrote when she felt like writing, not every day. When something important came up, or she had something on her mind, she jotted it down. I could do that. Even with my crazy schedule."

"Now I know what to get you for your birthday," her husband teased.

Montgomery laughed and turned to the professor. "Dr. Tremayne, since our ghost didn't put in an appearance today, I guess we'll have to give you Kamika's version of what she sounded like. Kamika, Lea, and Wendy heard the ghost screaming. It all sounded like noise and just the one word, 'Angus,' to Lea. However, since Kamika is multilingual in languages with different roots and alphabets and has a good ear for sounds, she was able to separate the sounds she heard into syllables. I asked her to repeat what she'd heard and recorded it."

He extracted his phone from his pocket and set it on the coffee table by the sofa, then hit play.

Dr. Tremayne leaned in and listened intently to the recording in which Kamika repeated what the ghost had said. Finally, the petite professor dug into her handbag and retrieved a pen and paper. "May I?" she asked, reaching for the phone.

Montgomery handed the device to her and watched silently, along with all the others in the room, as Dr. Tremayne transcribed the sounds on the recording into words, pausing the recording and restarting it several times.

At last, Dr. Tremayne looked up with a satisfied smile. "I know what she is saying, but the language could be only a few hundred years old. The people who told the story to Mae might have muddled similar incidents down through the centuries or made a more modern story seem ancient to impress Mae." She picked up her notes and reviewed them quickly. "The ghost is calling for her brother Angus, yelling that their lord and lady had been betrayed and murdered by her own lover. Based on what she says, I can guess at the rest. She found Angus, and, instead of helping her, Angus stood by and watched as the traitor, who was her own lover, killed her. Her brother was in league with the traitor and betrayed her, too."

"She was betrayed by her lover and her brother and then murdered. Poor woman," said Wendy.

"Show me," said Kamika, leaning over Dr. Tremayne to see the words she'd written.

"Here," Dr. Tremayne pointed, "this word, *fhealltóir*, means traitor. This word, *deartháir*, is brother. You did an excellent job of breaking the sounds into syllables and grouping them. I only had to regroup a few syllables to understand the whole thing." She continued explaining the words to Kamika.

Montgomery turned to Wendy, Ryan, and Lea. "Mae and the Irish people who told her the story were right. The ghost warns of betrayal."

Lea nodded and said, "Maybe she'll stop appearing now. The betrayals have been exposed. Desty Miller was betraying Wendy, trying to steal her work while pretending to be her friend. The ghost should have nothing left to warn us about."

Wendy blinked back tears. "A trusted steward, a lover, a brother, a cousin, an advisor, a friend . . . how did they justify their actions to themselves? They must have known the pain they were causing." She sniffed and swiped at her eyes. "I hope the ghost is gone. If you're right about why she appears, that would mean, if we can avoid betrayal in the house, we'll never see her again!"

Ryan put a supportive arm around his wife. "The ghost could be like an alarm system, an echo that replays only when conditions are right."

Dr. Tremayne placed her empty drink glass down on the coffee table. "As much as I've enjoyed this, I need to get back to work. Thank you for showing me your incredible piece of history. I'll contact you about bringing some of my students here." She shook hands with Ryan and Wendy and said her goodbyes to the others.

Wendy escorted Dr. Tremayne to the door and saw her out.

Preparing to leave, Montgomery picked up his phone from the coffee table and said, "We've done all we can here in the castle." He paused, struck by a thought. "At this location . . ."

"What is it?" Lea asked.

"I had an idea, but it may not be workable. I'll have to think about it some more." The intent look on his face deepened as he thought. He turned back to the Hanovers. Any thoughts of leaving the premises were apparently forgotten. "Some evidence is probably locked in Desty Miller's electronic devices. The police will be working to break her encryption software to try to retrieve any evidence in her computers or email. I wish them luck. If what she used to protect her equipment is state of the art, developed outside the United States with no back doors, they might not be able to get into her devices."

"They might not be able to find who hired her?" Kamika asked.

Montgomery nodded. "Scurzo isn't talking. He asked for a lawyer and invoked his right to remain silent as soon as he found out Desty Miller was dead. He's facing kidnapping and murder charges."

Ryan looked curiously at Montgomery. "Jack told us that after Mr. Scurzo picked them up from the party, they played at a park while Scurzo talked on a phone to someone. Later, they went to the Millers' house. Scurzo told the boys to wait in the car while he checked with Desty to see if the boys could watch a movie with him. Jack said they didn't wait long before he returned to say that Desty had said yes to the movie. That must have been when he gagged Desty and left her there. He must have called us later. Surely, the police can trace who he was working for."

Montgomery shook his head. "They haven't been able to so far."

"I still can't believe Desty had that man kidnap Jack," Wendy said. "It doesn't seem possible that the person I knew would do that. She seemed like a good mother. She wouldn't have put Wyatt in danger." Wendy's voice began cracking. "How could I have misjudged her that badly?"

Her husband hugged her to his chest, and frowned perplexedly at Montgomery.

Montgomery softened his tone and said, "We don't know that Desty ever intended for anyone to get hurt. It's possible she didn't want the boys to be taken. Scurzo may have bound her to prevent her from stopping him. If she panicked and fought to get free, the sudden stress could have caused a heart attack, or she might have suffocated. Her death was unintentional. She might have been innocent of that part of the plan. She might have tried to stop Scurzo from taking Jack. We don't know what happened."

"Still, she did agree to steal from us! For money! She could have refused to be hired!" Wendy's body trembled with disbelief and disappointment.

Ryan squeezed his wife's hand. "She made unconscionable, unprincipled choices. If she'd been working as a hacker in industrial espionage, then she'd been making unethical and morally questionable choices for a long time in her business practice. Her sense of wrong wasn't what yours is."

"That's true for a lot of criminals," Montgomery said. "People aren't consistently good or consistently bad; sometimes they compartmentalize their lives. She separated her personal life from her business life. She was a good mother, and she was a good friend. You didn't misjudge her entirely. You never saw her business side, so you never had anything to judge. You only saw her personal side, where she was an attentive, loving mother and helpful friend." He paused, stunned. "That's it! That's my way in! Excuse me! I need to make a phone call!" Montgomery turned and began looking for something on his phone as he walked toward the door. Everyone else watch as he vanished through the door. An awkward silence ensued.

"How did the presentation go? Did they buy your software?" Lea asked Wendy, changing the subject and drawing attention away from Montgomery.

Wendy brushed away her tears and smiled weakly. "They loved it. They said we outdid all the competitors in ease of use and functionality. I should be hearing back from them soon with an offer. Then the real negotiations begin. After that, I'll be working closely with their offices to get them up to speed on the software and to integrate it into their existing platform."

"She did a beautiful job!" Ryan said proudly. He pulled his wife close and kissed her noisily on the cheek.

Lea asked, "Did the police identify whoever was supposed to tell Scurzo that you weren't at the meeting? Your competitors weren't at the presentation meeting, were they? So that person had to be within the company."

Wendy frowned. "We still have no idea who that is. While I'd rather not have to work with them, if they were involved for pay, it's possible a competitor asked someone to let them know how my presentation went. That would make more sense than that someone within the company was trying to stop me. The police questioned people, but once everyone knew a kidnapping was involved, how serious the situation was, everyone denied knowing anything. Even if that inside person was inadvertently aiding the kidnapper, he would want to cover his own rear."

Kamika frowned with her eyebrows drawn together and her nose wrinkled. "What about Mr. Miller? Does he know his wife's passwords? Would he help?"

Montgomery trotted into the room. "That's a good question, Kamika. As it turns out, he doesn't know her passwords, but he is willing to help. Kamika, Lea, we need to grab the scanners from the van. We're doing a scan on the Millers' house right now, if Lea is willing." Montgomery looked directly at Lea inquiringly.

She realized immediately what he was asking. Another source of information, besides the Miller house itself, was Desty Miller, whose troubled soul might or might not still be lingering in her home. However, Montgomery wouldn't have told Hugh Miller that—he would do a reading on the house while Lea looked around. Lea nodded back her agreement.

CHAPTER 21

"HOW DID YOU GET HUGH MILLER to agree to that?" Ryan asked as Wendy looked at Montgomery with surprise.

"I realized earlier that a reading on the Millers' house might reveal new avenues for the police to investigate, but I didn't think we'd be able to get Hugh Miller to allow it. Then it occurred to me that if Wendy couldn't see the twisted, unethical side of Desty Miller, Desty's husband might not have seen it either. He travels frequently as a charter pilot. She could have hidden that side of her work from him, as she hid it from you. I called and offered to help him find the truth."

Ryan put his arm around his wife's shoulder and hugged her. "What did Hugh say?"

"He doesn't know what to believe right now," Montgomery said. "He's grieving the loss of his wife and being told that he didn't know who she truly was. He doesn't know if his wife conspired to kidnap Jack, or if she tried to stop the kidnapper and was killed for her efforts. He wants to know the truth as much as we do. I offered to read the room where Desty was found. If she argued with her killer in there, we'll find evidence of it. We might be able to find the truth for all of you. If we're lucky, when we scan the room, we'll get the name of the person or company who hired them or a clue we could pass on to the police to be investigated." Montgomery omitted the detail about checking for Desty Miller's ghost. There would be time for that later, if needed.

"Can I come?" Wendy asked. "I'd like to be there."

"You can ask Mr. Miller. He's home now with Wyatt and a few relatives who came to help plan the funeral. Desty's funeral, by the way, is on hold. They're still waiting for her autopsy to be completed and for her body to be released for burial."

"I'll come, too," Ryan said. "Hugh's not going to want Wyatt there for this. I can watch Wyatt and Jack play outside while you complete your scans." He left the room to retrieve Jack while Wendy called Hugh Miller for permission to come with Montgomery.

Montgomery took Lea aside with a look of apology and whispered, "I know, I know," he said. "You hate to converse with recently departed murder victims. She may not even be there, right? And we have to do the scans at the least."

Lea shrugged, resigned to the plan. "It's our best shot, whether I like it or not. Let's go."

They decided that Wendy, Ryan, and Jack would approach the door first and offer their condolences to Hugh Miller while Montgomery, Kamika, and Lea prepared their scanning equipment.

Lea watched the neighbors greet each other. Wyatt stood sadly behind his dad as greetings were exchanged, but he brightened when invited to come outside to play with Jack. Kids handled death differently from adults. Given a chance to see a friend and leave the gloom in his house, eight-year-old Wyatt went to play, momentarily relieved of his grief by the distraction.

The conversation between Mr. Miller and the Hanovers seemed stiff and tense at first, but then, suddenly, the mood shifted. Mr. Miller stepped out the door and hugged Wendy as Ryan patted him consolingly on the shoulder. He then turned and introduced an older woman and man standing just behind him. Lea guessed them to be his parents, or perhaps Desty's.

By the time Lea, Kamika, and Montgomery arrived with their equipment, the children were throwing a baseball back and forth on the front lawn and the adults were discussing the funeral arrangements.

Seeing the Bad Vibes crew approaching, Hugh Miller said, "Mom, Dad, would you mind watching the boys outside? I need to talk to these people inside the house. I'll explain later."

"Of course. Do what you need to do," said the gray-haired man from whom, Lea could see, Hugh had obviously gotten his hawkish nose.

The woman, with wrinkles around the corners of her blue eyes and lines across her forehead, looked troubled. "What's this about?" she asked, taking a step toward Montgomery like a lioness defending her cub.

"Later, Joanie," her husband said as he reached out a hand to stop her. "Let Hugh deal with things his way."

Joanie gave Montgomery a distrustful glance, pursing her lips in disapproval, but she stepped away and turned her attention back to the boys.

"I'll stay out here with the boys," Ryan said.

Joanie eyed Ryan as if she hadn't decided what to think of him yet while her husband smiled complacently, but Hugh said, "Thanks, Ryan. We'll let you know what we find."

Inside the house, Hugh led them into the living room where his wife had been bound and gagged a few days earlier. The room was designed for relaxation, with an overstuffed recliner and a deep sofa in front of a television mounted on the wall. The furniture, though of good quality, showed wear and tear from a child's use, including sticky spots on the armrests. A shelf of pile of slightly askew puzzles and games sat to one side of the room. The coffee table in front of the sofa held a plastic cup of water on a cork coaster and an array of gaming controllers. The carpet needed vacuuming. Someone, probably Wyatt, had dropped dry cereal on the floor and couch across from the television.

Hugh's blue eyes darted around the room dejectedly. "I still can't believe Desty would be involved in any of this. What the police told me was . . . unbelievable." His eyes glistened. "I need to know anything you can tell me." He wiped his hand over the dark, unshaven stubble on his haggard face. The gravity of the situation settled heavily on his shoulders, bowing them with grief.

Lea looked around the room intently. She saw a flash of Desty Miller lying on the floor next to the sofa, bound and gagged. The woman's eyes were frantic, with the whites showing all the way around her dark irises. Lea could feel her panic, desperation, and fear imprinted on the space. The flash ended, leaving only the dark emotional residue. Lea turned on her sound scanner and said to Montgomery, "Let's get started," to let him and Kamika know that Desty Miller wasn't in the room.

Hugh Miller and Wendy stood in the hallway as Lea and Montgomery methodically scanned the walls for residual sound patterns and Kamika tracked the incoming data on a tablet. Once the scanning was complete, Lea and Montgomery looked over Kamika's shoulders to review the scan data and choose likely areas of data to analyze.

Montgomery tapped the screen with one chubby index finger. "Here, here, and here."

Kamika tapped a few buttons in response. "Here we go!"

Lea beckoned Mr. Miller closer. "We have some results coming in. The analysis program will convert the patterns to words and syllables for us."

Montgomery read from the screen of the tablet. "A female voice yelled, 'No, no, no' and 'not involving children,' and then she said, 'not part of the original job.' A male voice said, 'pay off will be huge' and 'not your decision.' Then it looks like they moved across the room. She said, 'Give me my son now.' He said, 'get . . . back when . . . over.' She yells, 'now.' He yells, 'How . . . think . . . end? My part . . . always riskier.'" Montgomery tapped another area on the screen and looked around the room. "This next part is closer to the hall, toward the front door. Hang on. It's analyzing."

Tears leaked down Hugh Miller's cheeks. "At least she didn't agree to the kidnapping! That's a relief."

"Here's the last part." Montgomery read from the screen, "The male voice yelled, 'You're as dirty as I . . . helped me break into the castle' and 'can't let them identify me.' And she yelled, 'No one was supposed to get hurt . . . only supposed to take software. I never agreed to stop . . . meeting. Wyatt won't talk.' The man yelled, 'after . . . out . . . the country.'"

"That makes sense," Lea said. "Desty told Scurzo that the castle was unlocked. He could have watched the castle from here to see people leave before he went in and attacked Wendy and stole her software. The original job was to steal software. Desty never agreed to stopping Wendy from going to the meeting and didn't want the boys taken. Scurzo took that job on his own. Then later, after Scurzo took the boys, he knew that Wyatt could identify him. He came here either to get Desty to help him or to keep her from turning him in. Scurzo was going to leave the boys locked somewhere until after he got out of the country. Desty fought with him. He couldn't risk that she might report him to the police, so he tied her up and left her."

"Lea, do you see anything else worth checking on here?" Montgomery pointed at the tablet.

Lea searched the screen. "No. Nothing else."

Montgomery looked around the room. "The most likely sequence of events, then, is this. Scurzo hit Desty to stun her so he could tie her up and gag her. If he'd meant to kill her, he wouldn't have tied her up. Logically, that means he didn't want to kill her and the boys. Her death was accidental. Remember, he texted her, expecting she was alive. Maybe he hit her too hard, or her fear sent her into cardiac arrest, or she accidentally suffocated. Hopefully the autopsy results will tell us more." A look of disappointment crossed Montgomery's face. "While we have an idea of what happened here, we are no closer to identifying who hired Desty and Scurzo. Neither of them said anything about who hired them."

Wendy hugged Hugh Miller. "This gives me my friend back. She was my friend, even if she made some bad choices. She never planned for me or the boys to be hurt. I'm going to go tell Ryan what we found." She turned and left the room.

"An emotional energy scan wouldn't add anything. We don't need to do it," Montgomery said.

Montgomery and Kamika began to pack the scanning equipment.

Lea sighed and looked around the room. "Mr. Miller? Would you mind if I walked through the house?"

Hugh Miller gave her a bewildered look. "Why?"

Montgomery responded, prevaricating slightly, "Lea is very sensitive to emotional energy in rooms. It could help."

Hugh Miller shrugged in defeat and sorrow, lacking the energy to care. "Go ahead."

Lea walked up the stairs off the hallway to the second floor. At the top, she quickly found the master bedroom, Wyatt's room, a bathroom, and a guest room with suitcases in it. Lea could sense the grief beginning to seep into the atmosphere over what had been a typically happy space. The last room Lea looked into was an office. Stepping inside, Lea immediately sensed that she was not alone. She could feel regret, remorse, and an overwhelming wish for forgiveness.

Desty Miller's indistinct form hovered by her desk.

Lea had never faced the spirit of someone she had met in life. "Hello, Mrs. Miller," Lea said as softly and calmly as she could, although her pulse was racing. She sensed the vague form turning toward her more than she could actually see it. "Can you tell me who hired you? Who paid Scurzo to take the boys?"

"Please tell Hugh! I tried to stop him! Please tell Hugh that I'm sorry!" The words came softly, across a distance. Lea had to strain to understand.

"We know. Hugh knows, too. I'll tell him whatever you want," Lea said. "Can you help us finish this? Can you tell me who hired you?"

"Tell Wendy I'm sorry. I never thought it would end this way!"

A wave of remorse rolled through the air like a wave of smoke, covering Lea and constricting her chest. "She knows," Lea said, fighting to breathe and watching Mrs. Miller's form waver and begin to lose shape. "You aren't done here! Wait! Please tell me who hired you!"

"All in my laptop . . ."

"Wait. The police have your laptop, but they can't unlock the data!" Lea called and took a desperate step toward the wavering form.

"Look under the African violet," said the vanishing voice, as what Lea thought was an arm gestured at the windowsill. Then she was gone. The cloud of remorse evaporated, leaving wisps of penitence in the air behind it.

Lea looked at the purple-blossomed plant on the windowsill. The violet wasn't going anywhere, so she went and called downstairs to Montgomery. "I've got something! Come to Mrs. Miller's office." Lea didn't wait; she went back to look under the plant.

Lifting the plant, she was disappointed. Nothing was hidden under it. Nothing was attached to the rounded, special pot. Water sloshed inside the pot as she lifted it. The container was designed to allow the plant to suck water from beneath since directly watering the plant would kill it. She peered at the bottom of the pot. Nothing was written on it either. Perplexed she set the plant down.

Montgomery, Kamika, and Hugh Miller entered the room.

"What's up?" Montgomery asked.

"She said to look under the African violet, but I can't find anything." Lea brushed her dark hair out of her face and tucked it into the cloth on her head.

"Did you look inside the pot?" Kamika asked.

"What? You mean dump the plant out?" Lea asked, surprised.

"No, the pot is made of two separate pieces, so one part sits inside the other. Lift out the part with the plant." Kamika walked over and demonstrated. "See!" She held the flowering plant above its rounded, water-filled base.

Lea looked into the water. "There isn't anything here."

Kamika lifted the plant above her head to see the bottom of the unglazed pottery container. Water dripped into her face, but she ignored it. "There's something scratched into the pottery."

"Let me see," Montgomery said. He looked and found a twenty-digit combination of capital and lowercase letters, numbers, and symbols. "A password!"

Hugh Miller stood rigidly in the doorway, an expression of alarm on his face. "Hold on! What do you mean 'she said' to look there?"

Kamika and Montgomery looked at Lea. Montgomery raised his eyebrows, silently offering to take the lead, but Lea ignored him and turned her attention to Mr. Miller.

"Your wife's spirit was here when I entered the room. She wanted you and Wendy to know that she was sorry, that she never meant for any of this to happen. I asked if she could tell us who hired her. She told me that the password was under the flower pot on the windowsill." Lea spoke softly and gently, as if her words were dynamite that might provoke an explosion. She was used to anger, even rage, from people who didn't believe what they were hearing.

Instead, Mr. Miller's face crumpled into overwhelming sorrow. Both hands went to his light, wavy hair, and he bent over as if he'd been punched in the gut. "Is she trapped here? Can she not go to heaven? Is she being punished for what she did? Was she in pain?"

"I don't think she was in pain. I don't know where she is now. All the spirits I've ever spoken to were still here because they desperately wanted to tell someone something or resolve some issue. If I had to guess, I'd say that they kept themselves here, unable to move on. For the most part, they vanish once they're reassured that their messages have been delivered, which is what happened with your wife." Lea pushed the rolling desk chair toward the grieving man in the hope he would sit before he fell. From the corner of her eye, she saw Kamika vanish from the room.

Hugh Miller sank into the chair and wiped his damp eyes. "She was here to apologize?"

"Yes. She wanted you to know that she tried to stop Scurzo. She helped resolve this case by giving me a password."

"That's good to know. She was trying to make amends." Hugh Miller took a deep, ragged breath, steadying himself. "Then all I can do now is pray for her soul."

"Yes, sir," Lea said. "We can't do anything else."

Kamika returned to the room, breathless, sloshing a glass of water in her hand. "Here, Mr. Miller. Have some water."

He looked up at her concerned face and tried to smile, managing only a swift upturn of his lips. "Thank you." He took the glass from her and sipped at it slowly.

"If you prefer something stronger than water, I'll get it for you," Kamika offered. "But you'll have to tell me where you keep it."

Mr. Miller smiled wanly but amused. "No, thank you. I'm saving that for tonight when Desty's parents arrive from the East Coast. We'll all need something with a kick to it then."

Montgomery snapped a picture of the bottom of the flowerpot with his phone, "I'm sending this to a detective on the case. He'll get it to the tech guys who are working on Desty's laptop." He tapped rapidly on his phone, sending an email with the attached picture.

Hugh Miller took a deep breath. "Let's go downstairs. The others will be wondering what's going on in here." He heaved himself from the desk chair and straightened his shoulders, bracing himself against the weight of his grief.

CHAPTER 22

FOUR DAYS LATER, ON TUESDAY, MONTGOMERY, Lea, and Kamika arrived at their favorite Italian restaurant in historic downtown Georgetown. It was late afternoon, and all three were clad in black. They'd attended the funeral of Modesty Eustacia Miller, held in a chapel at the nearby Oak Leaf Funeral Home. The official autopsy results listed suffocation as the cause of death. The coroner speculated that her extreme emotional distress had led to the production of mucus that had clogged her nasal passages. With tape over her mouth and her nose clogged, she had been unable to breathe.

Montgomery went to speak to the hostess while Lea and Kamika stood in the waiting area by the door. "Have I ever told you how much I dislike funerals?" Kamika asked.

"No." She shot Kamika a bewildered look. "You said this was your first funeral."

"It was. I'm adding funerals to the list of things I absolutely dislike attending, right between gynecology appointments and going to the dentist." Kamika shuddered dramatically. "All that crying and grief messes with my head. A strawberry daiquiri would improve my mood!"

"Sounds good to me," Lea said. "I'll join you, but make mine a margarita. Look, here come Patrick and Dr. Tremayne." She gestured toward the parking lot, where the two could be seen exiting their respective cars. "I didn't know Dr. Tremayne was coming."

"Montgomery must have invited her," Kamika said with a speculative grin.

In a few moments, the hostess seated them all around a table, provided them with water and menus, and left them to consider their orders.

Lea updated Patrick on the Hanover case. "The police used the password we found to open Desty's files on her laptop. They found that someone working for a competitor of Wendy's called Molinard Travel Applications paid Desty to steal Wendy's software code. Once Scurzo got the software, the person sent a second request asking Desty and Scurzo to prevent Wendy from going to her meeting by any means necessary. Desty refused. Scurzo agreed in exchange for a big payoff."

Patrick grimaced. "The person at Molinard must have seen Wendy's code, realized it was a better program than theirs, and tried to eliminate her from the competition. Have the police arrested anyone yet?"

Lea shook her head. "The police are tracing the emails from the company to identify who sent them. Scurzo still isn't talking, and we don't know how many people were involved. However, it's a small company of only five guys. They may all have been in on the corporate espionage and kidnapping, or only one or two of them. We'll have to wait and see what evidence is found and who gets arrested."

Montgomery broke into the conversation. "By the way, Lea, the test results came back yesterday on that glass bottle of liquid you and Kamika found. It was a foxglove plant extract of digitalis. That stuff could have caused the elder Mr. Hanover to have a heart attack."

The waitress returned to take their orders. Once that was done, Montgomery cleared this throat. "Everyone, I have an announcement to make."

Lea, Kamika, Patrick, and Dr. Tremayne all turned to look at him.

"I'm expanding Montgomery Investigations, opening a branch office in Houston in two months." He paused, taking in three stunned faces and one smiling one. "And Patrick is going to oversee the opening and training of the new employees."

"You're hiring Patrick!" Kamika said with glee.

"To work in Houston?" Lea added, not quite so happily.

"No, no. He'll be my right hand, traveling between our local offices and the branch offices in Houston, Dallas, and San Antonio, as we get them all up and running. Houston is only the first! I'm not making Patrick move to Houston, though he will be traveling quite a bit at first."

Lea smiled in relief and looked at Patrick. "Why didn't you tell me?"

Patrick gave her an apologetic look. "Montgomery didn't want the word out until everything was formally approved. The final building leases and permits were signed yesterday."

"Congratulations!" she said.

Patrick leaned forward and kissed her. "I may even get to work with you from time to time." He brushed a strand of dark hair off her cheek and tucked it gently into the Roman-style cloth around her head.

Kamika did a little dance in her seat, her curls bobbing on her forehead as she moved. "Hooray! Lea, can you imagine doing an investigation with Patrick? That would be a blast!"

Dr. Tremayne watched the happy group around her and then leaned toward Montgomery. "You have a great group of people working for you, Montgomery."

"I only work with the best," he said with a wink. He stared at her for a second, as if he'd suddenly realized something. "You know, there's something you can help with, Jenny. Lea has an issue with one of her professors, and you could tell her how to proceed."

"Tell me about it." Dr. Tremayne leaned in toward Lea with a smile.

Lea explained about her advisor publishing her work as his own.

Dr. Tremayne was shocked and then angry. "What a rat! He can't do that! I know exactly how to approach this and where to start. We need to meet with the dean. By the time this is over, I may be your primary advisor. I meet all the prerequisites to step in since the other fellow died, and, believe me, I don't retreat in the face of an academic fight!"

Lea gave her a grateful look. "You would do that? Step in? Thank you! I appreciate your help!"

"Absolutely! That professor obviously thought you were an easy target! We'll show him that he chose the wrong pigeon for plucking!"

Kamika whispered to Lea, "Why would anyone want to pluck a pigeon?"

Lea burst out laughing. "It's an expression, silly."

Kamika grinned from ear to ear. "I know."

❦

Two months later, on a Monday morning, Kamika and Lea found themselves looking out the window of their company van at a familiar, massive, stone edifice.

"It's even more immense than I remembered it," Kamika said.

"It is enormous. Let's grab the gear and get to work. The space is huge, remember."

"I remember. Do you think the ghost will appear today?" Kamika asked with a hint of worry.

Lea stared at the building and let its historic atmosphere roll over her. "Who knows?" She sighed, thinking of the centuries of people who had left their marks upon the stones. "I hope not." She gathered her equipment bag onto her shoulder and walked toward the stairs.

"I feel sorry for Jack and Wyatt," Kamika said. "Those two are genuine friends."

The heavy wooden door at the top opened before Lea and Kamika finished climbing the stairs.

"Welcome back!" Wendy stood in the doorway smiling. Her oversized t-shirt didn't hide the growing bulge beneath it.

"How are you feeling?" Lea asked.

"I have some morning sickness, usually in the evenings, but not too bad." She patted her tummy. "Our little peanut is being gentle on me."

"Have you told Jack he's going to have a baby brother or sister?" Kamika asked.

"Yes." Wendy laughed. "He wanted to know if he could order a brother. Ryan told him that we get what we get."

"So we're taking another crack at neutralizing the garage and game room space?" Lea said. "Have you had any sightings of the crying woman since we last met?"

"No! We're going with the theory that she is an alarm that replays only under certain conditions. I hope we never have a situation that inspires her to appear again." Wendy looked down the street toward the house her son had spent so much time visiting.

Lea followed her gaze. "Are the Millers still living there?"

"No. Hugh Miller sold the house and moved closer to his family. Raising Wyatt alone will be hard enough, but it's even harder if he wants to keep working as a pilot. Hugh came by and apologized to us. He said Wyatt wanted to see Jack in the future for playdates. It won't be as easy now that they aren't so close, but we'll find a way." She shook her head, her mouth drooping at the corners. "It's still difficult for me to understand the choices Desty made."

Lea thought back to the ghost she'd encountered. "People don't always foresee consequences very well. She certainly never meant for your son to be kidnapped."

As they walked to the garage, Kamika asked, "Is everything for your business going well?"

"Yes!" Wendy's face brightened. "I'm working to integrate my software into their existing platform. I should be done before this little peanut comes along. We found out that a receptionist was supposed to report to Scurzo if I came to the meeting. She was fired on the spot, though she insisted she had no idea about the plot against me. And the police traced emails from Desty's computer back to the chief technology officer at Molinard Travel Applications. The other four people in the company claim that they had no idea what he had done. The police let me know that they arrested him last week. Once Scurzo copied my laptop, the Molinard CTO discovered that my software was better than theirs. He was in debt and really needed the money from the sale of their company. He didn't realize he'd be up to his neck in kidnapping and murder when he hired Scurzo to prevent me from presenting my software."

"What an idiot!" Lea shook her head at the stupidity of the unknown CTO.

When Wendy opened the door to the garage, Kamika and Lea found a space completely transformed from what it had been.

"Wow!" Kamika said as she walked through a doorway that hadn't been there previously. "You put in the dividing walls between the garage and game room that Montgomery recommended. It's a separate room now! I love the bright colors you chose for it!"

"If you have any recommendations for improvements, I'd love to hear them," Wendy said, deferring to Kamika's expertise.

"I'll write something for you if I notice anything. It looks like you did a fabulous job. We'll get started on the infusions in the new wall board."

Wendy left them, and Lea and Kamika worked for several hours, infusing joy into the space that had once inspired such terror. When they finished the game room, they moved on to the laundry room and storage rooms.

"How does it feel to you now?" Kamika asked as they finished the last door.

"Happy, as long as I don't go too near the stairs to the dungeon."

"Are we doing that next?" Kamika eyed the stairs warily. "I don't remember seeing it on the work order."

"No!" said the voice of Ryan from behind them. He stood in the door between the game room and garage. "We aren't going to waste the time and effort on an impossible task." He walked toward them and stood looking around. "I wish I could say I felt a difference in here now that you're done, but I don't. I'll be happy if Wendy does though."

"Are you giving up on using the basement space after all?" Lea asked. "Sealing it off?"

"No. But if we decide to store anything in there, I'm the one taking it there and retrieving it." He smiled. "I don't mind. Wendy shouldn't carry anything heavy up and down the stairs right now anyway."

"Have you found any more hidden treasure or cash?" Kamika asked as Lea began packing the equipment.

"No, nothing else. What we found was more than enough hidden treasure for one building. We actually didn't keep the cash you found. Wendy's niece, Carol's daughter, needed some expensive therapy treatments. We gave the money to Carol to help defray costs. Finding the money made it easier for her and her husband to accept our help. We've tried to help them pay medical bills before this, and they've declined. This time, since the money was essentially a windfall, not anyone's hard-earned salary, we were able to talk them into taking it. That was a relief to Wendy. She's wanted to help her niece for a while."

"That's great!" Kamika said.

"We're finished here," said Lea, heaving a bag of equipment onto her shoulder. "I don't know how long it will last, but this space should be more comfortable for a while. Keep the betrayers and traitors out of the house, and it could last years! Call us when Jack's room needs attention."

Ryan walked them back to their van. "Thank you again for everything."

Lea and Kamika waved goodbye from the van as it began moving on its route to their next assignment.

ASTRAL VIBES
A Bad Vibes Removal Services Short Story

"**Y**OU WANT ME TO MISS WATCHING the first total solar eclipse visible in the United States in my lifetime because of a ghost?" Lea rolled her eyes, sipped her cup of coffee, and sighed. "Okay, tell me about it." She knew from experience, trying to refuse Montgomery's requests would be pointless.

Montgomery, her boss, grinned at her from the doorway, where the overhead lights reflected off his balding pate. He stepped into the breakroom of Bad Vibes Removal Services. "Your coworkers, Keeley and Jose, have done emotional atmosphere resets at the client's house twice because certain rooms were giving him sudden chills and making his hair stand on end. They doubled-coated the walls both times with static to cover the residual emotional energy, which they thought was from the previous owner. After the second reset failed, I scanned the residence and found heavy amounts of lingering fear and anger."

Lea could see where he was going. "The emotional residue is either so strong that it's bleeding through their neutralization layers, or something keeps reestablishing the layers. You think the client has a ghost, and you want me to check because I'm the only one you know who can see ghosts. What does that have to do with my vacation to see the eclipse?"

Montgomery, who owned both Bad Vibes Removal Services and Montgomery Investigations, walked over and sat his massive bulk in a chair at the breakroom table. On the surface, he looked like a good-humored, tubby Friar Tuck. Those who knew him best knew that he was energetic, intelligent, ambitious, and persistent. "The client, whose name is Mel Strauss, says the former owner was an astronomer who died at home of a heart attack at the age of fifty-two. And he says that the room feels the worst right after a lunar or solar eclipse takes place anywhere in the world. This next eclipse will be a total eclipse and will be visible across a huge swath of the United States. Mr. Strauss thinks that might be the date on which we can best resolve this."

Lea gave Montgomery a puzzled look. "Why should we wait until the eclipse to try to sort this thing out? If the problem really is a ghost, I might be able to do something about it right now. Then I won't have to miss my vacation."

"You mean the ghost might be there all the time, but eclipse dates are when it's noticeable?

Lea grinned at Montgomery over her cup of coffee. "Yes!"

"I'll call Mr. Strauss and set something up. I'm sure he'd like the matter resolved sooner rather than later." Montgomery heaved himself up out of the chair. "I'll be your partner on this one, since Kamika's out sick," he called over his shoulder as he left the room.

Kamika was Lea's partner at work. They worked as a team doing atmosphere resets in businesses and residences. Lea missed Kamika's sense of humor. Hopefully, Kamika would recover quickly from the nasty summer cold she'd contracted. Lea finished her coffee and went to prepare the equipment for the case. If she knew Montgomery's powers of persuasion, they would be driving to the client's home within the hour.

❋

"Your hairdo looks modern," Montgomery said as they traveled in his self-driving van to Mr. Strauss's house less than an hour later. He studied her critically with confusion.

Lea looked up from the article she was reading and laughed. "It almost is. This style is only a couple hundred years old and was worn by unmarried women in China. I'm studying China right now. You may see some of the more elaborate styles next week, depending on how much time I have." Lea tucked an escaped strand of black hair behind her ear. As her master's degree courses in ancient world cultures at the University of Texas progressed, she tried different hairstyles and fashion habits to better understand her subjects' daily lives. She'd sampled ancient Egyptian and ancient Roman hairstyles while studying those civilizations, and she had just started a class on ancient China, where hairstyle revealed social status and ethnicity. Today, she wore her hair with bangs in the front and the rest pulled into a long, low ponytail that was bound at the bottom, a style common for unmarried women during the early Qing dynasty. She still needed to obtain a decorative bead for the end of the ponytail to make it authentic.

"Well, the ponytail looks nice," Montgomery said.

"Does the client know we're looking for ghosts?" Lea asked.

"No. I only told him that I had an employee who might be able to help diagnose the problem in his house more accurately."

"Okay." Lea had always been sensitive to the emotional energy in buildings—serenity in churches; guilt, anger, and despair in old jails; fear and anxiety in dentists' offices. She'd gone to work for Bad Vibes Removal Services so that she could help others be more comfortable in their homes in a way that she hadn't been. However, she was so sensitive that frequently she could see those who had left the emotional energy behind: sometimes, as echoes of whole scenes; other times, as ghosts.

The van parked in front of a limestone farmhouse which was surrounded by rolling fields covered with oak, cedar, prickly pear cactus, and wild grasses. They were in the heart of the Texas Hill Country, fifty miles west of Austin. Montgomery and Lea exited the vehicle and mounted the steps onto the front porch.

Lea examined the structure of the house and realized it had to be well over a century old. It oozed history. She hoped it only had one ghost. Given the house's age, there might be more.

Montgomery knocked on the door.

A graying, age-spotted man with vivid blue eyes under white brows answered the door. "Montgomery, welcome." He turned his eyes to Lea, who wore jeans and a t-shirt, and studied her. "And this is your house-diagnosing expert?"

"Yes, this is Lea." Montgomery turned to Lea and gave her a quick wink. "Lea, this is Mel Strauss. He bought this house about eighteen months ago when he retired."

"Pleased to meet you, sir," Lea said, extending her hand to shake his. "Would you mind if I look around?"

"Come in, come in. Go right ahead," Mr. Straus said after he shook Lea's hand. He retreated into the house and held the door open for them to pass by him.

Lea stepped into a living room with windows on three sides and a double doorway at the rear leading to the back of the house. The room had been designed to allow for maximum airflow in a time before air conditioners. The flooring was oak plank, and the walls were a smooth white. And, to Lea's sensitive brain, the room felt neutral. Montgomery's static treatments had worked well in this room.

Lea walked to the connecting room at the back of the house and found a modern kitchen. She guessed that the room had probably been used for something else when the house was built. The original kitchen would have been in a separate building in order to lessen the threat of fire danger to the house. A stairwell on the right-hand side had been added when a second floor had been built onto the house.

Montgomery and Mr. Strauss followed Lea into the kitchen.

"The downstairs doesn't seem to have any problems," Lea said, turning to Mr. Strauss. "Are the rooms you want reset upstairs?"

"Yep." The man's blue eyes twinkled under his bushy brows. "How did you know?"

"Let's say I'm really sensitive to atmosphere," she said, smiling back at him.

Mr. Strauss led them to the stairs. "Be careful on these stairs. They're a bit uneven."

Lea walked up the stairwell first. She could feel the air getting heavier as she went. At first, she thought it was because the house would be warmer upstairs due to heat rising from below. Then she noticed a squeezing sensation that forced her to take shallow breaths. She felt fear. "Well," Lea said to the men behind her, "I notice that the problem starts here, on the stairs."

"Really?" said Mr. Strauss. "I never notice anything until I go into the bedrooms."

Lea mounted the last step and came into a hallway that ran the length of the house. She saw that the first room to the right was a bedroom. Two more doors were visible. "What's the third door? You only mentioned two bedrooms."

Mr. Strauss came up the stairs behind her. "The middle door is the bathroom, between the bedrooms. Oddly, the bathroom has never bothered me. Only the bedrooms."

When Montgomery joined them, puffing a little from the climb, Lea entered the first bedroom door. She stopped a few feet into the room to survey it. The space was a sparsely furnished guest room containing only a double bed, a nightstand with a lamp, and a small dresser. By one window stood a large telescope. In one corner of the room, next to where a telescope now stood, a previous owner had added a closet. Lea's sense of fear increased until goosebumps appeared on her arms. "This room definitely has a problem."

"Yep," said Mr. Strauss. "You feel it too? Nice to know I'm not crazy."

Montgomery asked Lea, "Any ideas as to the source?"

"I'm not sure yet." Lea turned to their client. "Mr. Strauss, did the telescope come with the house?

"Yep. The dang thing is so big that none of the previous owner's family wanted to try to move it down the stairs. They didn't want it. They said the astronomer valued it over people, and I was welcome to it. It's extremely heavy."

"Why did you think a solar eclipse would make this room worse?" she asked.

"Well, one night, we had a partial lunar eclipse. I heard about it on the news and decided to see it with the telescope. The feeling in the room that night scared me so much I couldn't stay in here. I figured if a partial lunar eclipse made it that bad in here, a total solar one would be even worse."

Lea stepped toward the closet and noticed her goosebumps increasing. "Do you mind if I look in the closet?"

"Look all you want. I keep boxes of old tax and health records in there."

Lea crossed the wood floor and stopped in front of the closet. She hesitated a moment before opening the door. The fear had turned into terror. The source was in the closet. Slowly, she turned the knob.

Lea pulled the door open and felt a wall of terror. Something terrible had happened in the closet. Lea turned to face Montgomery and Mr. Strauss. "This closet is the source of the problem. It feels like death in here. If Keeley and Jose didn't neutralize the closet, we should try to get a sound reading to figure out what we're dealing with."

Montgomery stood in front of the closet with his arms crossed on his chest. "I reviewed their report before we came. They didn't treat the closet because the boxes were in the way. We'll need to move the boxes."

Mr. Strauss's white, bushy eyebrows went up curiously. "What are you going to do?"

Montgomery turned to face him. "We'll examine the walls for sound evidence of whatever happened in there." While running his investigations company, Montgomery had invented the equipment to read the imprint left by sound waves at the molecular level in walls. He discovered he could read what had been said at a crime scene if it was yelled or spoken loudly enough for the sound waves to imprint. At the same time, he'd found he could identify emotional energy imprints. Then he'd learned to obliterate those sound and emotion patterns, giving birth to Bad Vibes Removal Services. He hoped to eventually convince law enforcement agencies to use his inventions at active crime scenes. In the meantime, he used the sound-scanning equipment to aid his private-investigations clients and the obliterating equipment to help those who had moved into previously owned dwellings that contained negative emotional energy.

✄

Lea and Montgomery retrieved their sound-scanning equipment from the van and returned to the upstairs bedroom. They found Mr. Strauss removing boxes from the closet.

"That's the last one," Mr. Strauss said, pushing a box of files under the double bed to join those already there.

Montgomery handed his tablet to Lea. "Get the programs up and running. I'll do the scan."

Lea opened the scanning data analysis program. Montgomery slowly moved the scanner up and down, carefully scanning strips of the closet's walls.

"Looks good," Lea said. "The data's coming in."

Montgomery finished his scan, put down the equipment, and joined Lea in watching the data appear on the tablet.

Lea glanced up as he joined her. "We've got a shotgun blast: a huge sound imprint near the door and reverberation around that small space."

"I see it," said Montgomery. "Hopefully that didn't obliterate all other patterns."

"Here near the ceiling, I see something. Let me focus the analysis program." She tapped on the tablet. "There."

Montgomery read the results over her shoulder. "Someone yelled, 'No, Bollivar. Don't shoot.' And something else. It's still processing. Looks like a different vocal tone, maybe the shooter. He said, 'lights . . . ruining . . . research, Brennon.' We've got names. That should be helpful."

Mr. Strauss stared at the closet. "Bollivar was the previous owner who died of a heart attack. Does that mean Bollivar shot someone in the closet? Is that what that means?"

Montgomery nodded. "That's what it looks like."

Lea finished studying the data on the tablet and then handed it to Montgomery. "I don't see anything else." She glanced at the telescope by the window. "Bollivar was an astronomer. He was researching something, and someone named Brennon had lights that were interfering with his work. Light pollution is a problem in astronomy. Brennon must have lived nearby."

Montgomery began typing on the tablet. "I'm doing a search for anyone named Brennon in this area." He paused. "Here's an article. Someone named Ike Brennon was reported missing by his family a year and a half ago." He glanced at Mr. Strauss. "Is that around the time Mr. Bollivar died?"

Mr. Strauss nodded. "That's right."

Montgomery skimmed the news article. "Here's something else. Ike Brennon was a little league coach who had installed stadium lights on his property to allow the kids to practice there. That would certainly be light pollution for an astronomer." Montgomery tapped on his tablet. "I don't see anything about him being found, not even his body." He paused. "Here's Bollivar's obituary. He died the same week Ike Brennon went missing."

Lea looked out the window at the acreage surrounding the house. "What if Bollivar killed Brennon here and buried him on the property? Then Bollivar had a heart attack, maybe from the stress and strain of what he'd done."

Montgomery's eyebrows went up thoughtfully. "That's a good theory. We can do some work to check it. If the murder occurred in this closet, physical evidence may still be here: blood seepage into the floorboards, evidence of spatter. Blood is hard to clean up." He looked at Mr. Strauss. "We might need to remove a few of the floorboards."

Mr. Strauss pursed his lips in a determined, flat line. "Take up the whole floor if you want."

Montgomery retrieved tools from the van, got down on his knees in the closet, and went to work removing one of the floorboards. Almost immediately, he said, "I've found something." A brownish-red substance covered one edge of the board, and more lay in a dried pool beneath it. Montgomery pointed it out to Mr. Strauss. "Here's our evidence: dried blood."

The old man's face went pale, and he nodded.

Montgomery stood up and dusted himself off. "I wish the sound reading was acceptable in court as evidence. But it's a moot point since Bollivar is dead."

Mr. Strauss frowned thoughtfully and said, "Brennon's family will want to know what happened to him. They might bring a civil suit against the estate, maybe for wrongful death or something. The estate had plenty of money from the sale of this property. I know what I paid for it. Your sound readings might help in that kind of lawsuit."

"A civil suit. Hmm, maybe." Montgomery collected his tools and packed them back in his equipment bag.

Mr. Strauss turned away from the closet. "So, now do we look for the body? We don't know that it's even here. He could have dumped it anywhere."

"True," said Montgomery, getting out his phone. "But given the open fields and lack of neighbors, Bollivar wouldn't need to go far to dispose of the body. Moving a body somewhere else leaves evidence in a car and involves the risk of driving around with a body. Imagine if he got stopped by police. No, the easiest thing for Bollivar to do would be to bury his victim here. I need to make a call or two to get us some help. In the meantime, Lea can assess the other bedroom."

❦

Lea turned the knob to the second bedroom door and entered. Her eyes searched the room. Like the other bedroom, it had a bed, dresser, and nightstand. However, this room showed signs of occupation by its owner. Mr. Strauss had hung family photos on the wall, left books and loose coins on the nightstand, and kicked off shoes near the closet.

Mr. Strauss followed her into the room. "What do you think?"

"This room doesn't have fear imprinted on it, like the other one. This one is more complex: anger, despair, and guilt." Lea walked over to the closet and tugged the door open. Mr. Strauss's shirts and slacks were hung neatly inside. A pair of dress shoes and some slippers sat on a shoe rack.

Mr. Strauss stood with his hands on his hips, watching her curiously. "Do you think anyone got killed in here?"

Lea closed the closet door. "No. But the emotions in this room are so strongly imprinted on the space that the source may still be here. I'm going to try something that's worked for me before." Lea looked around the room and spoke loudly. "Mr. Bollivar? Are you here?" Lea felt a prickling on her neck, as though someone were watching her. She turned toward the bed and saw the barely visible outline of a man. "Is that you, Mr. Bollivar?"

"I don't see anything," said Mr. Strauss, frowning and squinting slightly. "Where are you looking?"

Lea pointed to the general area of the figure. "I see a form near the bed, but it isn't very distinct."

Mr. Strauss looked stunned. "You mean a ghost?"

"Yes."

Lea sensed anger. A picture from the wall crashed to the floor. Mr. Strauss flinched in surprise. The air around Lea throbbed with rage. The figure by the bed loomed larger and moved toward her.

Lea's whole body tensed. She took a deep breath and shouted, "Calm down and stop that, Mr. Bollivar! We're here to find Ike Brennon's body. We know that you lost your temper and killed him because his lights interfered with your research."

The throb of anger melted away, and the figure seemed to shrink. Lea sensed guilt and remorse. "You're sorry that you killed him. That's good. I'll bet you always had trouble controlling your temper, didn't you? We're going to find his body. Then his family will know what happened to him. They may bring a lawsuit for wrongful death against your estate. They could be compensated for your actions. You don't have to stay here. The problem here will be resolved."

The air shimmered and wavered slightly as the outline of the man vanished completely.

Lea shook slightly as adrenalin coursed through her body. She steadied herself and inhaled slowly to calm her erratic heartbeat. She glanced at Mr. Strauss. "I think he's gone. He wouldn't, or couldn't, speak to me, so I can't make any guarantees. All we can do is neutralize the room with static again and hope it works. If you still feel uncomfortable after that, you can call us back."

Mr. Strauss looked unnerved but recovered quickly. He raised his bushy eyebrows and cleared his throat to gather his voice. "Okay," he said, glancing at the broken picture frame on the floor. "Hopefully, no more pictures will be jumping off the walls." He bent down to pick up the pieces.

Lea managed an encouraging smile. "I hope so, too. Let's see if Montgomery's prepared to look for that body."

❦

Later that afternoon, Lea, Montgomery, and Mr. Strauss observed as a friend of Montgomery's flew his drone over the property looking for ground depressions or disturbed areas in the fields that might indicate a gravesite. Montgomery held a laptop and watched as the video streaming from the drone's camera appeared on the screen. They'd been working for three hours and had identified five possible places where a body could be buried.

"That covers the whole property," said Mr. Strauss as the drone operator brought his vehicle in for a landing. "Do we have to dig up each site?"

Montgomery looked up from his laptop. "No. I've got a friend arriving shortly with a dog that can help us out. Once we confirm which site, if any, has the body, we can call the police."

"A dog?" Mr. Strauss turned his questioning blue eyes on Montgomery.

"A cadaver dog," Montgomery said.

They all turned as the sound of a car arriving caught their attention.

"And here's the dog now." Montgomery walked over to greet a tall woman getting out of a red sport-utility vehicle. A sturdy, black Labrador retriever sat on the back seat.

Montgomery introduced his friend Cassie, who volunteered for search and rescue with her dog, Knight. The drone operator collected his belongings, shook hands with everyone, and departed. Montgomery, Cassie, and Knight set out to walk the property and inspect the sites identified by the drone.

Since Montgomery didn't want too many people walking around the potential crime scenes, Lea and Mr.

Strauss retired to the house to have a glass of tea while they waited. Within ten minutes, Lea received a text. "Montgomery says the dog signaled for remains at the second site," she said.

A short time later, the search party returned and joined Lea and Mr. Strauss in the kitchen. Montgomery explained what they had done. "We checked all the sites. Knight identified the second one and none of the others. At this point, we can involve the local police force. I have a friend in homicide. I'm going to call him now."

Cassie said her goodbyes and left with her dog. Montgomery followed her outside to make his calls.

A few moments later, Montgomery trotted back into the house. "Well, my friend says he'll take the cadaver dog's nose as evidence, and they'll bring a team out to take a look. He said not to dig ourselves. He should be here soon."

Half an hour later, the police contingent arrived. Montgomery showed a detective the blood in the closet and explained their theory of what had happened to Ike Brennon. Then he escorted the police to the possible burial site the dog had identified.

As evening fell, Montgomery returned to the kitchen to give Lea and Mr. Strauss an update. "They started digging and found human remains. Bollivar didn't dig a very deep hole to bury the body."

※

The next day, Lea sat in the Bad Vibes office breakroom, sipping her black coffee, telling her friend Kamika about the case of Ike Brennon.

"I get sick for one day, and you go on a ghost case without me. Next time, wait for me. You could have waited until today," Kamika said, shaking her bronze, corkscrew curls in annoyance.

Lea laughed and shook her head in disagreement. "Tell that to Montgomery. You know how persistent he is when he wants to solve something. Besides, now that it's over, I won't have to miss my vacation."

"Did I hear my name?" asked Montgomery, standing in the breakroom door.

Lea waved at Montgomery. "Kamika thinks we should have waited for her before going to see Mr. Strauss."

The big man grinned at Kamika. "Sorry, Kamika. I do have news on that case, though. The police found a shotgun, wrapped in a bedsheet and buried with the body. Records show it belonged to Mr. Bollivar. They still have to formally identify the body, but a driver's license found on the body said Ike Brennon. The police are contacting Brennon's family to get dental records, or, failing that, a DNA match."

Lea put down her coffee mug and looked questioningly at Montgomery. "Would the police mind if you tell Ike's family what we found?"

Montgomery perched his bulk on a chair next to her. "Since it won't interfere with their investigation, the police shouldn't mind. Yes, I'm going to pay the family a visit with our findings."

"If they file a civil suit, will it help your technology get accepted by law enforcement?" Lea asked.

"Maybe. Who knows? At this point, there's enough physical evidence, between the gun they found and the blood in the closet, that they won't necessarily need our sound-scan findings. But I can hope." Montgomery stood. "Well, ladies, what are you dawdling around here for? Don't you have houses and dentists' offices to reset? You're not on vacation yet."

"We're going," said Kamika, jumping up and grabbing Lea's arm. "Come on. Maybe we'll find more ghosts today."

AUTHOR'S NOTE

THANK YOU FOR READING *The Walls Can Talk.* I hope you enjoyed reading the book as much as I enjoyed writing it. If you have a moment, please leave a review of the book on your preferred retailer's site. If you have any comments or questions, you can contact me through my website, nmcedeno.com.

ABOUT THE AUTHOR

N. M. CEDEÑO LIVES IN TEXAS and writes mystery short stories and novels. Her mysteries vary from traditional mysteries, to romantic suspense, to science fiction in genre. Her debut novel, *All in Her Head*, was published in 2014 by Lucky Bat Books, followed by her second novel, *For the Children's Sake,* in 2015. *For the Children's Sake* was selected as a finalist for a First Chapter Book Award by the East Texas Writer's Guild in 2016. Another science fiction short mystery, *A Reasonable Expectation of Privacy,* was published by Analog Science Fiction and Fact Magazine in 2012. For more information, please visit nmcedeno.com.

OTHER STORIES BY N. M. CEDEÑO

If you enjoyed this story, you may also like:

Bad Vibes Removal Services: Short Story Collection

NEAR FUTURE MYSTERY SHORT STORIES:
A Reasonable Expectation of Privacy
In the Interest of Public Safety
Pariah

NOVELS
All in Her Head
For the Children's Sake

CONNECT WITH N. M. CEDEÑO

To connect with N. M. Cedeño please visit
nmcedeno.com.

CPSIA information can be obtained
at www.ICGtesting.com
Printed in the USA
LVOW10s1154160418
573642LV00004B/642/P